EVIL ROOTS

EVIL ROOTS

Killer Tales of the Botanical Gothic

Edited by
DAISY BUTCHER

This collection first published in 2019 by
The British Library
96 Euston Road
London NW1 2DB

Introduction and notes © Daisy Butcher 2019

Dates attributed to each story relate to first publication.

Cataloguing in Publication Data
A catalogue record for this publication is available from the British Library

ISBN 978 0 7123 5229 1
Limited edition ISBN 978 0 7123 5335 9
e-ISBN 978 0 7123 6490 4

Frontispiece illustration by Enrique Bernardou
The illustrations throughout the book are by Lauren Forrester of TwentyEight
Cover design by Mauricio Villamayor with illustration by Enrique Bernardou

Text design and typesetting by Tetragon, London
Printed in England by CPI Group (UK) Ltd, Croydon, CR0 4YY

Contents

Dedicated to my grandfather, Charles Mason

INTRODUCTION

Unlike its contemporaries the vampire, werewolf, ghost or mummy, the killer plant has never received enough recognition as its own subgenre of gothic/horror. Despite this, the man-eating plant was a true literary phenomenon of the nineteenth century, inspiring esteemed gothic writers such as Nathaniel Hawthorne, Arthur Conan Doyle and H. G. Wells to write short stories. The nineteenth century created a unique environment for the killer plant to grow, with imperialism's far-reaching networks, the emphasis on exploration and the popularity of gothic stories. Writers were able to feed off the era's anxieties and interests to create a horror which stemmed from their deepest fears and their greatest desires. With the rise of imperial global access, rare and exotic plant specimens became available for the rich Victorian collector.

During the nineteenth century the exotic plants market truly boomed as it became a sensation and obsession rivalling that of the better-known Egyptomania of the time. This exclusive pastime provided playthings and curios for the mega-rich as it was recorded at the end of the nineteenth century that a single bulb of the rare specimen *Odontoglossum crispum Cooksoniae* sold for the equivalent of £300,000.[*] The expeditions to fetch these specimens were long, dangerous and expensive. To justify high prices and add value to their wares, stories were told of the dangers of the jungles: from cannibal natives to man-eating trees, news and hoaxes of these kind were rampant during the era. Just like the vampire being invited inside,

[*] Endersby, Jim. 2016. *Orchid: A Cultural History*. University of Chicago Press & Kew Publishing. Chicago and London.

the monstrous plant was now closer to home than ever as they lived in their collectors' hothouses. Carnivorous plants in general were widely collected but orchids were especially coveted, causing the killer orchid to become a sub-genre of its own among man-eating plants. Their bodily appearance and descriptions oozed sexuality and femininity, which transformed the flower into the *femme fatale* of the killer plant world as collectors died for their beauty.

A major influence on the literature and arts featuring plant horror was that of Charles Darwin's work on carnivorous plants. His two essays *Insectivorous Plants* (1875) and *The Power of Movement in Plants* (1877) became incredibly important to the rise of the man-eating plant as he revolutionised the ways in which plants were perceived. No longer seeing insectivorous plants as mere objects without agency, he observed their methods as purposeful and almost sentient as they appeared to use their environment to their advantage to catch their prey. This in turn inspired the idea of the blood-thirsty vegetable, the plant with murderous intent which moves and kills at will. The seemingly passive poisoners from previous stories now became dangerously active in the short stories of the mid- to late nineteenth century. No longer wallflowers, the plants were given starring roles controlling tentacle-like appendages, growing legs or even mouths as you will see in the stories included in this collection.

As well as Darwin's work specifically on the carnivorous plant, this specific strain of gothic short story creates fear through the concept of devolution or degeneration. As Darwin illustrated the idea of natural selection, survival of the fittest with humans at the top of the evolutionary food chain, the idea that plants would rise up to threaten us inspired terror. The literary critic Cheryl Blake Price attributes the effectiveness of the Victorian killer plant to "ecophobia". Not only was there a sense of distrust of the natural world, but there was also a deep-rooted fear of foreign environments and sense of the unknown lurking in colonial jungles.[*] Moreover, this particular strain of botanical-themed gothic fiction highlights fears of hybridity and liminal figures not easily categorised. This can be seen within the one fungus tale within the collection, "The Voice in the Night" by William Hope Hodgson. Just as the fungus has been difficult to categorise in the plant/animal kingdoms, in Hodgson's tale the parasite and host become virtually indistinguishable. More generally, across the other man-eating plant tales the killer plants become more animalistic in their mobility and hunting as they evolve.

This collection spans from 1844 to 1932 and a shift towards the more familiar plant horror such as *Little Shop of Horrors* can be seen as the plants move away from poisonous women in "Rappaccini's Daughter" to tropes of early science fiction in the later texts that feature parasites and tentacles. In my selection I have attempted to include a spread of the many different strands of killer plant from vines, trees, orchids and venus fly traps to fungi. I am aware that fungi are classified in their own kingdom and therefore not considered a plant, but I believe they are part of the same conversation and elicit the same fear as the man-eating plant. With this in mind I have chosen to include "The Voice in the Night" in my collection as it is the hybridity and the blurring of the lines between animal and plant which prove effective in these stories.

With this selection of short stories, it is interesting to trace the beginning of the genre and how the man-eating plant has developed into the monster we know it as today. In modern times, the killer plant has become a staple of the videogame world as a classic enemy encountered in nearly every forest, swamp or jungle level. Moreover,

---

[*] Price, Cheryl Blake. 2013. "Vegetable Monsters: Man Eating Trees in *Fin de-Siècle* Fiction", *Victorian Literature and Culture*. Vol.41, 311–327.

the predatory plant has also featured in internationally renowned horror/science fiction film and TV, from the Demogorgon of the Duffer Brothers' *Stranger Things* (2016–) on Netflix to the anthropomorphic and mutated plants in Alex Garland's feature *Annihilation* (2018) based on Jeff Vandermeer's novel and characters such as Marvel's Groot and DC Comics' Swamp Thing.

As a gothicist, I have chosen stories with a more Botanical Gothic feel to them rather than alien/outer space narratives. It is worth noting, however, that I do agree that the killer plant shares a lot of similarities with the alien in terms of its symbolism and I would even argue that alien horror owes a lot to the legacy of killer plants. Overall, the killer plant deserves more recognition as its own genre of eco-horror and is especially relevant today as there is more awareness of the effects of deforestation and climate change. These fantasies provide a sense of repercussion when nature fights back.

DAISY BUTCHER

FURTHER READING

Endersby, Jim. 2016. *Orchid: A Cultural History*. University of Chicago Press & Kew Publishing. Chicago and London.

Price, Cheryl Blake. 2013. "Vegetable Monsters: Man Eating Trees in *Fin de-Siècle* Fiction", *Victorian Literature and Culture*. Vol.41, 311–327.

Keetley, Diane and Tenga, Angela. 2017. *Plant Horror: Approaches to the Monstrous Vegetal in Fiction and Film*. London.

RAPPACCINI'S DAUGHTER

Nathaniel Hawthorne

Born in Salem, Massachusetts in 1804, Nathaniel Hawthorne was a prolific novelist and short story writer perhaps most famous for *The Scarlet Letter.* First published in the *United States Magazine and Democratic Review*, December 1844, Hawthorne's "Rappaccini's Daughter" opens this anthology as one of the oldest short stories in the genre. The story is set in Padua, which is known for having the world's first botanical garden established in 1545, and follows botanist Giacomo Rappaccini's garden of poisonous plants. One day a student from the university of Padua, Giovanni, falls for a maiden called Beatrice in the luscious garden across from his accommodation. However, Giovanni's visits to the flower garden cause him to learn some troubling information about his beloved's true nature.

This story blazes the trail for the Botanical Gothic stories which follow and cements an interconnectedness between femininity, flowers and death which can be seen too in Lucy H. Hooper's 1889 tale "Carnivorine" in this collection. The titular daughter is the product of her father's experimentation with poisonous plants and their toxic properties, luring the male onlooker with her beauty just as the carnivorous flower lures its insect prey.

 young man, named Giovanni Guasconti, came, very long ago, from the more southern region of Italy, to pursue his studies at the University of Padua. Giovanni, who had but a scanty supply of gold ducats in his pocket, took lodgings in a high and gloomy chamber of an old edifice, which looked not unworthy to have been the palace of a Paduan noble, and which, in fact, exhibited over its entrance the armorial bearings of a family long since extinct. The young stranger, who was not unstudied in the great poem of his country, recollected that one of the ancestors of this family, and perhaps an occupant of this very mansion, had been pictured by Dante as a partaker of the immortal agonies of his Inferno. These reminiscences and associations, together with the tendency to heart-break natural to a young man for the first time out of his native sphere, caused Giovanni to sigh heavily, as he looked around the desolate and ill-furnished apartment.

"Holy Virgin, signor," cried old dame Lisabetta, who, won by the youth's remarkable beauty of person, was kindly endeavouring to give the chamber a habitable air, "what a sigh was that to come out of a young man's heart! Do you find this old mansion gloomy? For the love of heaven, then, put your head out of the window, and you will see as bright sunshine as you have left in Naples."

Guasconti mechanically did as the old woman advised, but could not quite agree with her that the Lombard sunshine was as cheerful as that of southern Italy. Such as it was, however, it fell upon a garden beneath the window, and expended its fostering influences on a variety of plants, which seemed to have been cultivated with exceeding care.

"Does this garden belong to the house?" asked Giovanni.

"Heaven forbid, signor!—unless it were fruitful of better potherbs than any that grow there now," answered old Lisabetta. "No: that garden is cultivated by the own hands of Signor Giacomo Rappaccini, the famous Doctor, who, I warrant him, has been heard of as far as Naples. It is said that he distils these plants into medicines that are as potent as a charm. Oftentimes you may see the signor Doctor at work, and perchance the signora his daughter, too, gathering the strange flowers that grow in the garden."

The old woman had now done what she could for the aspect of the chamber, and, commending the young man to the protection of the saints, took her departure.

Giovanni still found no better occupation than to look down into the garden beneath his window. From its appearance, he judged it to be one of those botanic gardens, which were of earlier date in Padua than elsewhere in Italy, or in the world. Or, not improbably, it might once have been the pleasure-place of an opulent family; for there was the ruin of a marble fountain in the centre, sculptured with rare art, but so woefully shattered that it was impossible to trace the original design from the chaos of remaining fragments. The water, however, continued to gush and sparkle into the sunbeams as cheerfully as ever. A little gurgling sound ascended to the young man's window, and made him feel as if a fountain were an immortal spirit, that sang its song unceasingly, and without heeding the vicissitudes around it; while one century embodied it in marble, and another scattered the perishable garniture on the soil. All about the pool into which the water subsided grew various plants, that seemed to require a plentiful supply of moisture for the nourishment of gigantic leaves, and, in some instances, flowers gorgeously magnificent. There was one shrub in particular, set in a marble vase in the midst of the pool, that bore a profusion of purple blossoms, each of which had the lustre and richness of a gem; and the whole together made a show so resplendent that it seemed enough to illuminate the garden, even had there been no sunshine. Every portion of the soil was peopled with plants and herbs, which, if less beautiful, still bore tokens of assiduous care; as if all had their individual virtues, known to the scientific mind that fostered them. Some were placed in urns, rich with old carving, and others in common garden-pots; some crept serpent-like along the ground, or climbed on high, using whatever means of ascent was offered them. One plant had wreathed itself round a statue of Vertumnus, which was thus quite veiled and shrouded in a drapery of hanging foliage, so happily arranged that it might have served a sculptor for a study.

While Giovanni stood at the window, he heard a rustling behind a screen of leaves, and became aware that a person was at work in the garden. His figure soon emerged into view, and showed itself to be that of no common labourer, but a tall, emaciated, sallow, and sickly-looking man, dressed in a scholar's garb of black. He was beyond the middle term of life, with grey hair, a thin grey beard, and a face singularly marked with intellect and cultivation, but which could never, even in his more youthful days, have expressed much warmth of heart.

Nothing could exceed the intentness with which this scientific gardener examined every shrub which grew in his path; it seemed as if he was looking into their inmost nature, making observations in regard to their creative essence, and discovering why one leaf grew in this shape, and another in that, and wherefore such and such flowers differed among themselves in hue and perfume. Nevertheless, in spite of the deep intelligence on his part, there was no approach to intimacy between himself and these vegetable existences. On the contrary, he avoided their actual touch, or the direct inhaling of their odours, with a caution that impressed Giovanni most disagreeably;

for the man's demeanour was that of one walking among malignant influences, such as savage beasts, or deadly snakes, or evil spirits, which, should he allow them one moment of licence, would wreak upon him some terrible fatality. It was strangely frightful to the young man's imagination, to see this air of insecurity in a person cultivating a garden, that most simple and innocent of human toils, and which had been alike the joy and labour of the unfallen parents of the race. Was this garden, then, the Eden of the present world?—and this man, with such a perception of harm in what his own hands caused to grow, was he the Adam?

The distrustful gardener, while plucking away the dead leaves, or pruning the too luxuriant growth of the shrubs, defended his hands with a pair of thick gloves. Nor were these his only armour. When, in his walk through the garden, he came to the magnificent plant that hung its purple gems beside the marble fountain, he placed a kind of mask over his mouth and nostrils, as if all this beauty did but conceal a deadlier malice. But finding his task still too dangerous, he drew back, removed the mask, and called loudly, but in the infirm voice of a person affected with inward disease:

"Beatrice!—Beatrice!"

"Here am I, my father! What would you?" cried a rich and youthful voice from the window of the opposite house; a voice as rich as a tropical sunset, and which made Giovanni, though he knew not why, think of deep hues of purple or crimson, and of perfumes heavily delectable—"Are you in the garden?"

"Yes, Beatrice," answered the gardener, "and I need your help."

Soon there emerged from under a sculptured portal the figure of a young girl, arrayed with as much richness of taste as the most splendid of the flowers, beautiful as the day, and with a bloom so deep and vivid, that one shade more would have been too much.

She looked redundant with life, health, and energy; all of which attributes were bound down and compressed, as it were, and girdled tensely, in their luxuriance, by her virgin zone. Yet Giovanni's fancy must have grown morbid, while he looked down into the garden; for the impression which the fair stranger made upon him was as if here were another flower, the human sister of those vegetable ones, as beautiful as they—more beautiful than the richest of them, but still to be touched only with a glove, nor to be approached without a mask. As Beatrice came down the garden-path, it was observable that she handled and inhaled the odour of several of the plants, which her father had most sedulously avoided.

"Here, Beatrice!" said the latter,—"see how many needful offices require to be done to our chief treasure. Yet, shattered as I am, my life might pay the penalty of approaching it so closely as circumstances demand. Henceforth, I fear, this plant must be consigned to your sole charge."

"And gladly will I undertake it," cried again the rich tones of the young lady, as she bent towards the magnificent plant, and opened her arms as if to embrace it. "Yes, my sister, my splendour, it shall be Beatrice's task to nurse and serve thee; and thou shalt reward her with thy kisses and perfume-breath, which to her is as the breath of life!"

Then, with all the tenderness in her manner that was so strikingly expressed in her words, she busied herself with such attentions as the plant seemed to require; and Giovanni, at his lofty window, rubbed his eyes, and almost doubted whether it were a girl tending her favourite flower, or one sister performing the duties of affection to another. The scene soon terminated. Whether Doctor Rappaccini had finished his labours in the garden, or that his watchful eye had caught the stranger's face, he now took his daughter's arm and retired. Night was already closing in; oppressive exhalations seemed to proceed from the plants, and steal upward past the open window; and Giovanni, closing the lattice, went to his couch, and dreamed of a rich flower and beautiful girl. Flower and maiden were different and yet the same, and fraught with some strange peril in either shape.

But there is an influence in the light of morning that tends to rectify whatever errors of fancy, or even of judgment, we may have incurred during the sun's decline, or among the shadows of the night, or in the less wholesome glow of moonshine. Giovanni's first movement on starting from sleep was to throw open the window, and gaze down into the garden which his dreams had made so fertile of mysteries. He was surprised, and a little ashamed to find how real and matter-of-fact an affair it proved to be, in the first rays of the sun, which gilded the dew-drops that hung upon leaf and blossom, and while giving a brighter beauty to each rare flower, brought everything within the limits of ordinary experience. The young man rejoiced, that, in the heart of the barren city, he had the privilege of overlooking this spot of lovely and luxuriant vegetation. It would serve, he said to himself, as a symbolic language, to keep him in communion with nature. Neither the sickly and thought-worn Doctor Giacomo Rappaccini, it is true, nor his brilliant daughter, were now visible; so that Giovanni could not determine how much of the singularity which he attributed to both, was due to their own qualities, and how much to his wonder-working fancy. But he was inclined to take a most rational view of the whole matter.

In the course of the day, he paid his respects to Signor Pietro Baglioni, professor of medicine in the University, a physician of eminent repute, to whom Giovanni had brought a letter of introduction. The Professor was an elderly personage, apparently of genial nature, and habits that might almost be called jovial; he kept the young man to dinner, and made himself very agreeable by the freedom and liveliness of his conversation, especially when warmed by a flask or two of Tuscan wine. Giovanni, conceiving that men of science, inhabitants of the same city, must needs be on familiar terms with one another, took an opportunity to mention the name of Dr Rappaccini. But the Professor did not respond with so much cordiality as he had anticipated.

"Ill would it become a teacher of the divine art of medicine," said Professor Pietro Baglioni, in answer to a question of Giovanni, "to withhold due and well-considered praise of a physician so eminently skilled as Rappaccini. But, on the other hand, I should answer it but scantily to my conscience, were I to permit a worthy youth like yourself, Signor Giovanni, the son of an ancient friend, to imbibe erroneous ideas respecting a man who might hereafter chance to hold your life and death in his hands. The truth is, our worshipful Doctor Rappaccini has as much science as any member of the faculty—with perhaps one single exception—in Padua, or all Italy. But there are certain grave objections to his professional character."

"And what are they?" asked the young man.

"Has my friend Giovanni any disease of body or heart, that he is so inquisitive about physicians?" said the Professor, with a smile. "But as for Rappaccini, it is said of him—and I, who know the man well, can answer for its truth—that he cares infinitely more for science than for mankind. His patients are interesting to him only as subjects for some new experiment. He would sacrifice human life, his own among the rest, or whatever else was dearest to him, for the sake of adding so much as a grain of mustard-seed to the great heap of his accumulated knowledge."

"Methinks he is an awful man, indeed," remarked Guasconti, mentally recalling the cold and purely intellectual aspect of Rappaccini.

"And yet, worshipful Professor, is it not a noble spirit? Are there many men capable of so spiritual a love of science?"

"God forbid," answered the Professor, somewhat testily—"at least, unless they take sounder views of the healing art than those adopted by Rappaccini. It is his theory, that all medicinal virtues are comprised within those substances which we term vegetable poisons. These he cultivates with his own hands, and is said even to have produced new varieties of poison, more horribly deleterious than Nature, without the assistance of this learned person, would ever have plagued the world with. That the Signor Doctor does less mischief than might be expected, with such dangerous substances, is undeniable. Now and then, it must be owned, he has effected—or seemed to effect—a marvellous cure. But, to tell you my private mind, Signor Giovanni, he should receive little credit for such instances of success—they being probably the work of chance—but should be held strictly accountable for his failures, which may justly be considered his own work."

The youth might have taken Baglioni's opinions with many grains of allowance, had he known that there was a professional warfare of long continuance between him and Doctor Rappaccini, in which the latter was generally thought to have gained the advantage. If the reader be inclined to judge for himself, we refer him to certain black-letter tracts on both sides, preserved in the medical department of the University of Padua.

"I know not, most learned Professor," returned Giovanni, after musing on what had been said of Rappaccini's exclusive zeal for science—"I know not how dearly this physician may love his art; but surely there is one object more dear to him. He has a daughter."

"Aha!" cried the Professor, with a laugh. "So, now our friend Giovanni's secret is out. You have heard of this daughter, whom all the young men in Padua are wild about, though not half a dozen have ever had the good hap to see her face. I know little of the Signora Beatrice, save that Rappaccini is said to have instructed her deeply in his science, and that, young and beautiful as fame reports her, she is already qualified to fill a professor's chair. Perchance her father destines her for mine! Other absurd rumours there be, not worth talking about, or listening to. So now, Signor Giovanni, drink off your glass of Lacryma."

Guasconti returned to his lodgings somewhat heated with the wine he had quaffed, and which caused his brain to swim with strange fantasies in reference to Doctor Rappaccini and the beautiful Beatrice. On his way, happening to pass by a florist's, he bought a fresh bouquet of flowers.

Ascending to his chamber, he seated himself near the window, but within the shadow thrown by the depth of the wall, so that he could look down into the garden with little risk of being discovered. All beneath his eye was a solitude. The strange plants were basking in the sunshine, and now and then nodding gently to one another, as if in acknowledgment of sympathy and kindred. In the midst, by the shattered fountain, grew the magnificent shrub, with its purple gems clustering all over it; they glowed in the air, and gleamed back again out of the depths of the pool, which thus seemed to overflow with coloured radiance from the rich reflection that was steeped in it. At first, as we have said, the garden was a solitude. Soon, however—as Giovanni had half-hoped, half-feared, would be the case—a figure appeared beneath the antique sculptured portal, and came down between the rows of plants, inhaling their various perfumes, as if she were one of those beings of old classic fable, that lived upon sweet odours. On again beholding Beatrice, the young man was even startled to perceive how much her beauty exceeded his recollection of it; so brilliant, so vivid in its character, that she glowed amid the sunlight, and, as Giovanni whispered to himself, positively illuminated the more shadowy intervals of the garden path. Her face being now more revealed than on the former occasion, he was struck by its expression of simplicity and sweetness; qualities that had not entered into his idea of her character, and which made him ask anew, what manner of mortal she might be. Nor did he fail again to observe, or imagine, an analogy between the beautiful girl and the gorgeous shrub that hung its gem-like flowers over the fountain; a resemblance which Beatrice seemed to have indulged a fantastic humour in heightening, both by the arrangement of her dress and the selection of its hues.

Approaching the shrub, she threw open her arms, as with a passionate ardour, and drew its branches into an intimate embrace; so intimate, that her features were hidden in its leafy bosom, and her glistening ringlets all intermingled with the flowers.

"Give me thy breath, my sister," exclaimed Beatrice; "for I am faint with common air! And give me this flower of thine, which I separate with gentlest fingers from the stem, and place it close beside my heart."

With these words, the beautiful daughter of Rappaccini plucked one of the richest blossoms of the shrub, and was about to fasten it in her bosom. But now, unless Giovanni's draughts of wine had bewildered his senses, a singular incident occurred. A small orange-coloured reptile, of the lizard or chameleon species, chanced to be creeping along the path, just at the feet of Beatrice. It appeared to Giovanni—but, at the distance from which he gazed, he could scarcely have seen anything so minute—it appeared to him, however, that a drop or two of moisture from the broken stem of the flower descended upon the lizard's head. For an instant, the reptile contorted itself violently, and then lay motionless in the sunshine. Beatrice observed this remarkable phenomenon, and crossed herself, sadly, but without surprise; nor did she therefore hesitate to arrange the fatal flower in her bosom. There it blushed, and almost glimmered with the dazzling effect of a precious stone, adding to her dress and aspect the one appropriate charm, which nothing else in the world could have supplied. But Giovanni, out of the shadow of his window, bent forward and shrank back, and murmured and trembled.

"Am I awake? Have I my senses?" said he to himself. "What is this being?—beautiful, shall I call her?—or inexpressibly terrible?"

Beatrice now strayed carelessly through the garden, approaching closer beneath Giovanni's window, so that he was compelled to thrust his head quite out of its concealment, in order to gratify the intense and painful curiosity which she excited. At this moment, there came a beautiful insect over the garden wall; it had perhaps wandered through the city and found no flowers nor verdure among those antique haunts of men, until the heavy perfumes of Doctor Rappaccini's shrubs had lured it from afar. Without alighting on the flowers, this winged brightness seemed to be attracted by Beatrice, and lingered in the air and fluttered about her head. Now here it could not be but that Giovanni Guasconti's eyes deceived him. Be that as it might, he fancied that while Beatrice was gazing at the insect with childish delight, it grew faint and fell at her feet!—its bright wings shivered! it was dead!—from no cause that he could discern, unless it were the atmosphere of her breath. Again Beatrice crossed herself and sighed heavily, as she bent over the dead insect.

An impulsive movement of Giovanni drew her eyes to the window. There she beheld the beautiful head of the young man—rather a Grecian than an Italian head, with fair, regular features, and a glistening of gold among his ringlets—gazing down upon her like a being that hovered in mid-air. Scarcely knowing what he did, Giovanni threw down the bouquet which he had hitherto held in his hand.

"Signora," said he, "there are pure and healthful flowers. Wear them for the sake of Giovanni Guasconti!"

"Thanks, Signor," replied Beatrice, with her rich voice, that came forth as if it were like a gush of music; and with a mirthful expression half childish and half woman-like. "I accept your gift, and would fain recompense it with this precious purple flower; but if I toss it into the air, it will not reach you. So Signor Guasconti must even content himself with my thanks."

She lifted the bouquet from the ground, and then as if inwardly ashamed at having stepped aside from her maidenly reserve to respond to a stranger's greeting, passed swiftly homeward through the garden. But, few as the moments were, it seemed to Giovanni when she was on the point of vanishing beneath the sculptured portal, that his beautiful bouquet was already beginning to wither in her grasp. It was an idle thought; there could be no possibility of distinguishing a faded flower from a fresh one, at so great a distance.

For many days after this incident, the young man avoided the window that looked into Doctor Rappaccini's garden, as if something ugly and monstrous would have blasted his eye-sight, had he been betrayed into a glance. He felt conscious of having put himself, to a certain extent, within the influence of an unintelligible power, by the communication which he had opened with Beatrice. The wisest course would have been, if his heart were in any real danger, to quit his lodgings and Padua itself, at once; the next wiser, to have accustomed himself, as far as possible, to the familiar and day-light view of Beatrice; thus bringing her rigidly and systematically within the limits of ordinary experience. Least of all, while avoiding her sight, should Giovanni have remained so near this extraordinary being, that the proximity and possibility even of intercourse, should give a kind of substance and reality to the wild vagaries which his imagination ran riot continually in producing. Guasconti had not a deep heart—or at all events, its depths were not sounded now—but he had a quick fancy, and an ardent southern temperament, which rose every instant to a higher fever-pitch. Whether or no Beatrice possessed those terrible attributes—that fatal breath—the affinity with those so beautiful and deadly flowers—which were indicated by what Giovanni had witnessed, she had at least instilled a fierce and subtle poison into his system. It was not love, although her rich beauty was a madness to him; nor horror, even while he fancied her spirit to be imbued with the same baneful essence that seemed to pervade her physical frame; but a wild offspring of both love and horror that had each parent in it, and burned like one and shivered like the other. Giovanni knew not what to dread; still less did he know what to hope; yet hope and dread kept a continual warfare in his breast, alternately vanquishing one another and starting up afresh to renew the contest. Blessed are all simple emotions, be they dark or bright! It is the lurid intermixture of the two that produces the illuminating blaze of the infernal regions.

Sometimes he endeavoured to assuage the fever of his spirit by a rapid walk through the streets of Padua, or beyond its gates; his footsteps kept time with the throbbings of his brain, so that the walk was apt to accelerate itself to a race. One day, he found himself arrested; his arm was seized by a portly personage who had turned back on recognising the young man, and expended much breath in overtaking him.

"Signor Giovanni!—stay, my young friend!" cried he. "Have you forgotten me? That might well be the case, if I were as much altered as yourself."

It was Baglioni, whom Giovanni had avoided, ever since their first meeting, from a doubt that the Professor's sagacity would look too deeply into his secrets. Endeavouring to recover himself, he stared forth wildly from his inner world into the outer one, and spoke like a man in a dream.

"Yes; I am Giovanni Guasconti. You are Professor Pietro Baglioni. Now let me pass!"

"Not yet—not yet, Signor Giovanni Guasconti," said the Professor, smiling, but at the same time scrutinising the youth with an earnest glance. "What, did I grow up side by side with your father, and shall his son pass me like a stranger, in these old streets of Padua? Stand still, Signor Giovanni; for we must have a word or two before we part."

"Speedily, then, most worshipful Professor—speedily!" said Giovanni, with feverish impatience. "Does not your worship see that I am in haste?"

Now, while he was speaking, there came a man in black along the street, stooping and moving feebly, like a person in inferior health. His face was all overspread with a most sickly and sallow hue, but yet so pervaded with an expression of piercing and active intellect, that an observer might easily have overlooked the merely physical attributes, and have seen only this wonderful energy. As he passed, this person exchanged a cold and distant salutation with Baglioni, but fixed his eyes upon Giovanni with an intentness that seemed to bring out whatever was within him worthy of notice. Nevertheless, there was a peculiar quietness in the look, as if taking merely a speculative, not a human interest, in the young man.

"It is Doctor Rappaccini!" whispered the Professor, when the stranger had passed. "Has he ever seen your face before?"

"Not that I know," answered Giovanni, starting at the name.

"He *has* seen you!—he must have seen you!" said Baglioni, hastily. "For some purpose or other, this man of science is making a study of you. I know that look of his! It is the same that coldly illuminates his face, as he bends over a bird, a mouse, or a butterfly, which, in pursuance of some experiment, he has killed by the perfume of a flower—a look as deep as nature itself, but without nature's warmth of love. Signor Giovanni, I will stake my life upon it, you are the subject of one of Rappaccini's experiments!"

"Will you make a fool of me?" cried Giovanni, passionately. "*That*, Signor Professor, were an untoward experiment."

"Patience, patience!" replied the imperturbable Professor. "I tell thee, my poor Giovanni, that Rappaccini has a scientific interest in thee. Thou hast fallen into fearful hands! And the Signora Beatrice? What part does she act in this mystery?"

But Guasconti, finding Baglioni's pertinacity intolerable, here broke away, and was gone before the Professor could again seize his arm. He looked after the young man intently, and shook his head.

"This must not be," said Baglioni to himself. "The youth is the son of my old friend, and shall not come to any harm from which the arcana of medical science can preserve him. Besides, it is too insufferable an impertinence in Rappaccini thus to snatch the lad out of my own hands, as I may say, and make use of him for his infernal experiments. This daughter of his! It shall be looked to. Perchance, most learned Rappaccini, I may foil you where you little dream of it!"

Meanwhile, Giovanni had pursued a circuitous route, and at length found himself at the door of his lodgings. As he crossed the threshold, he was met by old Lisabetta, who smirked and smiled, and was evidently desirous to attract his attention; vainly, however, as the ebullition of his feelings had momentarily subsided into a cold and dull vacuity. He turned his eyes full upon the withered face that was puckering itself into a smile, but seemed to behold it not. The old dame, therefore, laid her grasp upon his cloak.

"Signor!—Signor!" whispered she, still with a smile over the whole breadth of her visage, so that it looked not unlike a grotesque carving in wood, darkened by centuries—"Listen, Signor! There is a private entrance into the garden!"

"What do you say?" exclaimed Giovanni, turning quickly about, as if an inanimate thing should start into feverish life. "A private entrance into Doctor Rappaccini's garden!"

"Hush! hush!—not so loud!" whispered Lisabetta, putting her hand over his mouth. "Yes; into the worshipful Doctor's garden, where you may see all his fine shrubbery. Many a young man in Padua would give gold to be admitted among those flowers."

Giovanni put a piece of gold into her hand.

"Show me the way," said he.

A surmise, probably excited by his conversation with Baglioni, crossed his mind, that this interposition of old Lisabetta might perchance be connected with the intrigue, whatever were its nature, in which the Professor seemed to suppose that Doctor Rappaccini was involving him. But such a suspicion, though it disturbed Giovanni, was inadequate to restrain him. The instant he was aware of the possibility of approaching Beatrice, it seemed an absolute necessity of his existence to do so. It mattered not whether she were angel or demon; he was irrevocably within her sphere, and must obey the law that whirled him onward, in ever lessening circles, towards a result which he did not attempt to foreshadow. And yet, strange to say, there came across him a sudden doubt, whether this intense interest on his part were not delusory—whether it were really of so deep and positive a nature as to justify him in now thrusting himself into an incalculable position—whether it were not merely the fantasy of a young man's brain, only slightly, or not at all, connected with his heart!

He paused—hesitated—turned half about—but again went on. His withered guide led him along several obscure passages, and finally undid a door, through which, as it was opened, there came the sight and sound of rustling leaves, with the broken sunshine glimmering among them. Giovanni stepped forth, and forcing himself through the entanglement of a shrub that wreathed its tendrils over the hidden entrance, he stood beneath his own window, in the open area of Doctor Rappaccini's garden.

How often is it the case, that, when impossibilities have come to pass, and dreams have condensed their misty substance into tangible realities, we find ourselves calm, and even coldly self-possessed, amid circumstances which it would have been a delirium of joy or agony to anticipate! Fate delights to thwart us thus. Passion will choose his own time to rush upon the scene, and lingers sluggishly behind, when an appropriate adjustment of events would seem to summon his appearance. So was it now with Giovanni. Day after day, his pulses had throbbed with feverish blood, at the improbable idea of an interview with Beatrice, and of standing with her, face to face, in this very garden, basking in the oriental sunshine of her beauty, and snatching from her full gaze the mystery which he deemed the riddle of his own existence. But now there was a singular and untimely equanimity within his breast. He threw a glance around the garden to discover if Beatrice or her father were present, and perceiving that he was alone, began a critical observation of the plants.

The aspect of one and all of them dissatisfied him; their gorgeousness seemed fierce, passionate, and even unnatural. There was hardly an individual shrub which a wanderer, straying by himself through a forest, would not have been startled to find growing wild, as if an unearthly face had glared at him out of the thicket. Several, also, would have shocked a delicate instinct by an appearance of artificialness, indicating that there had been such commixture, and, as it were, adultery of various vegetable species, that the production was no longer of God's making, but the monstrous offspring of man's depraved fancy, glowing with only an evil mockery of beauty. They were probably the result of experiment, which, in one or two cases, had succeeded in mingling plants individually lovely into a compound possessing the questionable and ominous character that distinguished the whole growth of the garden. In fine, Giovanni recognised but two or three plants in the collection, and those of a kind that he well knew to be poisonous. While busy with these contemplations, he heard the rustling of a silken garment, and turning, beheld Beatrice emerging from beneath the sculptured portal.

Giovanni had not considered with himself what should be his deportment; whether he should apologise for his intrusion into the garden, or assume that he was there with the privity, at least, if not by the desire, of Doctor Rappaccini or his daughter. But Beatrice's manner placed him at his ease, though leaving him still in doubt by what agency he had gained admittance. She came lightly along the path, and met him near the broken fountain. There was surprise in her face, but brightened by a simple and kind expression of pleasure.

"You are a connoisseur in flowers, Signor," said Beatrice with a smile, alluding to the bouquet which he had flung her from the window. "It is no marvel, therefore, if the sight of my father's rare collection has tempted you to take a nearer view. If he were here, he could tell you many strange and interesting facts as to the nature and habits of these shrubs, for he has spent a life-time in such studies, and this garden is his world."

"And yourself, lady"—observed Giovanni—"if fame says true, you, likewise, are deeply skilled in the virtues indicated by these rich blossoms, and these spicy perfumes. Would you deign to be my instructress, I should prove an apter scholar than under Signor Rappaccini himself."

"Are there such idle rumours?" asked Beatrice, with the music of a pleasant laugh. "Do people say that I am skilled in my father's science of plants? What a jest is there! No; though I have grown up among these flowers, I know no more of them than their hues and perfume; and sometimes, methinks I would fain rid myself of even that small knowledge. There are many flowers here, and those not the least brilliant, that shock and offend me, when they meet my eye. But, pray, Signor, do not believe these stories about my science. Believe nothing of me save what you see with your own eyes."

"And must I believe all that I have seen with my own eyes?" asked Giovanni pointedly, while the recollection of former scenes made him shrink. "No, Signora, you demand too little of me. Bid me believe nothing, save what comes from your own lips."

It would appear that Beatrice understood him. There came a deep flush to her cheek; but she looked full into Giovanni's eyes, and responded to his gaze of uneasy suspicion with a queen-like haughtiness.

"I do so bid you, Signor!" she replied. "Forget whatever you may have fancied in regard to me. If true to the outward senses, still it may be false in its essence. But the words of Beatrice Rappaccini's lips are true from the heart outward. Those you may believe!"

A fervour glowed in her whole aspect, and beamed upon Giovanni's consciousness like the light of truth itself. But while she spoke, there was a fragrance in the atmosphere around her rich and delightful, though evanescent, yet which the young man, from an indefinable reluctance, scarcely dared to draw into his lungs. It might be the odour of the flowers. Could it be Beatrice's breath, which thus embalmed her words with a strange richness, as if by steeping them in her heart? A faintness passed like a shadow over Giovanni, and flitted away; he seemed to gaze through the beautiful girl's eyes into her transparent soul, and felt no more doubt or fear.

The tinge of passion that had coloured Beatrice's manner vanished; she became gay, and appeared to derive a pure delight from her communion with the youth, not unlike what the maiden of a lonely island might have felt, conversing with a voyager from the civilised world. Evidently her experience of life had been confined within the limits of that garden. She talked now about matters as simple as the daylight or summer clouds, and now asked questions in reference to the city, or Giovanni's distant home, his friends, his mother, and his sisters; questions indicating such seclusion, and such lack of familiarity with modes and forms, that Giovanni responded as if to an infant. Her spirit gushed out before him like a fresh rill, that was just catching its first glimpse of the sunlight, and wondering, at the reflections of earth and sky which were flung into its bosom. There came thoughts, too, from a deep source, and fantasies of a gem-like brilliancy, as if diamonds and rubies sparkled upward among the bubbles of the fountain. Ever and anon, there gleamed across the young man's mind a sense of wonder, that he should be walking side by side with the being who had so wrought upon his imagination—whom he had idealised in such hues of terror—in whom he had positively witnessed such manifestations of dreadful attributes—that he should be conversing with Beatrice like a brother, and should find her so human and so maiden-like. But such reflections were only momentary; the effect of her character was too real, not to make itself familiar at once.

In this free intercourse, they had strayed through the garden, and now, after many turns among its avenues, were come to the shattered fountain, beside which grew the magnificent shrub with its treasury of glowing blossoms. A fragrance was diffused from it, which Giovanni recognised as identical with that which he had attributed to Beatrice's breath, but incomparably more powerful. As her eyes fell upon it, Giovanni beheld her press her hand to her bosom, as if her heart were throbbing suddenly and painfully.

"For the first time in my life," murmured she, addressing the shrub, "I had forgotten thee!"

"I remember, signora," said Giovanni, "that you once promised to reward me with one of these living gems for the bouquet, which I had the happy boldness to fling to your feet. Permit me now to pluck it as a memorial of this interview."

He made a step towards the shrub, with extended hand. But Beatrice darted forward, uttering a shriek that went through his heart like a dagger. She caught his hand, and drew it back with the whole force of her slender figure. Giovanni felt her touch thrilling through his fibres.

"Touch it not!" exclaimed she, in a voice of agony. "Not for thy life! It is fatal!"

Then, hiding her face, she fled from him, and vanished beneath the sculptured portal. As Giovanni followed her with his eyes, he beheld the emaciated figure and pale intelligence of Doctor Rappaccini, who had been watching the scene, he knew not how long, within the shadow of the entrance.

No sooner was Guasconti alone in his chamber, than the image of Beatrice came back to his passionate musings, invested with all the witchery that had been gathering around it ever since his first glimpse of her, and now likewise imbued with a tender warmth of girlish womanhood. She was human: her nature was endowed with all gentle and feminine qualities; she was worthiest to be worshipped; she was capable, surely, on her part, of the height and heroism of love. Those tokens, which he had hitherto considered as proofs of a frightful peculiarity in her physical and moral system, were now either forgotten, or, by the subtle sophistry of passion, transmuted into a golden crown of enchantment, rendering Beatrice the more admirable, by so much as she was the more unique. Whatever had looked ugly, was now beautiful; or, if incapable of such a change, it stole away and hid itself among those shapeless half-ideas, which throng the dim region beyond the daylight of our perfect consciousness. Thus did Giovanni spend the night, nor fell asleep, until the dawn had begun to awake the slumbering flowers in Doctor Rappaccini's garden, whither his dreams doubtless led him. Up rose the sun in his due season, and flinging his beams upon the young man's eyelids, awoke him to a sense of pain. When thoroughly aroused, he became sensible of a burning and tingling agony in his hand—in his right hand—the very hand which Beatrice had grasped in her own, when he was on the point of plucking one of the gem-like flowers. On the back of that hand there was now a purple print, like that of four small fingers, and the likeness of a slender thumb upon his wrist.

Oh, how stubbornly does love—or even that cunning semblance of love which flourishes in the imagination, but strikes no depth of root into the heart—how stubbornly does it hold its faith, until the moment come, when it is doomed to vanish into thin mist! Giovanni wrapt a handkerchief about his hand, and wondered what evil thing had stung him, and soon forgot his pain in a reverie of Beatrice.

After the first interview, a second was in the inevitable course of what we call fate. A third; a fourth; and a meeting with Beatrice in the garden was no longer an incident in Giovanni's daily life, but the whole space in which he might be said to live; for the anticipation and memory of that ecstatic hour made up the remainder. Nor was it otherwise with the daughter of Rappaccini. She watched for the youth's appearance, and flew to his side with confidence as unreserved as if they had been playmates from early infancy—as if they were such playmates still. If, by any unwonted chance, he failed to come at the appointed moment, she stood beneath the window, and sent up the rich sweetness of her tones to float around him in his chamber, and echo and reverberate throughout his heart—"Giovanni! Giovanni! Why tarriest thou? Come down!" And down he hastened into that Eden of poisonous flowers.

But, with all this intimate familiarity, there was still a reserve in Beatrice's demeanour, so rigidly and invariably sustained, that the idea of infringing it scarcely occurred to his imagination. By all appreciable signs, they loved; they had looked love, with eyes that conveyed the holy secret from the depths of one soul into the depths of the other, as if it were too sacred to be whispered by the way; they had even spoken love, in those gushes of passion when their spirits darted forth in articulated breath, like tongues of long-hidden flame; and yet there had been no seal of lips, no clasp of hands, nor any slightest caress, such as love claims and hallows. He had never touched one of the gleaming ringlets of her hair; her garment—so marked was the physical barrier between them—had never been waved against him by a breeze. On the few occasions when Giovanni had seemed tempted to overstep the limit, Beatrice grew so sad, so stern, and withal wore such a look of desolate separation, shuddering at itself, that not a spoken word was requisite to repel him. At such times, he was startled at the horrible suspicions that rose, monster-like, out of the caverns of his heart, and stared him in the face; his love grew thin and faint as the morning-mist; his doubts alone had substance. But when Beatrice's face brightened again, after the momentary shadow, she was transformed at once from the mysterious, questionable being, whom he had watched with so much awe and horror; she was now the beautiful and unsophisticated girl, whom he felt that his spirit knew with a certainty beyond all other knowledge.

A considerable time had now passed since Giovanni's last meeting with Baglioni. One morning, however, he was disagreeably surprised by a visit from the Professor, whom he had scarcely thought of for whole weeks, and would willingly have forgotten still longer. Given up, as he had long been, to a pervading excitement, he could tolerate no companions, except upon condition of their perfect sympathy with his present state of feeling. Such sympathy was not to be expected from Professor Baglioni.

The visitor chatted carelessly, for a few moments, about the gossip of the city and the University, and then took up another topic.

"I have been reading an old classic author lately," said he, "and met with a story that strangely interested me. Possibly you may remember it. It is of an Indian prince, who sent a beautiful woman as a present to Alexander the Great. She was as lovely as the dawn, and gorgeous as the sunset; but what especially distinguished her was a certain rich perfume in her breath—richer than a garden of Persian roses. Alexander, as was natural to a youthful conqueror, fell in love at first sight with this magnificent stranger. But a certain sage physician, happening to be present, discovered a terrible secret in regard to her."

"And what was that?" asked Giovanni, turning his eyes downward to avoid those of the Professor.

"That this lovely woman," continued Baglioni, with emphasis, "had been nourished with poisons from her birth upward, until her whole nature was so imbued with them, that she herself had become the deadliest poison in existence. Poison was her element of life. With that rich perfume of her breath, she blasted the very air. Her love would have been poison!—her embrace death! Is not this a marvellous tale?"

"A childish fable," answered Giovanni, nervously starting from his chair. "I marvel how your worship finds time to read such nonsense, among your graver studies."

"By the bye," said the Professor, looking uneasily about him, "what singular fragrance is this in your apartment? Is it the perfume of your gloves? It is faint, but delicious, and yet, after all, by no means agreeable. Were I to breathe it long, methinks it would make me ill. It is like the breath of a flower—but I see no flowers in the chamber."

"Nor are there any," replied Giovanni, who had turned pale as the Professor spoke; "nor, I think, is there any fragrance, except in your worship's imagination. Odours, being a sort of element combined of the sensual and the spiritual, are apt to deceive us in this manner. The recollection of a perfume—the bare idea of it—may easily be mistaken for a present reality."

"Ay; but my sober imagination does not often play such tricks," said Baglioni; "and were I to fancy any kind of odour, it would be that of some vile apothecary drug, wherewith my fingers are likely enough to be imbued. Our worshipful friend Rappaccini, as I have heard, tinctures his medicaments with odours richer than those of Araby. Doubtless, likewise, the fair and learned Signora Beatrice would minister to her patients with draughts as sweet as a maiden's breath. But woe to him that sips them!"

Giovanni's face evinced many contending emotions. The tone in which the Professor alluded to the pure and lovely daughter of Rappaccini was a torture to his soul; and yet, the intimation of a view of her character, opposite to his own, gave instantaneous distinctness to a thousand dim suspicions, which now grinned at him like so many demons. But he strove hard to quell them, and to respond to Baglioni with a true lover's perfect faith.

"Signor Professor," said he, "you were my father's friend—perchance, too, it is your purpose to act a friendly part towards his son.

I would fain feel nothing towards you save respect and deference. But I pray you to observe, Signor, that there is one subject on which we must not speak. You know not the Signora Beatrice. You cannot, therefore, estimate the wrong—the blasphemy, I may even say—that is offered to her character by a light or injurious word."

"Giovanni!—my poor Giovanni!" answered the Professor, with a calm expression of pity, "I know this wretched girl far better than yourself. You shall hear the truth in respect to the poisoner Rappaccini, and his poisonous daughter. Yes; poisonous as she is beautiful! Listen! for even should you do violence to my grey hairs, it shall not silence me. That old fable of the Indian woman has become a truth, by the deep and deadly science of Rappaccini, and in the person of the lovely Beatrice!"

Giovanni groaned, and hid his face.

"Her father," continued Baglioni, "was not restrained by natural affection from offering up his child, in this horrible manner, as the victim of his insane zeal for science. For—let us do him justice—he is as true a man of science as ever distilled his own heart in an alembic. What, then, will be your fate? Beyond a doubt, you are selected as the material of some new experiment. Perhaps the result is to be death—perhaps a fate more awful still! Rappaccini, with what he calls the interest of science before his eyes, will hesitate at nothing."

"It is a dream!" muttered Giovanni to himself; "surely, it is a dream!"

"But," resumed the Professor, "be of good cheer, son of my friend! It is not yet too late for the rescue. Possibly, we may even succeed in bringing back this miserable child within the limits of ordinary nature, from which her father's madness has estranged her. Behold this little silver vase! It was wrought by the hands of the renowned Benvenuto Cellini, and is well worthy to be a love-gift to the fairest dame in Italy.

But its contents are invaluable. One little sip of this antidote would have rendered the most virulent poisons of the Borgias innocuous. Doubt not that it will be as efficacious against those of Rappaccini. Bestow the vase, and the precious liquid within it, on your Beatrice, and hopefully await the result."

Baglioni laid a small, exquisitely wrought silver phial on the table, and withdrew, leaving what he had said to produce its effect upon the young man's mind.

"We will thwart Rappaccini yet!" thought he, chuckling to himself, as he descended the stairs. "But, let us confess the truth of him, he is a wonderful man!—a wonderful man, indeed! A vile empiric, however, in his practice, and therefore not to be tolerated by those who respect the good old rules of the medical profession!"

Throughout Giovanni's whole acquaintance with Beatrice, he had occasionally, as we have said, been haunted by dark surmises as to her character. Yet, so thoroughly had she made herself felt by him as a simple, natural, most affectionate and guileless creature, that the image now held up by Professor Baglioni, looked as strange and incredible, as if it were not in accordance with his own original conception. True, there were ugly recollections connected with his first glimpses of the beautiful girl; he could not quite forget the bouquet that withered in her grasp, and the insect that perished amid the sunny air, by no ostensible agency save the fragrance of her breath. These incidents, however, dissolving in the pure light of her character, had no longer the efficacy of facts, but were acknowledged as mistaken fantasies, by whatever testimony of the senses they might appear to be substantiated. There is something truer and more real, than what we can see with the eyes, and touch with the finger. On such better evidence had Giovanni founded his confidence in Beatrice, though rather by the necessary force of her high attributes, than by any deep and generous faith on his part. But, now, his spirit was incapable of sustaining itself at the height to which the early enthusiasm of passion had exalted it; he fell down, grovelling among earthly doubts, and defiled therewith the pure whiteness of Beatrice's image. Not that he gave her up; he did but distrust. He resolved to institute some decisive test that should satisfy him, once for all, whether there were those dreadful peculiarities in her physical nature, which could not be supposed to exist without some corresponding monstrosity of soul. His eyes, gazing down afar, might have deceived him as to the lizard, the insect, and the flowers. But if he could witness, at the distance of a few paces, the sudden blight of one fresh and healthful flower in Beatrice's hand, there would be room for no further question. With this idea, he hastened to the florist's, and purchased a bouquet that was still gemmed with the morning dew-drops.

It was now the customary hour of his daily interview with Beatrice. Before descending into the garden, Giovanni failed not to look at his figure in the mirror; a vanity to be expected in a beautiful young man, yet, as displaying itself at that troubled and feverish moment, the token of a certain shallowness of feeling and insincerity of character. He did gaze, however, and said to himself, that his features had never before possessed so rich a grace, nor his eyes such vivacity, nor his cheeks so warm a hue of superabundant life.

"At least," thought he, "her poison has not yet insinuated itself into my system. I am no flower to perish in her grasp!"

With that thought, he turned his eyes on the bouquet, which he had never once laid aside from his hand. A thrill of indefinable horror shot through his frame, on perceiving that those dewy flowers were already beginning to droop; they wore the aspect of things that had been fresh and lovely, yesterday. Giovanni grew white as marble, and stood motionless before the mirror, staring at his own reflection there, as at the likeness of something frightful. He remembered Baglioni's remark about the fragrance that seemed to pervade the chamber. It must have been the poison in his breath! Then he shuddered—shuddered at himself! Recovering from his stupor, he began to watch, with curious eye, a spider that was busily at work, hanging its web from the antique cornice of the apartment, crossing and re-crossing the artful system of interwoven lines, as vigorous and active a spider as ever dangled from an old ceiling. Giovanni bent towards the insect, and emitted a deep, long breath. The spider suddenly ceased its toil; the web vibrated with a tremor originating in the body of the small artisan. Again Giovanni sent forth a breath, deeper, longer, and imbued with a venomous feeling out of his heart; he knew not whether he were wicked, or only desperate. The spider made a convulsive gripe with his limbs, and hung dead across the window.

"Accursed! accursed!" muttered Giovanni, addressing himself. "Hast thou grown so poisonous, that this deadly insect perishes by thy breath?"

At that moment, a rich, sweet voice came floating up from the garden:

"Giovanni! Giovanni! It is past the hour! Why tarriest thou? Come down!"

"Yes," muttered Giovanni again—"she is the only being whom my breath may not slay! Would that it might!"

He rushed down, and, in an instant, was standing before the bright and loving eyes of Beatrice. A moment ago, his wrath and despair had been so fierce that he could have desired nothing so much as to wither her by a glance. But, with her actual presence, there came influences which had too real an existence to be at once shaken off; recollections of the delicate and benign power of her feminine nature, which had so often enveloped him in a religious calm; recollections of many a holy and passionate out-gush of her heart, when the pure fountain had been unsealed from its depths, and made visible in its transparency to his mental eye; recollections which, had Giovanni known how to estimate them, would have assured him that all this ugly mystery was but an earthly illusion, and that, whatever mist of evil might seem to have gathered over her, the real Beatrice was a heavenly angel. Incapable as he was of such high faith, still her presence had not utterly lost its magic. Giovanni's rage was quelled into an aspect of sullen insensibility. Beatrice, with a quick spiritual sense, immediately felt that there was a gulf of blackness between them, which neither he nor she could pass. They walked on together, sad and silent, and came thus to the marble fountain, and to its pool of water on the ground, in the midst of which grew the shrub that bore gem-like blossoms. Giovanni was affrighted at the eager enjoyment—the appetite, as it were—with which he found himself inhaling the fragrance of the flowers.

"Beatrice," asked he, abruptly, "whence came this shrub?"

"My father created it," answered she, with simplicity.

"Created it! created it!" repeated Giovanni. "What mean you, Beatrice?"

"He is a man fearfully acquainted with the secrets of nature," replied Beatrice; "and, at the hour when I first drew breath, this plant sprang from the soil, the offspring of his science, of his intellect, while I was but his earthly child. Approach it not!" continued she, observing with terror that Giovanni was drawing nearer to the shrub. "It has qualities that you little dream of. But I, dearest Giovanni—I grew up and blossomed with the plant, and was nourished with its breath. It was my sister, and I loved it with a human affection: for—alas! hast thou not suspected it?—there was an awful doom."

Here Giovanni frowned so darkly upon her that Beatrice paused and trembled. But her faith in his tenderness reassured her, and made her blush that she had doubted for an instant.

"There was an awful doom," she continued—"the effect of my father's fatal love of science—which estranged me from all society of my kind. Until Heaven sent thee, dearest Giovanni, oh! how lonely was thy poor Beatrice!"

"Was it a hard doom?" asked Giovanni, fixing his eyes upon her.

"Only of late have I known how hard it was," answered she, tenderly. "Oh, yes; but my heart was torpid, and therefore quiet."

Giovanni's rage broke forth from his sullen gloom like a lightning-flash out of a dark cloud.

"Accursed one!" cried he, with venomous scorn and anger—"and finding thy solitude wearisome, thou hast severed me, likewise, from all the warmth of life, and enticed me into thy region of unspeakable horror!"

"Giovanni!" exclaimed Beatrice, turning her large bright eyes upon his face. The force of his words had not found its way into her mind; she was merely thunderstruck.

"Yes, poisonous thing!" repeated Giovanni, beside himself with passion—"thou hast done it! Thou hast blasted me! Thou hast filled my veins with poison! Thou hast made me as hateful, as ugly, as loathsome and deadly a creature as thyself—a world's wonder of hideous monstrosity! Now—if our breath be happily as fatal to ourselves as to all others—let us join our lips in one kiss of unutterable hatred, and so die!"

"What has befallen me?" murmured Beatrice, with a low moan out of her heart. "Holy Virgin, pity me, a poor heart-broken child!"

"Thou! dost thou pray?" cried Giovanni, still with the same fiendish scorn. "Thy very prayers, as they come from thy lips, taint the atmosphere with death. Yes, yes; let us pray! Let us to church, and dip our fingers in the holy water at the portal! They that come after us will perish as by a pestilence. Let us sign crosses in the air! It will be scattering curses abroad in the likeness of holy symbols!"

"Giovanni," said Beatrice calmly, for her grief was beyond passion, "Why dost thou join thyself with me thus in those terrible words? I, it is true, am the horrible thing thou namest me. But thou!—what hast thou to do, save with one other shudder at my hideous misery, to go forth out of the garden, and mingle with thy race, and forget that there ever crawled on earth such a monster as poor Beatrice?"

"Dost thou pretend ignorance?" asked Giovanni, scowling upon her. "Behold! This power have I gained from the pure daughter of Rappaccini!"

There was a swarm of summer-insects flitting through the air, in search of the food promised by the flower-odours of the fatal garden. They circled round Giovanni's head, and were evidently attracted towards him by the same influence which had drawn them, for an instant, within the sphere of several of the shrubs. He sent forth a breath among them, and smiled bitterly at Beatrice, as at least a score of the insects fell dead upon the ground.

"I see it! I see it!" shrieked Beatrice. "It is my father's fatal science? No, no, Giovanni; it was not I! Never, never! I dreamed only to love thee, and be with thee a little time, and so to let thee pass away, leaving but thine image in mine heart. For, Giovanni—believe it—though my body be nourished with poison, my spirit is God's creature, and craves love as its daily food. But my father!—he has united us in this fearful sympathy. Yes; spurn me!—tread upon me!—kill me! Oh, what is death, after such words as thine? But it was not I! Not for a world of bliss would I have done it!"

Giovanni's passion had exhausted itself in its outburst from his lips. There now came across him a sense, mournful, and not without tenderness, of the intimate and peculiar relationship between Beatrice and himself. They stood, as it were, in an utter solitude, which would be made none the less solitary by the densest throng of human life. Ought not, then, the desert of humanity around them to press this insulated pair closer together? If they should be cruel to one another, who was there to be kind to them? Besides, thought Giovanni, might there not still be a hope of his returning within the limits of ordinary nature, and leading Beatrice—the redeemed Beatrice—by the hand? Oh, weak, and selfish, and unworthy spirit, that could dream of an earthly union and earthly happiness as possible, after such deep love had been so bitterly wronged as was Beatrice's love by Giovanni's blighting words! No, no; there could be no such hope. She must pass heavily, with that broken heart, across the borders—she must bathe her hurts in some fount of Paradise, and forget her grief in the light of immortality—and *there* be well!

But Giovanni did not know it.

"Dear Beatrice," said he, approaching her, while she shrank away, as always, at his approach, but now with a different impulse—"dearest Beatrice, our fate is not yet so desperate. Behold! There is a medicine, potent, as a wise physician has assured me, and almost divine in its efficacy. It is composed of ingredients the most opposite to those by which thy awful father has brought this calamity upon thee and me. It is distilled of blessed herbs. Shall we not quaff it together, and thus be purified from evil?"

"Give it me!" said Beatrice, extending her hand to receive the little silver phial which Giovanni took from his bosom. She added, with a peculiar emphasis: "I will drink—but do thou await the result."

She put Baglioni's antidote to her lips; and, at the same moment, the figure of Rappaccini emerged from the portal, and came slowly towards the marble fountain. As he drew near, the pale man of science seemed to gaze with a triumphant expression at the beautiful youth and maiden, as might an artist who should spend his life in achieving a picture or a group of statuary, and finally be satisfied with his success. He paused—his bent form grew erect with conscious power, he spread out his hand over them, in the attitude of a father imploring a blessing upon his children. But those were the same hands that had thrown poison into the stream of their lives! Giovanni trembled. Beatrice shuddered very nervously, and pressed her hand upon her heart.

"My daughter," said Rappaccini, "thou art no longer lonely in the world! Pluck one of those precious gems from thy sister shrub, and bid thy bridegroom wear it in his bosom. It will not harm him now! My science, and the sympathy between thee and him, have so wrought within his system, that he now stands apart from common men, as thou dost, daughter of my pride and triumph, from ordinary women. Pass on, then, through the world, most dear to one another, and dreadful to all besides!"

"My father," said Beatrice, feebly—and still, as she spoke, she kept her hand upon her heart—"wherefore didst thou inflict this miserable doom upon thy child?"

"Miserable!" exclaimed Rappaccini. "What mean you, foolish girl? Dost thou deem it misery to be endowed with marvellous gifts, against which no power nor strength could avail an enemy? Misery, to be able to quell the mightiest with a breath? Misery, to be as terrible as thou art beautiful? Wouldst thou, then, have preferred the condition of a weak woman, exposed to all evil, and capable of none?"

"I would fain have been loved, not feared," murmured Beatrice, sinking down upon the ground. "But now it matters not; I am going, father, where the evil, which thou hast striven to mingle with my being, will pass away like a dream—like the fragrance of these poison-ous flowers, which will no longer taint my breath among the flowers of Eden. Farewell, Giovanni! Thy words of hatred are like lead within my heart—but they, too, will fall away as I ascend. Oh, was there not, from the first, more poison in thy nature than in mine?"

To Beatrice—so radically had her earthly part been wrought upon by Rappaccini's skill—as poison had been life, so the power-ful antidote was death. And thus the poor victim of man's ingenuity and of thwarted nature, and of the fatality that attends all such efforts of perverted wisdom, perished there, at the feet of her father and Giovanni. Just at that moment, Professor Pietro Baglioni looked forth from the window, and called loudly, in a tone of triumph, mixed with horror, to the thunder-stricken man of science:

"Rappaccini! Rappaccini! And is *this* the upshot of your experiment?"

THE AMERICAN'S TALE

Arthur Conan Doyle

Best known for creating Sherlock Holmes, Arthur Conan Doyle is the author of the second story in this anthology. "The American's Tale" precedes the well-known detective by nearly a decade and allows Doyle to show off his impressive gothic writing. The story was published in the literary magazine *London Society*, Christmas Number, 1880. The story involves a quarrel between British citizens in America and a disgruntled American. After their altercation, the American Joe Hawkins heads out into the night and follows Tom Scott through the gulch towards his home with malicious intentions, only to disappear mysteriously.

This man-eating plant story is particularly unique as it hybridises genres, being part Western as well as part Gothic, and the reader is ultimately left to discern whether it was a true account or a mere tall tale. Conan Doyle exploits the evocative Venus flytrap plant with its toothy and jaw-like appearance and creates fear by effectively minimising the tough male characters; the flytraps are eight to ten feet wide and capable of engulfing an adult victim.

"IT air strange, it air," he was saying as I opened the door of the room where our social little semi-literary society met; "but I could tell you queerer things than that 'ere—almighty queer things. You can't learn everything out of books, sirs, nohow. You see, it ain't the men as can string English together, and as has had good eddications, as finds themselves in the queer places I've been in. They're mostly rough men, sirs, as can scarce speak aright, far less tell with pen and ink the things they've seen; but if they could they'd make some of you Europeans har riz with astonishment. They would, sirs, you bet!"

His name was Jefferson Adams, I believe; I know his initials were J. A., for you may see them yet deeply whittled on the right-hand upper panel of our smoking-room door. He left us this legacy, and also some artistic patterns done in tobacco juice upon our Turkey carpet; but beyond these reminiscences our American story-teller has vanished from our ken. He gleamed across our ordinary quiet conviviality like some brilliant meteor, and then was lost in the outer darkness. That night, however, our Nevada friend was in full swing; and I quietly lighted my pipe and dropped into the nearest chair, anxious not to interrupt his story.

"Mind you," he continued, "I haven't got no grudge against your men of science. I likes and respects a chap as can match every beast and plant, from a huckleberry to a grizzly, with a jaw-breakin' name; but if you wants real interestin' facts, something a bit juicy, you go to your whalers and your frontiersmen, and your scouts and Hudson Bay men, chaps who mostly can scarce sign their names."

51

There was a pause here, as Mr Jefferson Adams produced a long cheroot and lighted it. We preserved a strict silence in the room, for we had already learned that on the slightest interruption our Yankee drew himself into his shell again. He glanced round with a self-satisfied smile as he remarked our expectant looks, and continued through a halo of smoke:

"Now, which of you gentlemen has ever been in Arizona? None, I'll warrant. And of all English or Americans as can put pen to paper, how many has been in Arizona? Precious few, I calc'late. I've been there, sirs, lived there for years; and when I think of what I've seen there, why, I can scarce get myself to believe it now.

"Ah, there's a country! I was one of Walker's filibusters, as they chose to call us; and after we'd busted up, and the chief was shot, some on us made tracks and located down there. A reg'lar English and American colony, we was, with our wives and children, and all complete. I reckon there's some of the old folk there yet, and that they hain't forgotten what I'm a-going to tell you. No, I warrant they hain't, never on this side of the grave, sirs.

"I was talking about the country, though; and I guess I could astonish you considerable if I spoke of nothing else. To think of such a land being built for a few 'Greasers' and half-breeds! It's a misusing of the gifts of Providence, that's what I calls it. Grass as hung over a chap's head as he rode through it, and trees so thick that you couldn't catch a glimpse of blue sky for leagues and leagues, and orchids like umbrellas! Maybe some on you has seen a plant as they calls the 'fly-catcher' in some parts of the States?"

"Dionœa muscipula," murmured Dawson, our scientific man *par excellence*.

"Ah, 'Die near a municipal,' that's him! You'll see a fly stand on that 'ere plant, and then you'll see the two sides of a leaf snap up together and catch it between them, and grind it up and mash it to bits, for all the world like some great sea squid with its beak; and hours after, if you open the leaf, you'll see the body lying half-digested, and in bits. Well, I've seen those fly-traps in Arizona with leaves eight and ten feet long, and thorns or teeth a foot or more; why, they could— But darn it, I'm going too fast!

"It's about the death of Joe Hawkins I was going to tell you; 'bout as queer a thing, I reckon, as ever you heard tell on. There wasn't nobody in Arizona as didn't know of Joe Hawkins—'Alabama' Joe, as he was called there. A reg'lar out and outer, he was, 'bout the darnedest skunk as ever man clapt eyes on. He was a good chap enough, mind ye, as long as you stroked him the right way; but rile him anyhow, and he were worse nor a wildcat. I've seen him empty his six-shooter into a crowd as chanced to jostle him a-going into Simpson's bar when there was a dance on; and he bowied Tom Hooper 'cause he spilt his liquor over his weskit by mistake. No, he didn't stick at murder, Joe didn't; and he weren't a man to be trusted further nor you could see him.

"Now, at the time I tell on, when Joe Hawkins was swaggerin' about the town and layin' down the law with his shootin'-irons, there was an Englishman there of the name of Scott—Tom Scott, if I rec'lects aright. This chap Scott was a thorough Britisher (beggin' the present company's pardon), and yet he didn't freeze much to the British set there, or they didn't freeze much to him. He was a quiet, simple man, Scott was—rather too quiet for a rough set like that; sneakin', they called him, but he weren't that. He kept hisself mostly apart, and didn't interfere with nobody so long as he were left alone. Some said as how he'd been kinder ill-treated at home—been a Chartist, or something of that sort, and had to up stick and run; but he never spoke of it hisself, an' never complained. Bad luck or good, that chap kept a stiff lip on him.

"This chap Scott was a sort o' butt among the men about Arizona, for he was so quiet an' simple-like. There was no party either to take up his grievances; for, as I've been saying, the Britishers hardly counted him one of them, and many a rough joke they played on him. He never cut up rough, but was polite to all hisself. I think the boys got to think he hadn't much grit in him till he showed 'em their mistake.

"It was in Simpson's bar as the row got up, an' that led to the queer thing I was going to tell you of. Alabama Joe and one or two other rowdies were dead on the Britishers in those days, and they spoke their opinions pretty free, though I warned them as there'd be an almighty muss. That partic'lar night Joe was nigh half drunk, an' he swaggered about the town with his six-shooter, lookin' out for a quarrel. Then he turned into the bar, where he know'd he'd find some o' the English as ready for one as he was hisself. Sure enough, there was half a dozen lounging about, an' Tom Scott standin' alone before the stove. Joe sat down by the table, and put his revolver and bowie down in front of him. 'Them's my arguments, Jeff,' he says to me, 'if any white-livered Britisher dares give me the lie.' I tried to stop him, sirs; but he weren't a man as you could easily turn, an' he began to speak in a way as no chap could stand. Why, even a 'Greaser' would flare up if you said as much of Greaserland! There was a commotion at the bar, an' every man laid his hands on his wepins; but before they could draw, we heard a quiet voice from the stove: 'Say your prayers, Joe Hawkins; for, by Heaven, you're a dead man!' Joe turned round, and looked like grabbin' at his iron; but it weren't no manner of use. Tom Scott was standing up, covering him with his derringer, a smile on his white face, but the very devil shining in his eye. 'It ain't that the old country has used me over-well,' he says, 'but no man shall speak agin it afore me, and live.' For a second or two I could see his finger tighten round the trigger, an' then he gave a laugh, an' threw the pistol on the floor. 'No,' he says, 'I can't shoot a half-drunk man. Take your dirty life, Joe, an' use it better nor you have done. You've been nearer the grave this night than you will be ag'in until your time comes. You'd best make tracks now, I guess. Nay, never look back at me, man; I'm not afeard at your shootin'-iron. A bully's nigh always a coward.' And he swung contemptuously round, and relighted his half-smoked pipe from the stove, while Alabama slunk out o' the bar, with the laughs of the Britishers ringing in his ears. I saw his face as he passed me, and on it I saw murder, sirs—murder, as plain as ever I seed anything in my life.

"I stayed in the bar after the row, and watched Tom Scott as he shook hands with the men about. It seemed kinder queer to me to see him smilin' and cheerful-like; for I knew Joe's bloodthirsty mind, and that the Englishman had small chance of ever seeing the morning. He lived in an out-of-the-way sort of place, you see, clean off the trail, and had to pass through the Flytrap Gulch to get to it. This here gulch was a marshy, gloomy place, lonely enough during the day even; for it were always a creepy sort o' thing to see the great eight- and ten-foot leaves snapping up if aught touched them; but at night there were never a soul near. Some parts of the marsh, too, were soft and deep, and a body thrown in would be gone by the morning. I could see Alabama Joe crouchin' under the leaves of the great Flytrap in the darkest part of the gulch, with a scowl on his face and a revolver in his hand; I could see it, sirs, as plain as with my two eyes.

"'Bout midnight Simpson shuts up his bar, so out we had to go. Tom Scott started off for his three-mile walk at a slashing pace. I just dropped him a hint as he passed me, for I kinder liked the chap. 'Keep your derringer loose in your belt, sir,' I says, 'for you might chance to need it.' He looked round at me with his quiet smile, and then I lost sight of him in the gloom. I never thought to see him again. He'd hardly gone afore Simpson comes up to me and says: 'There'll be a nice job in the Flytrap Gulch to-night, Jeff; the boys say that Hawkins started half an hour ago to wait for Scott and shoot him on sight. I calc'late the coroner'll be wanted to-morrow.'

"What passed in the gulch that night? It were a question as were asked pretty free next morning. A drifter was in Ferguson's store after daybreak, and he said as he'd chanced to be near the gulch 'bout one in the morning. It warn't easy to get at his story, he seemed so uncommon scared; but he told us, at last, as he'd heard the fearfulest screams in the stillness of the night. There weren't no shots, he said, but scream after scream, kinder muffled, like a man with a serape over his head, an' in mortal pain. Abner Brandon, and me, and a few more was in the store at the time; so we mounted and rode out to Scott's house, passing through the gulch on the way. There weren' nothing partic'lar to be seen there—no blood nor marks of a fight, nor nothing; and when we gets up to Scott's house out he comes to meet us as fresh as a lark. 'Halloo, Jeff!' says he, 'no need for the pistols after all. Come in an' have a cocktail, boys.' 'Did ye see or hear nothing as ye came home last night?' says I. 'No,' says he; 'all was quiet enough. An owl kinder moaning in the Flytrap Gulch—that was all. Come, jump off and have a glass.' 'Thank ye,' says Abner. So off we gets, and Tom Scott rode into the settlement with us when we went back.

"An all-fired commotion was on in Main Street as we rode into it. The 'Merican party seemed to have gone clean crazed. Alabama Joe was gone, not a darned particle of him left. Since he went out to the gulch nary eye had seen him. As we got off our horses there was a considerable crowd in front of Simpson's, and some ugly looks at Tom Scott, I can tell you. There was a clickin' of pistols, and I saw as Scott had his hand in his bosom, too. There weren't a single English face about. 'Stand aside, Jeff Adams,' says Zebb Humphrey, as great a scoundrel as ever lived; 'you hain't got no hand in this game. Say, boys, are we, free Americans, to be murdered by any darned Britisher?' It was the quickest thing as ever I seed. There was a rush an' a crack; Zebb was down, with Scott's ball in his thigh, and Scott hisself was on the ground with a dozen men holding him. It weren't no use struggling, so he lay quiet. They seemed a bit uncertain what to do with him at first, but then one of Alabama's special chums put them up to it. 'Joe's gone,' he said; 'nothing ain't surer nor that, an' there lies the man as killed him. Some on you knows as Joe went on business to the gulch last night; he never came back. That 'ere Britisher passed through after he'd gone; they'd had a row, screams is heard 'mong the great flytraps. I say ag'in, he has played poor Joe some o' his sneakin' tricks, an' thrown him into the swamp. It ain't no wonder as the body is gone. But air we to stan' by and see English murderin' our own chums? I guess not. Let Judge Lynch try him, that's what I say.' 'Lynch him!' shouted a hundred angry voices—for all the rag-tag an' bobtail o' the settlement was round us by this time. 'Here, boys, fetch a rope, and swing him up. Up with him over Simpson's door!' 'See here, though,' says another, coming forward; 'let's hang him by the great flytrap in the gulch. Let Joe see as he's revenged, if so be as he's buried 'bout theer.' There was a shout for this, an' away they went, with Scott tied on his mustang in the middle, and a mounted guard, with cocked revolvers, round him; for we knew as there was a score or so Britishers about, as didn't seem to recognise Judge Lynch, and was dead on a free fight.

"I went out with them, my heart bleedin' for Scott, though he didn't seem a cent put out, he didn't. He were game to the backbone. Seems kinder queer, sirs, hangin' a man to a flytrap; but our'n were a reg'lar tree, and the leaves like a brace of boats with a hinge between 'em and thorns at the bottom.

"We passed down the gulch to the place where the great one grows, and there we seed it with the leaves, some open, some shut. But we seed something worse nor that. Standin' round the tree was some thirty men, Britishers all, an' armed to the teeth. They was waitin' for us, evidently, an' had a business-like look about 'em as if they'd come for something and meant to have it. There was the raw material there for about as warm a scrimmidge as ever I seed. As we rode up, a great red-bearded Scotchman—Cameron were his name—stood out afore the rest, his revolver cocked in his hand. 'See here, boys,' he says, 'you've got no call to hurt a hair of that man's head. You hain't proved as Joe is dead yet; and if you had, you hain't proved as Scott killed him. Anyhow, it were in self-defence; for you all know as he was lying in wait for Scott, to shoot him on sight; so I say ag'in, you hain't got no call to hurt that man; and what's more, I've got thirty-six-barrelled arguments against your doin' it.' 'It's an interestin' p'int, and worth arguin' out,' said the man as was Alabama Joe's special chum. There was a clickin' of pistols, and a loosenin' of knives, and the two parties began to draw up to one another, an' it looked like a rise in the mortality of Arizona. Scott was standing behind with a pistol at his ear if he stirred, lookin' quiet and composed as having no money on the table, when sudden he gives a start an' a shout as rang in our ears like a trumpet. 'Joe!' he cried, 'Joe! Look at him! In the flytrap!' We all turned an' looked where he was pointin'. Jerusalem! I think we won't get that picter out of our minds ag'in. One of the great leaves of the flytrap, that had been shut and touchin' the ground as it lay, was slowly rolling back upon its hinges. There, lying like a child in its cradle, was Alabama Joe in the hollow of the leaf. The great thorns had been slowly driven through his heart as it shut upon him. We could see as he'd tried to cut his way out, for there was a slit on the thick, fleshy leaf, an' his bowie was in his hand;

but it had smothered him first. He'd lain down on it likely to keep the damp off while he were a-waitin' for Scott, and it had closed on him as you've seen your little hothouse ones do on a fly; an' there he were as we found him, torn and crushed into pulp by the great, jagged teeth of the man-eatin' plant. There, sirs, I think you'll own as that's a curious story."

"And what became of Scott?" asked Jack Sinclair.

"Why, we carried him back on our shoulders, we did, to Simpson's bar, and he stood us liquors round. Made a speech, too—a darned fine speech—from the counter. Somethin' about the British lion an' the 'Merican eagle walkin' arm in arm forever an' a day. And now, sirs, that yarn was long, and my cheroot's out, so I reckon I'll make tracks afore it's later;" and with a "Good-night!" he left the room.

"A most extraordinary narrative!" said Dawson. "Who would have thought a Dionœa had such power!"

"Deuced rum yarn!" said young Sinclair.

"Evidently a matter-of-fact, truthful man," said the doctor.

"Or the most original liar that ever lived," said I. I wonder which he was.

CARNIVORINE

Lucy H. Hooper

Lucy H. Hooper's "Carnivorine" is perhaps one of the more obscure titles in this collection. It was published in *Peterson's Magazine* in 1889, and follows the tale of Ellis Graham, who searches for his dear friend Mrs Lambert's lost son Julius. After having lost contact with her son, she hears of his involvement with a lady called "Carnivorine". Concerned, she entrusts her friend to search for him in Europe where he had gone to conduct his scientific experiments. After tracking him down, Ellis Graham learns that Julius is on the brink of a remarkable discovery. "Carnivorine" encapsulates the killer plant horror theme of hybridity as Julius Lambert shares his theory of the mythic origins of carnivorous plants.

hen I, Ellis Graham, being a man of middle age, means, and leisure, determined upon starting, last autumn, for Rome, with a view to studying up the localities for my projected history of the Cenci family, I never expected assuredly that a momentous and important task, regarding other people's affairs and not my own, should be imposed upon me. Yet I could not well refuse the mission. I had known the Lambert family for many years, and had always cherished a warm friendship for Mr and Mrs Lambert—a friendship which, after the demise of the former, I had continued to his widow. And Julius, the elder son, had been quite a favourite of mine in his boyish days, though I could not altogether sympathise with his craze for scientific pursuits, and especially for botany. It must be confessed, however, that his researches into the formation and functions of the vegetable kingdom had led to some curious discoveries. But these discoveries had only served to arouse in his mind, as he grew to manhood, a wild ambition for further successes in the same line. I never exactly comprehended what course his investigations had taken, but I knew he was deeply interested in the Darwinian theories, and had set himself, in that connection, some inscrutable problem that he was trying to make out. He lived such a secluded life, shut up with his plants and his theories, that I had wholly lost sight of him for some years, though my visits to Mrs Lambert were still continued.

I was a good deal surprised, however, on the eve of my departure for Europe, to receive from my old friend a few hurried lines, begging that I would call to see her before I left and fixing the very next evening for my visit. I responded to the appeal, and found the usually serene and dignified lady in a state of unwonted emotion.

"I have sent for you, dear Mr Graham," she said, "to ask if you will undertake for me a very important mission. It is hardly right, I know, for me to make such a request of you, involving, as your consent will surely do, a good deal of trouble and the loss of a considerable portion of your time. But my peace of mind is at stake, and I do not know what else to do if you are not willing to help me."

"Anything that is in my power to execute, dear Mrs Lambert, I will gladly undertake," I answered. And, indeed, I was so much moved by her distress and by noticing the traces left upon her still fair features by wearing anxiety, that I was ready to promise anything or to undertake anything in her behalf.

"I want you to find Julius for me."

"Julius? Is he absent from home? I did not even know that he had gone away."

"Yes; he sailed for Europe three years ago. You know, his uncle left him a handsome fortune a little before that time, and he went abroad—to pursue, as he stated, his scientific experiments. I know that he believed himself to be on the verge of a great discovery; but, of what nature that discovery was, he never would reveal, even to me. As you may remember, I have never sympathised with him in his studies, so I suppose he did not consider me worthy of his confidence. Perhaps I did wrong. Maybe, if I had interested myself more in his pursuits, he would not have left me as he has done. He told me, before he went away, that his experiments must be perfected in thorough seclusion, and that he never meant to relinquish them till he had arrived at some great result. We heard from him, afterward, at Paris, and later on, at Milan; but he has not written to his brothers or to me for months."

"Have you no idea as to his whereabouts at present?"

"I have reason to think that he has taken up his abode somewhere in the neighbourhood of Rome. He was seen there, two winters ago, by Alan Spencer, the artist—who had quite a talk with him, but who could find out nothing from him respecting his residence or his pursuits."

"Did he seem well?"

"He looked tired and haggard, Mr Spencer said, but was otherwise well. The reason for my anxiety is—is—well, I may as well confess it to you at once: I fear that there is some entanglement in the case—a passion for some woman, who may entrap Julius into matrimony."

"And have you any foundation for this dread?"

"Only this: he let fall something to Mr Spencer about a personage called Carnivorine."

"What an extraordinary name! Did he give his friend any information concerning her?"

"No. He was singularly reticent on the subject, and seemed really distressed at having let even her name slip out unawares. He requested Mr Spencer never to mention it; but Alan has always been on very intimate terms with Richard and Maude, and, seeing how uneasy we were at Julius's long silence, he did not hesitate, not having made any promise of secrecy, to tell us the little that he knew. So, when you reach Rome, if you will try to find our lost Julius for us, I shall be more indebted to you than I can well tell you."

I promised to do my best, and Mrs Lambert, visibly relieved, added some details about her son's banker in Rome and also respecting the few persons that he knew in that city, and who might have learned something concerning him during the last few months. Also, she gave me the name and address of the herbalist before whose door—and, indeed, issuing from it—Alan Spencer had met Julius in such an unexpected fashion.

"You will write to me as soon as you have any news," she said, wistfully, to me, at parting. "And, above all, let me know everything you can find out about Carnivorine. Do not hesitate to tell me the worst—even if Julius has married this creature with the singular name."

I must confess that, when I first arrived in Rome, so many personal interests claimed me that I did not at once begin my search for Julius Lambert, as I had intended to do. There were so many of my old friends and old haunts to revisit, and such numbers of new and interesting statues in the studios of the Roman sculptors, both native and foreign, to go to see, and my negotiations with the artists who were to execute the illustrations for my history of the Cenci family took up so much time, that the weeks insensibly slipped away before I had taken any steps in the matter. I had had the time to receive more than one letter from Mrs Lambert on the subject before I commenced my investigations. I must acknowledge that I had come to the conclusion that the mystery, on investigation, would prove to be no mystery at all, and that Julius would be discovered in one of the minor hotels in Rome—too busy, or perhaps too much in love, to write. But, when I did finally set out in search of him, I found myself baffled at the very outset by an impenetrable wall of mystery. Nobody had seen him, and nobody knew anything about him. He had drawn all his funds from the banker's on his first arrival in the city. He had been in Rome some two years before, and had bought a collection of the curious insect-eating plants of South America from the old herbalist at whose door Alan Spencer had met him. That was all. If the earth had opened beneath his feet and had swallowed him up, he could not have vanished more utterly from human ken. I sought for him in every direction. I employed the services of a private detective. I offered a reward for any news of him. All was of no use. I succeeded in learning that he had not left Rome—and that was all I could find out.

Some months had elapsed, and I had pretty much abandoned the search in despair, when one day the fancy took me to go on a ride on horseback over the Campagna. I had long cherished the desire to explore the less frequented and scarcely known districts of that vast region, haunted by malaria and tenanted only by a few fever-stricken shepherds, that lies outside the beaten track of tourists and travellers beyond the city walls. As may be imagined, I found my excursion rather dreary. I rode on and on, passing now a flock of sheep watched over by a brigand-looking guardian and a fierce rough dog that looked ready, at a word or a sign from his master, to tear down my horse and throttle its rider, and then some huge arch of a ruined aqueduct that in the days of classic Rome had been musical with laughing water. Sometimes I came upon the shattered fragments of an abandoned hovel, or met with a herd of the grey-coated long-horned oxen of the region, beautiful placid-looking creatures, that gazed at me inquiringly out of their large soft eyes as I rode by, as though saying What is this stranger doing in this home of solitude and ruin? Still, I was interested by the very novelty of the dreary region, and I rode on and on, till the sun began to sink toward the western horizon. I have always considered myself fever-proof, but all the same, a ride after sunset over the Campagna is not the healthiest experiment in the world, so I wheeled my horse round and started to return to the city. And, as I did so, I became aware of the existence of a house at a very short distance. I might very well have passed it without noticing it, as it was so embowered in a mass of vegetation, vines, and bushes, as well as trees, that its shape and architecture were barely discernible. As I rode nearer, I saw that it was a modern villa of imposing dimensions, which had been suffered to fall into almost total ruin. Whether the freak of a speculator or the wild idea of some Campagna proprietor had caused the erection, in this lonely unhealthy place, of a costly country residence, there was no evidence to reveal. The grounds, once spacious and well laid out, were overrun with a thick undergrowth of plants and grasses. Here and there, a statue in white marble, streaked with damp and green with mould, showed under the shadow of the trees, and one, a graceful figure of a nymph, overthrown from its pedestal, lay prostrate amongst the rank grass. The façade of the house itself was adorned with moss-grown sculptures, and one of the pillars supporting the doorway had been broken away and its place was supplied by the trunk of a cypress. One-half of the building showed deserted and ruinous with its broken windows and decaying roof. But there were traces elsewhere of human habitation. The roof of the right wing had been mended, the windows were in good condition, and a gleam of firelight from the lower rooms gave a cheery aspect to that part of the edifice. And, oddly enough, in spite of the universal decay and dilapidation, there were traces not only of comfort, but of luxury, in one portion of the premises, which I noticed as I drew near. This was a large conservatory adjoining the inhabited portion of the house. It was in perfect order. Not a pane was missing in its glazed walls, through which I could discern the red glare of the stove-fires within, as well as the dull green of the foliage of the plants.

Both I and my horse were weary, so I decided that I would halt for an hour or so at this singular habitation, and try for a feed of oats for my horse, as well as for a flask of Chianti and a crust of bread for myself. I drew rein at the dilapidated doorway, and, just as I was about to announce my presence by a resounding knock from the butt-end of my riding-whip, the door was suddenly opened and a man came hurriedly forth. He started when he saw me, and was about to retreat into the house; but, by the red light of the waning sunset, I discerned his features and recognised him instantly. It was the man I had so long sought for and in vain—it was Julius Lambert.

"Julius!" I cried, as he was about to vanish through the doorway. "Julius Lambert! Is it thus that you treat an old friend who has come so far to visit you?"

He turned back at the sound of my voice. "So it is really you, Mr Graham," he said, hesitatingly. "How in the world did you ever find me or the Villa Anzieri? Nobody has come near it or me either, for over two years past. But come in—my man shall take charge of your horse—and you can tell me something about home matters."

I willingly relinquished the charge of my wearied steed to the black-eyed, bronze-complexioned, picturesque-looking young fellow who came in answer to his master's call, and I followed Julius into the house. I could hardly believe my senses, or that I had found my missing friend at last. It had all happened so simply and yet so strangely. Meanwhile Julius, after he had gotten over the first shock of my intrusion, seemed really glad to see me. He piled fresh wood on the fire, and gave orders that dinner should be served as soon as possible, and plied me with questions respecting his mother and his brother and sisters. As for himself, I found him looking far from well. He was never very stout, but he had grown lean and emaciated, and the yellowish pallor of his face gave evidence of the effects that the malaria of the Campagna had on his system. Dinner was served at last—a very palatable stew flavoured with red peppers and tomatoes, with the accompaniment of some fine oranges and grapes by way of dessert, and a flask or two of Chianti wine and one of the delicate Civita Lavinia. Throughout the repast, I noticed with pain that Julius talked in a feverish incoherent way, pressing me to eat or to drink, and hurrying questions and remarks about home matters, half the time without waiting for an answer.

At last, pushing my plate aside, I remarked:

"Now, Julius, I have told you everything that you wished to know. It is my turn now to ask for a little information. What have you been doing all this long time in this solitude?"

He moved uneasily in his chair, and his wandering glance avoided mine.

"Nothing," he muttered—"I have done—I am doing—nothing."

"Nonsense! You cannot persuade me of the truth of that assertion, so ardent an experimentalist as you have always been, and so interested in the cause of science. Confess, now—have you not made, or are you not on the verge of perfecting, some great discovery?"

I had touched the right chord. His eyes flashed, and his whole countenance grew bright with animation.

"Yes!" he cried. "I have succeeded at last in my researches. For years I have tried to perfect a demonstration of the link between the vegetable and the animal kingdom. If you have come to scoff at my discoveries, go—go at once! Otherwise, follow me—and be prepared for full conviction as to the truth of what I have said."

He rose as he spoke, and, taking me by the hand, he led me to a door at the extremity of the large room in which we had dined. This door he unlocked with a key which he took from his pocket. Night had closed in, and he completed his preparations by lighting a great torch of pine-branches.

"Wait on the threshold, as you value your life," he said to me, impressively. Then he threw open the door.

It was the entrance to the conservatory. The first thing that struck me was a sort of faint rustling sound like that of a trailing garment or

70

a sweeping bird's-wing. Then, by the light of the torch which Julius held on high, I discerned, in the centre of the room, a vast tub filled with masses of spongy moss, from which rose a strange plant—a hideous shapeless monster: a sort of vegetable hydra—or, rather, octopus—gigantic in size and repulsive in aspect and in colouring. So immense were its proportions, that it filled by itself the whole space of the conservatory. It consisted of a central bladder-shaped trunk or core, from which sprang countless branches—or, rather, arms—thick, leafless, of a livid green, and streaked with blotches of a dull crimson. Each arm terminated in an oval protuberance which had a resemblance to the human eye. Julius took, from a basket that stood near the door, a great slice of raw meat, and, fastening it to the end of a stick, he advanced it, taking infinite precautions to keep well out of reach of the circle of outstretched branches. Then I saw these great tentacle-like arms fold around their prey, which they transmitted to the central core; and then, closing around it, I saw it no more. It was this slow motion of the branches that had caused the rustling sound which had amazed me on my first entrance.

So repulsive was the aspect of this enormous creature, half plant and half animal, that I was glad to beat a retreat to the dining-room. Julius followed, flushed and elated at the healthful aspect of his monstrous creation.

"The plant you have just seen," he said, "is a Drosera, which, by dint of careful selection and persevering attention, I have developed into this unheard-of size. I have studied the discoveries of Warming and of Darwin concerning those strange plants, the Drosera and the Dionœa—which, though still vegetables, feed on the insects that they kill. It has been my desire for years to perfect the missing link and to develop the animal side of these curious vegetable natures. It has always been my theory that the hydra, the dragon, and other monstrous forms of animal life really did exist, and that, in the evolution of ages and by reason of geological changes on the surface of the earth, these creatures, deprived of their accustomed forms of nourishment, degenerated into trees and plants and took root in the earth. Some of them still preserve their primitive forms, as witness the dragon-tree of Java. It has been my aim and endeavour to resuscitate the animal in the plant. Chance threw in my way a Drosera of great size. I have fed it on animal food for years, and developed it into something that is not yet a dragon or a hydra, but which is surely something more than a plant. Had you ventured within reach of its branches, the grasp of a boa would not have been more swift or more deadly."

"And what further do you propose doing with your dreadful plant?"

"My aim now is to give it locomotion—to see it detach itself from the soil and go forth in search of prey."

"How can you contemplate the possibility of letting loose such a monster on the world?"

"For science, there is no such thing as a monster. Moreover, are there not crocodiles and anacondas and tigers upon earth, to say nothing of the shark and the octopus? Beside these, my creation—my Carnivorine—is a harmless creature."

I started as I heard the name. So this, then, was the object of my poor friend's affections—this ghastly shape, not yet wholly animal, yet scarcely vegetable, with the form of a plant and the appetites of a beast of prey?

Just then, Pietro, the man-servant, came in to announce that my horse was at the door. It was a beautiful moonlit night, promising a pleasant ride to the city. I took my leave of Julius, therefore, with something of the feeling of relief of a man who awakes from sleep after having been oppressed by a terrible nightmare. But I did not depart without leaving my address, and I begged Julius to let me know if his strange discovery took any new developments in the near future.

Weeks passed away, and I had nearly forgotten all about Julius and Carnivorine, when one day I received a letter from him, written in a strain of great exultation and excitement. "Come to me, dear friend," he wrote; "come at once! The hour of the perfecting of my experiment is at hand. Already, amid the masses that surround Carnivorine, I discern the stirring and striving of the roots, which are acquiring powers of independent locomotion. In a few days, the problem will be solved. I want you to be present as a witness of the phenomenon. My ambition is satisfied at last—my name shall be inscribed on the list of the great discoverers of the world of science. Come to me, and be at my side in the moment of my triumph."

It was not without difficulty that I once more made my way to the Villa Anzieri. It was late in the afternoon when I drew rein at the dilapidated doorway that I remembered so well. I knocked loudly at the door, but there was no response to my call. Looking around, I saw that the whole place wore an inexplicable air of desertion. No firelight was visible at the windows, and the red glare of the stove-fire no longer shone behind the dim panes of the hot-house. Finally, in vague alarm, finding that my shouts and knocking produced no response, I tied my horse to one of the door-posts, and, singling out a window of the large room in which we had dined on the occasion of my former visit, I swung myself up to it by the help of a thick stem of ivy, and peered into the room. The sight that I beheld within froze my soul with horror.

At the end of the room, near the entrance to the conservatory, rose the hideous form of Carnivorine, no longer planted in a tub, but supported on what seemed, to me, a pair of paddle-like feet or paws like those of some misshapen antediluvian animal. The powerful branches—or, rather, tentacles—were upraised and closely folded around some central object. And at the summit of these livid green, closely pressed, serpent-like stems appeared a ghastly object: it was a livid human head—the head of a corpse—and the pallid features were those of Julius Lambert!

With one stroke of my arm, I burst open the casement. I sprang into the room and hastened toward the dreadful object. The long arms quivered and began to unfold themselves. But, before the creature could put itself in motion, a shot from the revolver that I always carried during my Campagna wanderings pierced its central core. The tentacles fell apart, and the hideous plant sank prone upon the ground, bearing with it, in its fall, the crushed and lifeless form of Julius Lambert. A stream of reddish sap that looked like blood flowed from the shattered stem and mingled with the branches, stained as they were with a ruddier crimson—the life-blood of my unhappy friend.

I never discovered how or when the catastrophe took place. From the condition of the body, death must have taken place at least twenty-four hours before my arrival. The servants, brought face to face with such a shocking—and, to them, inexplicable—catastrophe, had fled from the house, taking with them whatever money or valuables they could lay their hands upon. I tried to trace them out, but in vain. As to the rest, it was all mere conjecture on my part. The uptorn earth and mosses in the tub in which Carnivorine had originally found an abode seemed to prove that a sudden development of the long-sought-for powers of locomotion in the creature had unexpectedly taken place, and that Julius had been seized either in the act of inspecting its condition or at the moment of offering it food. At all events, the vegetable-animal or animal-vegetable had made a solitary trial of its newly formed powers, and had found a solitary prey when the bullet from my pistol put an end to its existence.

Among the papers left behind by Julius was a series of memoranda respecting the experiments he had tried and the processes he had used to bring his dread creation to full perfection. These I destroyed without hesitation. It would not have been well to have suffered the race of the vegetable octopus to be extended and propagated by curious scientists in the future. Then, lest a new growth should spring from the stem or branches of the accursed tree, I hewed them to pieces with my own hand and burned the fragments to ashes. The annihilation of my friend's discovery may be a loss to science, but humanity will only have cause to rejoice in the total destruction of Carnivorine.

THE GIANT WISTARIA

Charlotte Perkins Gilman

Charlotte Perkins Gilman was an accomplished feminist short story writer best known for "The Yellow Wallpaper". Among her numerous short stories is "The Giant Wistaria", written in 1891 and published in *New England Magazine*. In one of the more gothic tales in the collection, a wealthy young couple and their friends rent a rustic manor excited by the prospect of it being haunted. Gilman's work is known for its feminist themes such as female entrapment and patriarchal control as well as featuring women at the centre of her stories. The history of the flowery house is discovered to be filled with scandal, shame and tragedy which is revealed to the new guests as they all experience the same vivid dream.

Gilman adds her own unique stamp onto the genre by implementing distinctly feminist and gothic themes such as patriarchal control and uses the domestic setting of the house for her tale. Temporality is also a key theme within the story as the narrative moves from centuries past to the present day where Gilman effectively juxtaposes past tragedy with modern frivolousness.

eddle not with my new vine, child! See! Thou hast already broken the tender shoot! Never needle or distaff for thee, and yet thou wilt not be quiet!"

The nervous fingers wavered, clutched at a small carnelian cross that hung from her neck, then fell despairingly.

"Give me my child, mother, and then I will be quiet!"

"Hush! hush! thou fool—some one might be near! See—there is thy father coming, even now! Get in quickly!"

She raised her eyes to her mother's face, weary eyes that yet had a flickering, uncertain blaze in their shaded depths.

"Art thou a mother and hast no pity on me, a mother? Give me my child!"

Her voice rose in a strange, low cry, broken by her father's hand upon her mouth.

"Shameless!" said he, with set teeth. "Get to thy chamber, and be not seen again to-night, or I will have thee bound!"

She went at that, and a hard-faced serving woman followed, and presently returned, bringing a key to her mistress.

"Is all well with her—and the child also?"

"She is quiet, Mistress Dwining, well for the night, be sure. The child fretteth endlessly, but save for that it thriveth with me."

The parents were left alone together on the high square porch with its great pillars, and the rising moon began to make faint shadows of the young vine leaves that shot up luxuriantly around them: moving shadows, like little stretching fingers, on the broad and heavy planks of the oaken floor.

"It groweth well, this vine thou broughtest me in the ship, my husband."

"Aye," he broke in bitterly, "and so doth the shame I brought thee! Had I known of it I would sooner have had the ship founder beneath us, and have seen our child cleanly drowned, than live to this end!"

"Thou art very hard, Samuel, art thou not afeard for her life? She grieveth sore for the child, aye, and for the green fields to walk in!"

"Nay," said he grimly, "I fear not. She hath lost already what is more than life; and she shall have air enough soon. Tomorrow the ship is ready, and we return to England. None knoweth of our stain here, not one, and if the town hath a child unaccounted for to rear in decent ways—why, it is not the first, even here. It will be well enough cared for! And truly we have matter for thankfulness, that her cousin is yet willing to marry her."

"Hast thou told him?"

"Aye! Thinkest thou I would cast shame into another man's house, un-knowing it? He hath always desired her, but she would none of him, the stubborn! She hath small choice now!"

"Will he be kind, Samuel? Can he—"

"Kind? What call'st thou it to take such as she to wife? Kind! How many men would take her, an' she had double the fortune? And being of the family already, he is glad to hide the blot forever."

"An' if she would not? He is but a coarse fellow, and she ever shunned him."

"Art thou mad, woman? She weddeth him ere we sail tomorrow, or she stayeth ever in that chamber. The girl is not so sheer a fool! He maketh an honest woman of her, and saveth our house from open shame. What other hope for her than a new life to cover the old? Let her have an honest child, an' she so longeth for one!"

He strode heavily across the porch, till the loose planks creaked again, strode back and forth, with his arms folded and his brows fiercely knit above his iron mouth.

Overhead the shadows flickered mockingly across a white face among the leaves, with eyes of wasted fire.

"O, George, what a house! What a lovely house! I am sure it's haunted! Let us get that house to live in this summer! We will have Kate and Jack and Susy and Jim of course, and a splendid time of it!"

Young husbands are indulgent, but still they have to recognise facts.

"My dear, the house may not be to rent; and it may also not be habitable."

"There is surely somebody in it. I am going to inquire!"

The great central gate was rusted off its hinges, and the long drive had trees in it, but a little footpath showed signs of steady usage, and up that Mrs Jenny went, followed by her obedient George. The front windows of the old mansion were blank, but in a wing at the back they found white curtains and open doors. Outside, in the clear May sunshine, a woman was washing. She was polite and friendly, and evidently glad of visitors in that lonely place. She "guessed it could be rented—didn't know." The heirs were in Europe, but "there was a lawyer in New York had the lettin' of it." There had been folks there years ago, but not in her time. She and her husband had the rent of their part for taking care of the place. "Not that they took much care on't either, but keepin' robbers out." It was furnished throughout, old-fashioned enough, but good; and "if they took it she could do the work for 'em herself, she guessed—if *he* was willin'!"

Never was a crazy scheme more easily arranged. George knew that lawyer in New York; the rent was not alarming; and the nearness to a rising sea-shore resort made it a still pleasanter place to spend the summer.

Kate and Jack and Susy and Jim cheerfully accepted, and the June moon found them all sitting on the high front porch.

They had explored the house from top to bottom, from the great room in the garret, with nothing in it but a rickety cradle, to the well in the cellar without a curb and with a rusty chain going down to unknown blackness below. They had explored the grounds, once beautiful with rare trees and shrubs, but now a gloomy wilderness of tangled shade.

The old lilacs and laburnums, the spirea and syringa, nodded against the second-storey windows. What garden plants survived were great ragged bushes or great shapeless beds. A huge wistaria vine covered the whole front of the house. The trunk, it was too large to call a stem, rose at the corner of the porch by the high steps, and had once climbed its pillars; but now the pillars were wrenched from their places and held rigid and helpless by the tightly wound and knotted arms.

It fenced in all the upper storey of the porch with a knitted wall of stem and leaf; it ran along the eaves, holding up the gutter that had once supported it; it shaded every window with heavy green; and the drooping, fragrant blossoms made a waving sheet of purple from roof to ground.

"Did you ever see such a wistaria!" cried ecstatic Mrs Jenny. "It is worth the rent just to sit under such a vine—a fig tree beside it would be sheer superfluity and wicked extravagance!"

"Jenny makes much of her wistaria," said George, "because she's so disappointed about the ghosts. She made up her mind at first sight to have ghosts in the house, and she can't find even a ghost story!"

"No," Jenny assented mournfully; "I pumped poor Mrs Pepperill for three days, but could get nothing out of her. But I'm convinced there is a story, if we could only find it. You need not tell me that a house like this, with a garden like this, and a cellar like this, isn't haunted!"

"I agree with you," said Jack. Jack was a reporter on a New York daily, and engaged to Mrs Jenny's pretty sister. "And if we don't find a real ghost, you may be very sure I shall make one. It's too good an opportunity to lose!"

The pretty sister, who sat next him, resented. "You shan't do anything of the sort, Jack! This is a *real* ghostly place, and I won't have you make fun of it! Look at that group of trees out there in the long grass—it looks for all the world like a crouching, hunted figure!"

"It looks to me like a woman picking huckleberries," said Jim, who was married to George's pretty sister.

"Be still, Jim!" said that young woman. "I believe in Jenny's ghost as much as she does. Such a place! Just look at this great wistaria trunk crawling up by the steps here! It looks for all the world like a writhing body—cringing—beseeching!"

"Yes," answered the subdued Jim, "it does, Susy. See its waist— about two yards of it, and twisted at that! A waste of good material!"

"Don't be so horrid, boys! Go off and smoke somewhere if you can't be congenial!"

"We can! We will! We'll be as ghostly as you please." And forthwith they began to see bloodstains and crouching figures so plentifully that the most delightful shivers multiplied, and the fair enthusiasts started for bed, declaring they should never sleep a wink.

"We shall all surely dream," cried Mrs Jenny, "and we must all tell our dreams in the morning!"

"There's another thing certain," said George, catching Susy as she tripped over a loose plank; "and that is that you frisky creatures must use the side door till I get this Eiffel tower of a portico fixed, or we shall have some fresh ghosts on our hands! We found a plank here that yawns like a trap-door—big enough to swallow you—and I believe the bottom of the thing is in China!"

The next morning found them all alive, and eating a substantial New England breakfast, to the accompaniment of saws and hammers on the porch, where carpenters of quite miraculous promptness were tearing things to pieces generally.

"It's got to come down mostly," they had said. "These timbers are clean rotted through, what ain't pulled out o' line by this great creeper. That's about all that holds the thing up."

There was clear reason in what they said, and with a caution from anxious Mrs Jenny not to hurt the wistaria, they were left to demolish and repair at leisure.

"How about ghosts?" asked Jack after a fourth griddle cake. "I had one, and it's taken away my appetite!"

Mrs Jenny gave a little shriek and dropped her knife and fork.

"Oh, so had I! I had the most awful—well, not dream exactly, but feeling. I had forgotten all about it!"

"Must have been awful," said Jack, taking another cake. "Do tell us about the feeling. My ghost will wait."

"It makes me creep to think of it even now," she said. "I woke up, all at once, with that dreadful feeling as if something were going to happen, you know! I was wide awake, and hearing every little sound for miles around, it seemed to me. There are so many strange little noises in the country, for all it is so still. Millions of crickets and things outside, and all kinds of rustles in the trees! There wasn't much wind, and the moonlight came through in my three great windows in three white squares on the black old floor, and those fingery wistaria leaves we were talking of last night just seemed to crawl all over them. And—O, girls, you know that dreadful well in the cellar?"

84

A most gratifying impression was made by this, and Jenny proceeded cheerfully:

"Well, while it was so horridly still, and I lay there trying not to wake George, I heard as plainly as if it were right in the room, that old chain down there rattle and creak over the stones!"

"Bravo!" cried Jack. "That's fine! I'll put it in the Sunday edition!"

"Be still!" said Kate. "What was it, Jenny? Did you really see anything?"

"No, I didn't, I'm sorry to say. But just then I didn't want to. I woke George, and made such a fuss that he gave me bromide, and said he'd go and look, and that's the last I thought of it till Jack reminded me—the bromide worked so well."

"Now, Jack, give us yours," said Jim. "Maybe it will dovetail in somehow. Thirsty ghost, I imagine; maybe they had prohibition here even then!"

Jack folded his napkin, and leaned back in his most impressive manner.

"It was striking twelve by the great hall clock—" he began.

"There isn't any hall clock!"

"O hush, Jim, you spoil the current! It was just one o'clock then, by my old-fashioned repeater."

"Waterbury! Never mind what time it was!"

"Well, honestly, I woke up sharp, like our beloved hostess, and tried to go to sleep again, but couldn't. I experienced all those moonlight and grasshopper sensations, just like Jenny, and was wondering what could have been the matter with the supper, when in came my ghost, and I knew it was all a dream! It was a female ghost, and I imagine she was young and handsome, but all those crouching, hunted figures of last evening ran riot in my brain, and this poor creature looked just like them. She was all wrapped up in a shawl, and had a big bundle under her arm—dear me, I am spoiling the story! With the air and gait of one in frantic haste and terror, the muffled figure glided to a dark old bureau, and seemed to be taking things from the drawers. As she turned, the moonlight shone full on a little red cross that hung from her neck by a thin gold chain—I saw it glitter as she crept noiselessly from the room! That's all."

"O Jack, don't be so horrid! Did you really? Is that all! What do you think it was?"

"I am not horrid by nature, only professionally. I really did. That was all. And I am fully convinced it was the genuine, legitimate ghost of an eloping chambermaid with kleptomania!"

"You are too bad, Jack!" cried Jenny. "You take all the horror out of it. There isn't a 'creep' left among us."

"It's no time for creeps at nine-thirty A.M., with sunlight and carpenters outside! However, if you can't wait till twilight for your creeps, I think I can furnish one or two," said George. "I went down cellar after Jenny's ghost!"

There was a delighted chorus of female voices, and Jenny cast upon her lord a glance of genuine gratitude.

"It's all very well to lie in bed and see ghosts, or hear them," he went on. "But the young householder suspecteth burglars, even though as a medical man he knoweth nerves, and after Jenny dropped off I started on a voyage of discovery. I never will again, I promise you!"

"Why, what *was* it?"

"Oh, George!"

"I got a candle—"

"Good mark for the burglars," murmured Jack.

"And went all over the house, gradually working down to the cellar and the well."

"Well?" said Jack.

"Now you can laugh; but that cellar is no joke by daylight, and a candle there at night is about as inspiring as a lightning-bug in the Mammoth Cave. I went along with the light, trying not to fall into the well prematurely; got to it all at once; held the light down and *then* I saw, right under my feet—(I nearly fell over her, or walked through her, perhaps)—a woman, hunched up under a shawl! She had hold of the chain, and the candle shone on her hands—white, thin hands—on a little red cross that hung from her neck—*vide* Jack! I'm no believer in ghosts, and I firmly object to unknown parties in the house at night; so I spoke to her rather fiercely. She didn't seem to notice that, and I reached down to take hold of her—then I came upstairs!"

"What for?"

"What happened?"

"What was the matter?"

"Well, nothing happened. Only she wasn't there! May have been indigestion, of course, but as a physician I don't advise any one to court indigestion alone at midnight in a cellar!"

"This is the most interesting and peripatetic and evasive ghost I ever heard of!" said Jack. "It's my belief she has no end of silver tankards, and jewels galore, at the bottom of that well, and I move we go and see!"

"To the bottom of the well, Jack?"

"To the bottom of the mystery. Come on!"

There was unanimous assent, and the fresh cambrics and pretty boots were gallantly escorted below by gentlemen whose jokes were so frequent that many of them were a little forced.

The deep old cellar was so dark that they had to bring lights, and the well so gloomy in its blackness that the ladies recoiled.

"That well is enough to scare even a ghost. It's my opinion you'd better let well enough alone," quoth Jim.

"Truth lies hid in a well, and we must get her out," said George. "Bear a hand with the chain?"

Jim pulled away on the chain, George turned the creaking windlass, and Jack was chorus.

"A wet sheet for this ghost, if not a flowing sea," said he. "Seems to be hard work raising spirits! I suppose he kicked the bucket when he went down!"

As the chain lightened and shortened there grew a strained silence among them; and when at length the bucket appeared, rising slowly through the dark water, there was an eager, half reluctant peering, and a natural drawing back. They poked the gloomy contents. "Only water."

"Nothing but mud."

"Something—"

They emptied the bucket upon the dark earth, and then the girls all went out into the air, into the bright warm sunshine in front of the house, where was the sound of saw and hammer, and the smell of new wood. There was nothing said until the men joined them, and then Jenny timidly asked:

"How old should you think it was, George?"

"All of a century," he answered. "That water is preservative—lime in it. Oh!—you mean?—Not more than a month; a very little baby!"

There was another silence at this, broken by a cry from the workmen. They had removed the floor and the side walls of the old porch, so that the sunshine poured down to the dark stones of the cellar bottom. And there, in the strangling grasp of the roots of the great wistaria, lay the bones of a woman, from whose neck still hung a tiny scarlet cross on a thin chain of gold.

THE FLOWERING OF THE STRANGE ORCHID

H. G. Wells

Famous for his science fiction writings such as *The Invisible Man, The War of the Worlds* and *The Island of Doctor Moreau,* H. G. Wells was one of the most notable short story authors during the end of the nineteenth and start of the twentieth centuries. "The Flowering of the Strange Orchid" is one of the best-known stories in the Botanical Gothic genre and chooses the evocative orchid as its focus. Orchids were one of the most collectable and expensive flowers during the Victorian era which inspired many orchid-related hothouse horrors. H. G. Wells's take on the story follows orchid collector Wedderburn, who yearns for some adventure in his humdrum life but gets more than he bargained for when tending his new floral specimen.

Wells's short story provides an insight into the world of exotic plant collecting during the nineteenth century as it proves how commonplace and all-consuming the hobby could be. Wells foreshadows the sinister nature of Wedderburn's prized orchid revealing how the collector died while retrieving it. The theme of death is also prevalent within the plant itself as its growing shoots and buds look strikingly similar to a dead man's fingers.

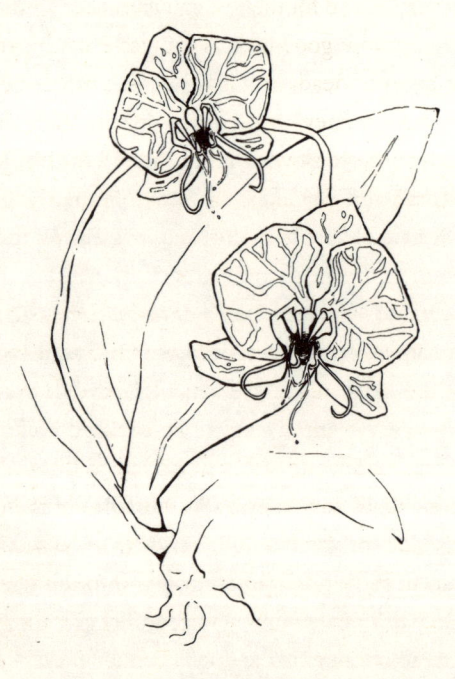

he buying of orchids always has in it a certain speculative flavour. You have before you the brown shrivelled lump of tissue, and for the rest you must trust your judgment, or the auctioneer, or your good luck, as your taste may incline. The plant may be moribund or dead, or it may be just a respectable purchase, fair value for your money, or perhaps—for the thing has happened again and again—there slowly unfolds before the delighted eyes of the happy purchaser, day after day, some new variety, some novel richness, a strange twist of the labellum, or some subtler coloration or unexpected mimicry.

Pride, beauty, and profit blossom together on one delicate green spike, and it may be, even immortality. For the new miracle of Nature may stand in need of a new specific name, and what so convenient as that of its discoverer? "Johnsmithia!" There have been worse names.

It was perhaps the hope of some such happy discovery that made Winter-Wedderburn such a frequent attendant at these sales—that hope, and also, maybe, the fact that he had nothing else of the slightest interest to do in the world. He was a shy, lonely, rather ineffectual man, provided with just enough income to keep off the spur of necessity, and not enough nervous energy to make him seek any exacting employments. He might have collected stamps or coins, or translated Horace, or bound books, or invented new species of diatoms. But, as it happened, he grew orchids, and had one ambitious little hothouse.

"I have a fancy," he said over his coffee, "that something is going to happen to me today."

He spoke—as he moved and thought—slowly.

"Oh, don't say THAT!" said his housekeeper, who was also his remote cousin. For "something happening" was a euphemism that meant only one thing to her.

"You misunderstand me. I mean nothing unpleasant... though what I do mean I scarcely know."

"Today," he continued, after a pause, "Peters' are going to sell a batch of plants from the Andamans and the Indies. I shall go up and see what they have. It may be I shall buy something good, unawares. That may be it."

He passed his cup for his second cupful of coffee.

"Are these the things collected by that poor young fellow you told me of the other day?" asked his cousin as she filled his cup.

"Yes," he said, and became meditative over a piece of toast.

"Nothing ever does happen to me," he remarked presently, beginning to think aloud. "I wonder why? Things enough happen to other people. There is Harvey. Only the other week, on Monday he picked up sixpence, on Wednesday his chicks all had the staggers, on Friday his cousin came home from Australia, and on Saturday he broke his ankle. What a whirl of excitement—compared to me."

"I think I would rather be without so much excitement," said his housekeeper. "It can't be good for you."

"I suppose it's troublesome. Still... you see, nothing ever happens to me. When I was a little boy I never had accidents. I never fell in love as I grew up. Never married... I wonder how it feels to have something happen to you, something really remarkable.

"That orchid-collector was only thirty-six—twenty years younger than myself when he died. And he had been married twice, and divorced once; he had had malarial fever four times, and once he broke his thigh. He killed a Malay once, and once he was wounded by a poisoned dart. And in the end he was killed by

92

jungle-leeches. It must have all been very troublesome, but then it must have been very interesting, you know, except, perhaps, the leeches."

"I am sure it was not good for him," said the lady, with conviction.

"Perhaps not." And then Wedderburn looked at his watch. "Twenty-three minutes past eight. I am going up by the quarter to twelve train, so that there is plenty of time. I think I shall wear my alpaca jacket—it is quite warm enough—and my grey felt hat and brown shoes. I suppose—"

He glanced out of the window at the serene sky and sunlit garden, and then nervously at his cousin's face.

"I think you had better take an umbrella if you are going to London," she said, in a voice that admitted of no denial. "There's all between here and the station coming back."

When he returned he was in a state of mild excitement. He had made a purchase. It was rarely that he could make up his mind quickly enough to buy, but this time he had done so.

"There are Vandas," he said, "and a Dendrobe and some Palaeonophis." He surveyed his purchases lovingly as he consumed his soup. They were laid out on the spotless tablecloth before him, and he was telling his cousin all about them as he slowly meandered through his dinner. It was his custom to live all his visits to London over again in the evening for her and his own entertainment.

"I knew something would happen today. And I have bought all these. Some of them—some of them—I feel sure, do you know, that some of them will be remarkable. I don't know how it is, but I feel just as sure as if someone had told me that some of these will turn out remarkable."

"That one"—he pointed to a shrivelled rhizome—"was not identified. It may be a Palaeonophis—or it may not. It may be a new

93

species, or even a new genus. And it was the last that poor Batten ever collected."

"I don't like the look of it," said his housekeeper. "It's such an ugly shape."

"To me it scarcely seems to have a shape."

"I don't like those things that stick out," said his housekeeper.

"It shall be put away in a pot tomorrow."

"It looks," said the housekeeper, "like a spider shamming dead."

Wedderburn smiled and surveyed the root with his head on one side. "It is certainly not a pretty lump of stuff. But you can never judge of these things from their dry appearance. It may turn out to be a very beautiful orchid indeed. How busy I shall be tomorrow! I must see tonight just exactly what to do with these things, and tomorrow I shall set to work.

"They found poor Batten lying dead, or dying, in a mangrove swamp—I forget which," he began again presently, "with one of these very orchids crushed up under his body. He had been unwell for some days with some kind of native fever, and I suppose he fainted. These mangrove swamps are very unwholesome. Every drop of blood, they say, was taken out of him by the jungle-leeches. It may be that very plant that cost him his life to obtain."

"I think none the better of it for that."

"Men must work though women may weep," said Wedderburn, with profound gravity.

"Fancy dying away from every comfort in a nasty swamp! Fancy being ill of fever with nothing to take but chlorodyne and quinine—if men were left to themselves they would live on chlorodyne and quinine—and no one round you but horrible natives! They say the Andaman islanders are most disgusting wretches— and, anyhow, they can scarcely make good nurses, not having the necessary training. And just for people in England to have orchids!"

"I don't suppose it was comfortable, but some men seem to enjoy that kind of thing," said Wedderburn. "Anyhow, the natives of his party were sufficiently civilised to take care of all his collection until his colleague, who was an ornithologist, came back again from the interior; though they could not tell the species of the orchid and had let it wither. And it makes these things more interesting."

"It makes them disgusting. I should be afraid of some of the malaria clinging to them. And just think, there has been a dead body lying across that ugly thing! I never thought of that before. There! I declare I cannot eat another mouthful of dinner!"

"I will take them off the table if you like, and put them in the window-seat. I can see them just as well there."

The next few days he was indeed singularly busy in his steamy little hot-house, fussing about with charcoal, lumps of teak, moss, and all the other mysteries of the orchid cultivator. He considered he was having a wonderfully eventful time. In the evening he would talk about these new orchids to his friends, and over and over again he reverted to his expectation of something strange.

Several of the Vandas and the Dendrobium died under his care, but presently the strange orchid began to show signs of life. He was delighted and took his housekeeper right away from jam-making to see it at once, directly he made the discovery.

"That is a bud," he said, "and presently there will be a lot of leaves there, and those little things coming out here are aerial rootlets."

"They look to me like little white fingers poking out of the brown," said his housekeeper. "I don't like them."

"Why not?"

"I don't know. They look like fingers trying to get at you. I can't help my likes and dislikes."

"I don't know for certain, but I don't THINK there are any orchids I know that have aerial rootlets quite like that. It may be my fancy, of course. You see they are a little flattened at the ends."

"I don't like 'em," said his housekeeper, suddenly shivering and turning away. "I know it's very silly of me—and I'm very sorry, particularly as you like the thing so much. But I can't help thinking of that corpse."

"But it may not be that particular plant. That was merely a guess of mine."

His housekeeper shrugged her shoulders. "Anyhow I don't like it," she said.

Wedderburn felt a little hurt at her dislike of the plant. But that did not prevent his talking to her about orchids generally, and this orchid in particular, whenever he felt inclined.

"There are such queer things about orchids," he said one day; "such possibilities of surprises. You know, Darwin studied their fertilisation, and showed that the whole structure of an ordinary orchid flower was contrived in order that moths might carry the pollen from plant to plant. Well, it seems that there are lots of orchids known the flower of which cannot possibly be used for fertilisation in that way. Some of the Cypripediums, for instance; there are no insects known that can possibly fertilise them, and some of them have never been found with seed."

"But how do they form new plants?"

"By runners and tubers, and that kind of outgrowth. That is easily explained. The puzzle is, what are the flowers for?"

"Very likely," he added, "MY orchid may be something extra-ordinary in that way. If so, I shall study it. I have often thought of making researches as Darwin did. But hitherto I have not found the time, or something else has happened to prevent it. The leaves are beginning to unfold now. I do wish you would come and see them!"

But she said that the orchid-house was so hot it gave her the headache. She had seen the plant once again, and the aerial rootlets, which were now some of them more than a foot long, had unfortunately reminded her of tentacles reaching out after something; and they got into her dreams, growing after her with incredible rapidity. So that she had settled to her entire satisfaction that she would not see that plant again, and Wedderburn had to admire its leaves alone. They were of the ordinary broad form, and deep, glossy green, with splashes and dots of deep red towards the base. He knew of no other leaves quite like them.

The plant was placed on a low bench near the thermometer, and close by was a simple arrangement by which a tap dripped on the hot-water pipes and kept the air steamy. And he spent his afternoons now with some regularity meditating on the approaching flowering of this strange plant.

And at last the great thing happened. Directly he entered the little glass house he knew that the spike had burst out, although his great Palaeonophis Lowii hid the corner where his new darling stood. There was a new odour in the air—a rich, intensely sweet scent, that overpowered every other in that crowded, steaming little greenhouse.

Directly he noticed this he hurried down to the strange orchid. And, behold! the trailing green spikes bore now three great splashes of blossom, from which this overpowering sweetness proceeded. He stopped before them in an ecstasy of admiration.

The flowers were white, with streaks of golden orange upon the petals; the heavy labellum was coiled into an intricate projection, and a wonderful bluish purple mingled there with the gold. He could see at once that the genus was altogether a new one. And the insufferable scent! How hot the place was! The blossoms swam before his eyes.

He would see if the temperature was right. He made a step towards the thermometer. Suddenly everything appeared unsteady. The bricks on the floor were dancing up and down. Then the white blossoms, the green leaves behind them, the whole greenhouse, seemed to sweep sideways, and then in a curve upward.

At half-past four his cousin made the tea, according to their invariable custom. But Wedderburn did not come in for his tea.

"He is worshipping that horrid orchid," she told herself, and waited ten minutes. "His watch must have stopped. I will go and call him."

She went straight to the hothouse, and, opening the door, called his name. There was no reply. She noticed that the air was very close, and loaded with an intense perfume. Then she saw something lying on the bricks between the hot-water pipes.

For a minute, perhaps, she stood motionless.

He was lying, face upward, at the foot of the strange orchid. The tentacle-like aerial rootlets no longer swayed freely in the air, but were crowded together, a tangle of grey ropes, and stretched tight, with their ends closely applied to his chin and neck and hands.

She did not understand. Then she saw from one of the exultant tentacles upon his cheek there trickled a little thread of blood.

With an inarticulate cry she ran towards him, and tried to pull him away from the leech-like suckers. She snapped two of these tentacles, and their sap dripped red.

Then the overpowering scent of the blossom began to make her head reel. How they clung to him! She tore at the tough ropes, and he and the white inflorescence swam about her. She felt she was fainting, knew she must not. She left him and hastily opened the nearest door, and, after she had panted for a moment in the fresh air, she had a brilliant inspiration. She caught up a flower-pot and smashed in the windows at the end of the greenhouse. Then she re-entered. She tugged now with renewed strength at Wedderburn's motionless body, and brought the strange orchid crashing to the floor. It still clung with the grimmest tenacity to its victim. In a frenzy, she lugged it and him into the open air.

Then she thought of tearing through the sucker rootlets one by one, and in another minute she had released him and was dragging him away from the horror.

He was white and bleeding from a dozen circular patches.

The odd-job man was coming up the garden, amazed at the smashing of glass, and saw her emerge, hauling the inanimate body with red-stained hands. For a moment he thought impossible things.

"Bring some water!" she cried, and her voice dispelled his fancies. When, with unnatural alacrity, he returned with the water, he found her weeping with excitement, and with Wedderburn's head upon her knee, wiping the blood from his face.

"What's the matter?" said Wedderburn, opening his eyes feebly, and closing them again at once.

"Go and tell Annie to come out here to me, and then go for Dr Haddon at once," she said to the odd-job man so soon as he had brought the water, and added, seeing he hesitated: "I will tell you all about it when you come back."

Presently, Wedderburn opened his eyes again, and, seeing that he was troubled by the puzzle of his position, she explained to him: "You fainted in the hothouse."

"And the orchid?"

"I will see to that," she said.

Wedderburn had lost a good deal of blood, but beyond that he had suffered no very great injury. They gave him brandy mixed with some pink extract of meat, and carried him upstairs to bed. His housekeeper told her incredible story in fragments to Dr Haddon. "Come to the orchid-house and see," she said.

The cold outer air was blowing in through the open door, and the sickly perfume was almost dispelled. Most of the torn aerial rootlets lay already withered amidst a number of dark stains upon the bricks. The stem of the inflorescence was broken by the fall of the plant, and the flowers were growing limp and brown at the edges of the petals. The doctor stooped towards it, then saw that one of the aerial rootlets still stirred feebly, and hesitated.

The next morning the strange orchid still lay there, black now and putrescent. The door banged intermittently in the morning breeze, and all the array of Wedderburn's orchids was shrivelled and prostrate. But Wedderburn himself was bright and garrulous upstairs in the glory of his strange adventure.

THE GUARDIAN OF MYSTERY ISLAND

Edmond Nolcini

Published in the famous nineteenth-century literary magazine *The Black Cat*, Nolcini's story takes a more nautical theme with young sailor Sam Lenartson as its protagonist. Unperturbed by fellow sailors' superstitions of a cursed island, he rows out to inspect it for himself. Stories surrounding the island involve a demonic hound guarding its secrets but Lenartson encounters a friendly mastiff that leads him to an abandoned house with a mysterious tenant.

Nolcini's story shares its maritime theme with William Hope Hodgson's "A Voice in the Night" and delves into the fear of the unknown in the form of exotic and uninhabited islands. The threat in this story transgresses boundaries as it showcases both vegetable and animal qualities. In this sense, Nolcini's tale exhibits the Darwinian fear of the breathing, moving, sentient and predatory plant which outgrows all human control.

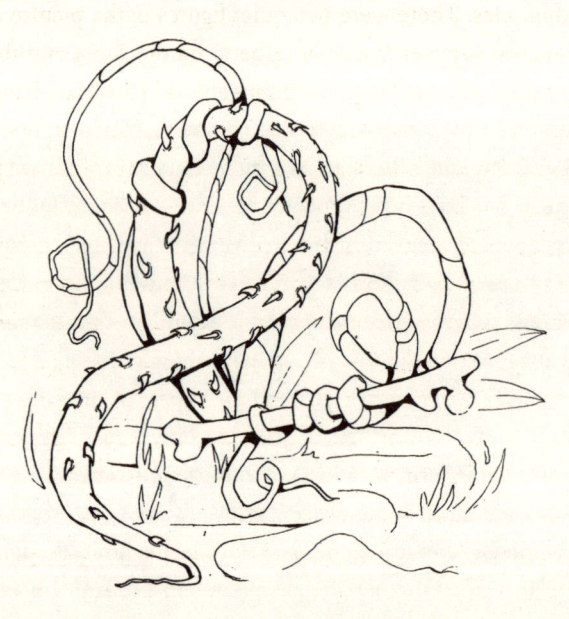

n the white slope of the sandy beach at Orr, a company of fishermen, just in from the night's catch, were variously employed in loading, disposing of their traps, or mending their nets. There were two quiet figures in the picture outlined in the clear summer atmosphere between the shore and the sea. A young man, who marked three points ahead in the line of intellectual development, was standing beside an overturned boat, upon which was seated an old fisherman, engaged in mending his net, and conveying to the attentive ear of his companion some interesting bits of information concerning the surrounding islands of the bay. There were relative values an artist would have appreciated, afforded by the contrast in dress and person of the two men. The fair, sensitive face of the young man, with his lithe and elegant figure coolly clad in white flannel, was a complement to the burly form of the sailor, roughly clothed, and with weather-stained features composing a simple but kindly countenance, well shaded under an oilskin hat.

"No land twixt her en Spain, sir."

"A period between continents," interrupted the young man jocosely.

"En I wouldn't go anighst her fur all the gold en the mint. Thar's plenty of land twixt her en us, thank God! Ye ken see she's the furtherest out nor all the islands."

"Yes, I see, Tom," replied the young man, directing a quizzical glance toward a small dark spot between the two spaces of blue. "She must be ten miles out."

"Nigh onter it."

"Well, what is out there to prevent a man from visiting your 'Mystery Island,' if he wants to?"

"Fur one thing, sir, Kidd's gold ez buried out thar, but thar hain't a feller on this yer coast dar's to go anighst it. Cauz the cove, what's only a narrer cut twixt two cliffs thet crawls inter sarpent ledges under the warter, makes it a damned nasty place ter git inter, even ef it warn't guarded—"

"Guarded? Guarded by whom?"

"A dorg, a confounded sperret dorg, with eyes like lighthouse lanterns, thet kin be seed ten miles out, whenever anything is goin' ter harpen. Whoever sees thet ar dorg might just's well make peace with God, fer he hain't likely ter stay round much longer 'mong men."

The young man, whose name was Lenartson—Sam Lenartson—laughed outright. It seemed the most ridiculous story he had ever heard credited by otherwise sensible men.

He determined at once to administer a rebuke to their foolish superstitions.

"Tom," he said, wheeling about impulsively, "give me a dory and a pair of oars, and I will go out there to-day and explode all your thrilling romance about the island."

"My God, sir!" Tom dropped his horny hands helplessly, an ashy pallor creeping over his face.

"Yer don't know, sir. Twenty years ago, sir, there was a party of young chaps from the city, who wouldn't hear to nuthin', went out there en never come back. Ye hain't lived round these parts en watched the signs. Thar's the awfullest rocket strikes this yer coast en a hurricane every time thet unarthly beast ez seed. 'Twould be like a helpin' ye to commit suicide; et's damned folly ter think uv et."

"Tom, you might just as well let me have your boat as to put me to the trouble of getting another, as I shall certainly go out to Mystery

Island, and I should like to go this morning. I vow solemnly to break the awful spell which has power over you only from your belief in it. And when I have entered the cove, braved the dog, and upset the kingdom of the devil supposed to be established there, not one of you fellows will dispute my right to Kidd's gold."

Tom's revolutions of thought were too slow to frame a new objection. Hypnotised by the spirit and energy of his companion, he rose from his seat, pointing doggedly at the boat.

"Ef ye will, ye will, I spoze; take her en go; ye don't go unwarned.

"Ye ken look out fur a squall," he shouted after the departing youth, who flung up his hat like a person taking leave of a party of particular friends, as he paddled out.

Sam was not by nature over-cautious, so that the admonition regarding the weather gave him no concern of mind as he floated past the beautiful islands of Casco Bay. One after another they disappeared behind him, as the island for which his oars were bent loomed up more definitely before him. Suddenly, conscious of a chill penetrating the atmosphere, he looked up, to remark a marshalling force of clouds that, unperceived by him, had been marching up the heavenly plain for the last half hour, and were now rapidly darkening with a summer shower.

An ominous lash of the wind struck the bosom of the great deep. With a startled throb, it lifted the boat sharply. Sam looked around him with critical and troubled eyes.

He was not far from the little cove, which presented itself as a sharply inclined sand-bar displayed between the cliffs that rose precipitously upon either side of it.

But the ledges upon either side of the passage rendered it so narrow and dangerous that they were called the Black Snakes. Around them the seething tide boiled like a witch's pot, flinging the white foam of the angry billows high against the cliffs, which returned it with such force that a boat carried in this direction must have been doomed to certain destruction.

Just as Lenartson was about to breast the wave that should have carried him safely into the little harbour, a fierce gust of wind from an unexpected quarter seized upon his light craft, and before he could make an effort to resist it, he was whirled about broadside upon one of the rising breakers. In this position, half capsized and waterlogged, blinded by the falling rain, his face wet by the salt spray, he must have been borne to certain death had not the capricious wind, playing with the frail craft like a paper toy, suddenly reversed it. Thus it was set upon the crest of a falling breaker in such a direction as to he flung into the cove, landing with a sharp collision some twenty feet up the beach.

The shock threw Lenartson face forward, where he lay for a moment half stunned. Then, as a flash of light and crash of thunder aroused him to a sense of danger, he sprang out of the boat, dragging it up the incline just in time to save it from the returning wave. After finding a broken stake, to which he secured his boat, he fled to the trees, seeking shelter from the rain among the tall and serried columns of pine and fir, whose thick mat of interlaced branches made the darkness almost impenetrable.

When, the shower ended, light through the breaking clouds penetrated the internal fastness, Lenartson discovered a rank growth of foliage not common to these islands nor the latitude in which they were located. Everywhere flowers and plants of variegated hues were massed in such rich profusion as to suggest the land of the deadly cobra, while even the more familiar trees had reached a height and breadth that seemed wholly foreign.

As he began to work his way through the thick undergrowth toward the interior, he came to the conclusion not only that the island was uninhabited, but that the place had not been marked by human footsteps for many years, as the small animals, and the birds that flew from cover, seemed quite fearless.

He had but just arrived at this conclusion when there rose upon the air the distinct bay of a dog, apparently not many feet away.

Evidently someone else had chosen the same day to pay a visit to the island.

Led by the sound of the animal's voice, he soon emerged upon what had been a small clearing, but at the present time was entirely covered with the second growth of trees, shooting up over an area of a hundred square feet. Here, amidst a medley of decayed stumps and underbrush, he saw a rude board hut, before which, with his nose in the air, sat the dog who had led him to question and investigation.

But, far from being the formidable creature of the fisherman's yarn, this noble wreck of the mastiff breed was ill fitted to hold midnight revels with hurricanes and to conjure with infernal powers, since every fibre of his poor old body seemed to call for blanket and a kennel.

His eyes, instead of appearing the baleful globes of fire that fishermen's fancies had made visible ten miles out at sea, were rather dim and piteous in their appeal for friendly recognition.

The poor creature had somehow missed his master—or such was Sam's conclusion—and in dog anguish thus lamented his misfortune.

"Hullo, old boy! have you lost him? Well, never mind, we'll set that straight directly."

Having convinced himself by a glance into the interior of the cabin, which was filled with spiders' webs and their crafty weavers, that it had not been used for many years, Lenartson turned once more to the dog.

"Come, Jack," he said, "let us go after your master."

With one of those peremptory barks that is interpreted as dog consent, the great lion-like creature bounded into the thicket.

This action served to reveal what had at one time been a path, but now, like every other effort of man here, indicated a contention with, and partial subjection to, the native wildness of the woodland.

Through bramble and briar they pushed along the overgrown path, the dog still ahead, until a space of light suddenly penetrated the open branches of the trees. A moment later, they emerged upon a plot of ground, where was revealed to Lenartson's astonished gaze a stately old mansion, built of stone, and enclosed by neglected terraces and overgrown gardens, upon which, at some time, had been bestowed much expense and care.

Now, however, the sharp tooth of time had gnawed into the vitals of the old place, from the broken chimneys and sunken flags of the walks to the defaced and fallen fence, rotting away beneath the mould of the drifting leaves.

The deserted house conveyed an air of melancholy to all of its surroundings.

It seemed a little singular to the young man, as he came upon this scene, that no person at Orr had ever mentioned its builders and occupants to him.

"Why not?" he wondered.

The dog left him no time to consider this point at length. He bounded up the steps, ran across the stone veranda, and leaped through the wide door into the hall, at the entrance of which rose a flight of winding stone stairs.

As Lenartson made haste to follow him, he had time to notice that the curtains at the lower windows were rendered almost invisible from the outside by the thick veil of dust encrusting the glass panes. He further felt the chill of a damp and mouldy house while ascending the stairs.

The upper hall presented a tableau in still life of open doors, dusty floor, and cobwebbed corners. His steps seemed to evoke a ghostly ring of answering echoes through the vacant halls. As the dog passed through one of the open doors leading off at the right of the staircase, Lenartson paused upon the threshold to listen to the laboured breathing of a sick or dying person.

Another moment, and his singular quest had brought him to the bedside of an old woman, lying beneath a heap of worn silk quilts and battered blankets, tossed about her emaciated figure in utmost confusion. The lips, thin, seamed, and crossed by yellow wrinkles, were parted above toothless gums in an almost vain struggle for breath. The talon-like fingers clutched nervously at the worn coverlid, as the great creature at Lenartson's side leaped upon the bed, lapping the withered cheek of his mistress; then settled down, with his head upon his paws, and his eyes fixed in appeal upon the stranger.

In bewilderment Lenartson glanced about the room, to observe, here as elsewhere, the absence of care denoted in the carpet of dust upon the oak floor, the array of cobwebs festooning the ceiling or woven across the brocade shades depending in sags from the four large windows of the room.

Here was a mystery of Mystery Island that made his blood boil with indignation. An old woman! Abandoned, it was evident, and dying thus, unattended except by a dog, her last earthly friend!

As he entered, she regarded him with no apparent recognition of a human presence, but turned the wandering glance of her wild, dark eyes toward a crucifix placed upon a table near the head of the bed. This crucifix was the only thing within reach of her vision to suggest solace to the dying, as there was neither bread upon the table to sustain her perishing frame, nor water to cool her parched lips.

"You are sick," affirmed the young man, with great pity vibrating in his voice; "what can I do for you?"

At the sound she sprang up in bed, and glared angrily upon him from dark and cavernous eyes. She stretched forth her long, lean arms, away from whose unlovely bones fell the tattered lace of her nightrobe.

"Pierre! Pierre!" she almost shrieked, as Lenartson shrank repulsed from the uninviting embrace. "At last! At last! Oh, my God, why did you leave me alone in this strange deserted land?"

She spoke in French, and Lenartson, understanding it well, thus discovered her lineage.

Then she had been deserted, this poor old creature—a refugee from a sunny land, abandoned to a life of wretchedness on this forsaken isle.

"Madame," he interrupted in reverent sympathy, "I am not Pierre; I am a stranger, providentially brought to you in this hour of need. What can I give you, food or drink, and where can either be found?"

With a supreme effort she pulled herself forward, a movement that called his attention to the glittering rings that hung upon her yellow, shrivelled hands.

"Ah! you would deceive me, and to what purpose, I ask?" She pointed in his face her old, skinny forefinger, an index of scorn shaken by wrath.

"Sir, I command you to leave me. If alone, well, so be it. If the King's head has fallen, it is a pretty piece of business these dogs have done. Never fear, the end will find France restored to reason. We shall make another King. No, sir! I decline your assistance in this matter. We are not a race of cowards."

As these scenes unshadowed themselves, she used first this tone of haughty complacency, and then, when the full horror of some fearful situation made itself felt, she threw up her arms with a cry of terror.

"What are they doing, these brutes in the street? It is she, my dear lady. Quick, give my cloak—this way—we must not be seen. The Bastille has fallen! It is the Conciergerie where they would carry our innocent, woe-white queen! It is dark, my dear—give me your hand—we are suspected, but we are also protected. Let us fly! The nobles are in the winepress, the people are on top—blood flows, curses darken the air. This is not France, it is a pandemonium; it is a mad-house: it is hell!"

Through this hurried, breathless speech of terror, Lenartson stood as if rooted the spot. At the close of it Madame sank, white with exhaustion, among the pillows. Then, as the dying candle fire flickered into a blaze, the old lips muttered:

"Have mercy, my lord! Do not leave me with these rough fellows even for so short a time. Do you believe the weak hand of a woman can protect such immense treasure? The earth where it lies buried is but an open storehouse, when, by your absence, the lock is removed from silence, and that devil, cupidity, which I see in each man's eye is free to manifest itself.

"Ah! the weed—the devil-weed! I had not thought about it. Plant it tomorrow upon yonder ledge that will lift it to the sun and air. Superstition will stay their greedy clutch for your gold, sir count. It will live—like the evil in men's hearts, it is too viperous to die."

She tossed herself uneasily. Great drops of perspiration stood upon her forehead.

"Pierre! Pierre!" she moaned, "It is not a devil-weed, it is a soul bound and restless; it is my soul shrieking silent maledictions to heaven.

"Ah, sir count, it was an awkward slip to take a woman from palaces and thrones to a hut in the woods; from association with princes to a company of thieves. But the gold tempted you, my poor count. For the promise of a title under the new régime we plotted—a pirate sold to you the secret of hidden treasure. He had sailed with the great captain; he knew it was here. We were an odd assemblage, I vow, but the house was built by stealth, of material brought in the ship—the treasure concealed. It was thought to be a secret, but when two have a secret it becomes public matter. Your devil-weed was planted to secure the gold. Your devil-weed—only a little evil, like the incipient causes of a revolution; the hand that cozened it into unholy life and nurtured its growth grew weak as the evil grew strong, to encompass the land. So, with the count's devil-plant, the treasure was no longer protected; it was buried and consumed by that thing which he brought from India—a little curling, crawling weed, concealed in a golden box, a cousin to the breathing plant, but an apostate, a wretched outcast from the world of flowers, embodying all their passion of growth and reproduction, yet endowed with the cruel instincts and power of a viper."

What was she talking about? There seemed so little coherency in what she said.

From what he could patch together of this ragged information, it led him to suppose she was a refugee from the French Revolution, who had sought these shores in company with her son, or whoever Pierre or the count might have been; that in their flight they had fallen in with a company of buccaneers, who had piloted them to this spot, where now lay concealed beneath some monstrous growth their hidden treasure. But, hark! she spoke again, placing her hand on the dog's head.

"Ah, Rollin, is it you? You are more faithful than men. They left me alone here to die—for I am dying—but in death I will not lie in quiet amidst this savagery of nature.

"Would it be possible, if my body were bound to this accursed soil, that my spirit could abandon the scene of its torture? No! no! I should traverse the earth until the resurrection of the dead. Like yonder devil-plant, to which my feet have worn a path through the wilderness, I should writhe and creep and live, forever.

"Back to France! O souls of the dead! if ye have ears for mortal complaint—if ye bear in your spirits a kinship and sympathy for human woe, I call upon you to witness the last cry of my embodied spirit for the land of its nativity: Bear me back to France!"

With a shriek of agony that made Lenartson's blood curdle, she threw her face, in the last desperate action of despair, forward upon her knees. Lay thus, with her features concealed, her arms stretched forth, and her hair straying loosely about her thin, white figure like a scant and shredded veil.

Lenartson, shocked and awakened from his trance, hastened to list her so as to give her air. Too late! The candle had flickered out. She was dead.

Gravely he composed the old limbs and worn features of the Grand Madame. What a sad romance. How singular that he should have witnessed the closing scenes of such a tragedy!

Having done what was possible, he determined to return to Orr, to give information of what had happened. And if it was true that treasure was concealed on this island, the final cry of the departed soul should be answered. She should be carried back to France. First, however, he must solve the final mystery of the gold and the devil-plant.

After a short search he discovered what appeared to be an overgrown path, which led out of the garden toward the interior, directly opposite to the one by which he had entered, and began at once to make his way through it.

At length he arrived at an open space where, for half a mile, the trees were dwarfed at every point of the circle where they approached it. In the centre of this enclosure of green earth, thus denuded of shrubs and trees, there was situated a long ledge, rising in some places to a height of thirty or forty feet. All about it the tall grass pliantly bent to the light touch of the wind. Covering the entire cliff, and often dripping to the ground along the face of it, was a peculiar mass, whose narrow, spiked leaves presented a living sea of green. The entire plant seemed to be endowed with voluntary motion, as without apparent cause it rose and fell like the jerky hunch of an inchworm, or the ceaseless motion of the waves of the sea.

Some of the limbs of the plant dropping over the head of the boulder were as large as the body of an anaconda. They were clothed in smooth, mottled bark somewhat resembling the skin of that reptile in colour. The limbs and stems were set about with a glossy corolla of leaves, about four inches between each cluster. From their centres depended a bunch of tendrils and a cluster of flame-like, star-shaped blossoms. Long, and dank, and dark, this beautiful devil-plant swung to and fro. At an interval of about ten seconds the limbs and tendrils contracted in such a manner as to bring all of the leaves together so as to entirely conceal the branches upon which they grew, then stretched forth again.

It was this singular motion, somewhat like that of the breathing plant, which caused the heaving, crawling motion of the whole mass above and the tremulous vibration of the limbs below.

Curiously fascinated, Lenartson crept somewhat nearer, hoping to determine something of the character of the plant's malign influence without perilous adventure.

As he approached nearer and nearer, fixing his eyes upon the plant with the suspicion of watching for an enemy in ambush, he kept pushing his foot cautiously through the long grass. "Was it here?" he speculated, "or over yonder, directly beneath that restless sea of leaves, the great treasure was buried?"

Suddenly he struck something concealed in the grass that leaped upon him, coiling with such a sharp, unexpected pressure about his feet and ankles, that, thus entangled, he was jerked from his feet, falling backward upon the earth. In this position, before he had time to struggle to his knees, he felt himself being rapidly drawn toward the cliff, upon which grew the great mass of the devil-plant, a limb of which, serpent-like, coiled and concealed in the grass, had caught his wary feet and was now rapidly coiling up his body, to bear him with angry jerks toward the great monster plant that, to Lenartson's horrified eyes, appeared to rise and approach him, full of malignant life. At that moment he remembered a fish knife which he happened to have in his pocket, and, seizing it, he commenced a desperate attack upon the vine as he struggled to his knees.

It was a short, sharply contested battle, in which the man realised that, once within the grasp of the great mass of deadly limbs and viperous tendrils of the great plant, there would be no more tomorrows for him upon the earth.

He succeeded none too soon in freeing himself from the obnoxious embrace of the fearful thing, whose wounded part continued by jerky hunches to retire toward the main body, trembling to receive it into its umbrageous bosom; while the severed portion about his legs, with a faint quiver as of departing life, uncoiled itself and dropped, with the soft thud of dead material, lengthwise upon the grass.

Filled with a great sense of gratitude and relief, not unmixed with horror, he made haste to beat a retreat toward the woodland, moving backward with his white face set suspiciously toward the enemy. When once assured that safe distance had been placed between them, he stood for some minutes watching the heaving body of green with its serpent arms flung over the cliff. He was deeply impressed by Madame's characterisation.

"It is not a plant! It is my soul shrieking maledictions to heaven."

What was it? He could not classify it as other than a rare specimen from a prehistoric period—a monstrous growth and prophecy in plant life of the mighty powers of intelligence destined to inherit and subdue the earth, significantly saved to this age for the study and wonder of man. In the unreckoned ages of its existence it had survived the sweep of universal conflagration; it had beheld the God-abandoned race perishing in the carburetted atmosphere, smothered in subterranean caverns, plunged in boiling oceans, or buried beneath mounds of burning cinders that followed the trail of the red serpent of the air. It had witnessed the age of darkness and cold, and now, a living chronicle of disaster, it had been captured by the daring hand of man and transplanted to a foreign shore.

It was five o'clock when Lenartson set out on his homeward journey. The sky was clear, the sea was calm, so that nothing occurred to withdraw his mind from meditating deeply upon ways and means by which the devil-plant might be overcome, the gold secured, and Madame's body returned to France.

He concluded that he would not speak to the people at Orr about the later portion of his adventure, as it would be likely to open inquiries that would lead to the discovery of the gold—a secret that he did not wish at present to reveal to them.

Late as he arrived, for it was after sunset, he found Bill Maynard awaiting him. The old fisherman greeted him with surprise and emotion, and on hearing a portion of the story, hastened to bear the tidings from house to house. In consequence, Lenartson found himself an hour later besieged at the hotel by a crowd of curious people, to whom he rehearsed the tale of the finding of the dog, his pursuit to the deserted house, and the impressive death-bed scene of the Grand Madame.

The kerosene lamp upon the clerk's desk made a narrow circle of light around the room. In the centre of it Lenartson occupied a wooden chair. He frequently changed his position as he talked.

Each strong-featured lad or bearded and weather-stained man kept his face attentively set toward the narrator. Each sharply silhouetted ghost upon the white-plastered wall showed scarcely a tremor of the immobile figures that surrounded him. Lenartson represented all the action of the company at the centre.

The young man being unpleasantly conscious of the profound impression made upon his own high-wrought sensibilities, attempted to assume an air of carelessness.

To cover a slight tremor of his limbs, which he could not wholly repress, he would push himself up on the back legs of his chair, and sit thus, with his hands in his pockets, talking almost waggishly. Then, almost irresistibly overcome by the intensity of his feelings, he would drop suddenly forward, with a tragic earnestness that made itself felt in every heart.

They comprehended at once how cruel superstition had made them to this poor old creature, the harrowing scenes of whose death-bed lost nothing by Lenartson's tragic recital, excepting her connection with the concealed gold and the devil-plant.

Finally, they agreed that a company of twenty men should accompany Lenartson in the morning to Mystery Island, for the purpose of bringing Madame's body to Orr, where for a time, at least, it should remain, peacefully interred.

They did not separate until about one o'clock, and then, few of them who had listened to the story slept much for the night. As for Lenartson, he threw himself dressed upon the bed, from which he frequently started up to pace the floor.

All night he was haunted by the cry of Madame's departed spirit for the land of its nativity.

It lay upon him, a fearful injunction he could but obey. The devil-plant must in some way be overcome, the vast treasure unearthed, and Madame's embalmed body returned to the dear, sunny land of her birth.

As the yacht was launched, he moved among them, a strangely silent figure, with set lips and pallid cheek, his hat pulled low over his brow, his gaze abstracted from present scenes, his soul filled in all its chambers of sense with that piteous cry.

When they arrived at Mystery Island the mid-day sun had ploughed his passage to the zenith without a cloud to vex his progress. They made haste to secure their boats, then dropped into Indian file, twenty men behind their leader, pushing and breaking their way through the overgrown path toward the old house in the woods.

The sharp clink of their stout heels sprang up behind them in startling echoes along the wide hall and stone stairway.

Upon the threshold of the room Lenartson had left yesterday, so full of tragic pictures memory would ever recall, he stopped a moment, looking over his shoulder into the pale and kindly faces behind him.

"Poor old Madame! It was here, boys, I left her yesterday after all was over."

Thus remarking, he turned his face inward and approached the bed. He stood before it aghast; the bed was empty! There was the yellow, crumpled linen, there were the soiled blankets and tattered coverlid which the long, thin, bejewelled fingers had plucked at yesterday. But she and the dog were gone!

For the space of ten seconds each man stood staring in helpless silence. Then one of them ventured to suggest that he had made a mistake in the room. No one thought of doubting him. His face was too plain an index of his astonishment.

"That's it," concluded Bill Maynard. "You gut addled. Let's try another room."

Lenartson, continuing to gaze in a bewildered way at the bed, shook his head. "No, it was right here, and no other place, that I passed through the experience I have related to you. There must be some other person on the premises, and all that talk about being deserted was Madame's lunacy. Let's look about."

As they commenced their investigation, the noise of their approach and departure startled the bats from their corners in the empty rooms. Everything was covered with dust and mould; even the chairs and floors were thickly encrusted. Through the holes in the roof the rain had beaten unchecked and the resulting fungus life consumed, as it grew, the wooden sills and doorways. Cobwebs hung in festoons from the ceiling, and cut in elaborate patterns of grey lace the corners of the rooms, in one of which a rabbit had made her nest and was rearing her young. Across the threshold of another a serpent slipped into the golden shimmer of the outer sunshine.

In a cupboard was found a china service, and a silver or pewter pot so black with long exposure to the air and moisture, its true metal could not at once be determined. And everywhere was the all-recording dust, covering the entire house like a pall cloth upon the face of the dead. There was no food, nor evidence of recent occupancy in the entire house.

Once again they looked at each other, and then to Lenartson, the question trembling upon each man's lips he feared to utter.

Superstition repossessed them. Lenartson, dazed and distressed, placed his hand against his forehead, struggling to think.

Ah! The devil-weed and the treasure! If these things existed in reality, it would establish the fact of his having spoken with a dying woman yesterday.

"Boys, I must leave you for half an hour. Will you wait for me here?"

"Out there," they consented gruffly, pointing to the garden. No man cared to remain within.

In feverish impatience he darted away from them, tearing his way along the gloomy woodland path toward the spot where that terrible thing grew.

At the point where the opening would reveal the cliff, he stopped short, struck by a chill of horror. Great drops of perspiration rolled over his face. His heart beat with stifling throbs in his bosom, while his hands clenched themselves unconsciously.

In this mood, appalled by awful doubt, he dashed out into the open space—then stopped short, an exclamation of joy bursting from his fevered lips. Thank God, it was there, and she had been!

Steeped in the still sunshine of the upper air, that monster plant still crawled over the grey head of the great boulder, emitting fiery sparks from its bosom, as with each lift of its huge body the round rings of its red blossoms flashed into view. The long, grey, snake-like limbs, bristling with their gay corolla of spiked leaves, swung, contracted, and lengthened, exactly as he had seen them yesterday.

Cautiously he crept forward, his nervous fingers clutching the handle of his knife, treading carefully through the long grass which appeared to grow here like some dangerous accomplice of the enemy.

Now he understood why no shrub or tree grew near the boulder. The devil-plant had, as it grew, grasped, one after another, every living thing which could afford resistance to its malignant clutch. It had made itself a supreme evil in the garden of God, annihilating all living beauty excepting the long, pliant grass, through which it might creep and glide towards the object to be destroyed.

Not a wonder Madame, who knew its nature, moaned. "It will encompass the land." And the treasure beneath it—Ugh! the whole thing grew uncanny. He commenced to feel that any attempt to recover a treasure upon which rested the curse of Madame's passion-withered lips would prove fatal. He could almost see the ghastly glistening of dead men's bones impaled in the meshes of that fearful thing. An accursed root had sprung out of the practical Maine soil, engrafted upon it from some kingdom of the damned.

A shadow crossed the sun, followed by another and still another in quick succession, like the swift lifting of gigantic wings.

The trees shivered. The air leaped at once into strong currents, gathering velocity and darkness as they travelled. The sky lowered with a blaze of fury, followed by deafening thunder and accompanied by the roar of the sea.

Lenartson felt himself raised bodily by the wind and dashed down again like chaff. In terror, lest the mighty breath of the tempest make him the plaything of yonder devil-weed, now tossing forward and flinging up its long, crawling arms into the sulphurous air, he grasped the trunk of a tree with his arms, and flung himself face down upon the ground.

Ships went down everywhere along the coast that day. Their own boat dragged her anchor and was driven upon the rocks. Houses were unroofed and blown about like paper toys. It was a day of doom. It was like the passionate protest of the dead in league with the elements.

"I would haunt the land forever. I will not lie on this accursed soil. Bear me back to France!"

Pale, and shaken, and drenched by the pitying floods of the sky, Lenartson crept back, when the tempest was past, to the old house, where he met a company of stern, white faces.

"Boys," he said brokenly, "I cannot talk of what has happened on this mysterious island. I only ask to be taken away. Bill Maynard, give me your hand, old boy. I am no longer able to jeer at your superstitions."

None seemed inclined to talk.

When at last they swung out upon the broad, blue breast of the ocean, under a sunny sky, every man thanked God he had left the place forever.

And although at times some bold lad dares to steer his skiff beneath the haunted cliff, where he declares the dog Rollin may still be seen on watch at the cove, there has been none other ambitious to investigate the mystery of Mystery Island.

The old house in the woods remains untenanted and unvisited. Dank and dark the devil-weed swings in the undisturbed silence of its green oasis.

The treasure buried upon the island is to many but a vague speculation. To Lenartson there appears no doubt as to the reality of the concealed treasure, and the Grand Madame is to him one of the most marvellous mysteries of life. Who was the Grand Madame? What was it that he saw at the old house? What did he hear? He had not slept and dreamed. Was it a visitation from the other world? A disturbed and earthbound soul enacting the closing scene of its mortality? If not, what? Where did the Grand Madame and the dog Rollin disappear?

THE ASH TREE

M. R. James

"The Ash Tree" was first published in James's collection *Ghost Stories of an Antiquary* and is similarly gothic to Gilman's "The Giant Wistaria" as both stories focus on a tragic past which comes back to haunt the present. M. R. James was one of the most famous ghost story writers of his time with a vast catalogue of short stories, many of which have been adapted for TV or film. "The Ash Tree" documents the experience of Sir Richard Fell, who inherits Castringham Hall as well as its curse, which caused the mysterious deaths of the previous owners. The ash tree of the title acts more as a vessel and instrument of dark magic than other plants in this collection, which are more active and murderous. With this in mind, "The Ash Tree" is a standout entry within this collection as it expresses a different strand of Botanical Gothic. The element of witch trials and subsequent revenge draws attention to the theme of female suffering as well as the intrinsic link between femininity and (super)nature.

veryone who has travelled over Eastern England knows the smaller country-houses with which it is studded—the rather dank little buildings, usually in the Italian style, surrounded with parks of some eighty to a hundred acres. For me they have always had a very strong attraction: with the grey paling of split oak, the noble trees, the meres with their reed-beds, and the line of distant woods. Then, I like the pillared portico—perhaps stuck on to a red-brick Queen Anne house which has been faced with stucco to bring it into line with the "Grecian" taste of the end of the eighteenth century; the hall inside, going up to the roof, which hall ought always to be provided with a gallery and a small organ. I like the library, too, where you may find anything from a Psalter of the thirteenth century to a Shakespeare quarto. I like the pictures, of course; and perhaps most of all I like fancying what life in such a house was when it was first built, and in the piping times of landlords' prosperity, and not least now, when, if money is not so plentiful, taste is more varied and life quite as interesting. I wish to have one of these houses, and enough money to keep it together and entertain my friends in it modestly.

But this is a digression. I have to tell you of a curious series of events which happened in such a house as I have tried to describe. It is Castringham Hall in Suffolk. I think a good deal has been done to the building since the period of my story, but the essential features I have sketched are still there—Italian portico, square block of white house, older inside than out, park with fringe of woods, and mere. The one feature that marked out the house from a score of others is gone. As you looked at it from the park, you saw on the right a great old ash tree growing within half a dozen yards of the wall, and almost or quite touching the building with its branches. I suppose it had stood there ever since Castringham ceased to be a fortified place, and since the moat was filled in and the Elizabethan dwelling-house built. At any rate, it had well-nigh attained its full dimensions in the year 1690.

In that year the district in which the Hall is situated was the scene of a number of witch trials. It will be long, I think, before we arrive at a just estimate of the amount of solid reason—if there was any—which lay at the root of the universal fear of witches in old times. Whether the persons accused of this offence really did imagine that they were possessed of unusual power of any kind; or whether they had the will at least, if not the power, of doing mischief to their neighbours; or whether all the confessions, of which there are so many, were extorted by the mere cruelty of the witch-finders—these are questions which are not, I fancy, yet solved. And the present narrative gives me pause. I cannot altogether sweep it away as mere invention. The reader must judge for himself.

Castringham contributed a victim to the *auto-da-fé*. Mrs Mothersole was her name, and she differed from the ordinary run of village witches only in being rather better off and in a more influential position. Efforts were made to save her by several reputable farmers of the parish. They did their best to testify to her character, and showed considerable anxiety as to the verdict of the jury.

But what seems to have been fatal to the woman was the evidence of the then proprietor of Castringham Hall—Sir Matthew Fell. He deposed to having watched her on three different occasions from his window, at the full of the moon, gathering branches "from the ash tree near my house." She had climbed into the branches, clad only in her shift, and was cutting off small twigs with a peculiarly curved knife, and as she did so she seemed to be talking to herself. On each occasion Sir Matthew had done his best to capture the woman, but she had always taken alarm at some accidental noise he had made, and all he could see when he got down to the garden was a hare running across the path in the direction of the village.

On the third night he had been at pains to follow at his best speed, and had gone straight to Mrs Mothersole's house; but he had had to wait a quarter of an hour battering at her door, and then she had come out very cross, and apparently very sleepy, as if just out of bed; and he had no good explanation to offer of his visit.

Mainly on this evidence, though there was much more of a less striking and unusual kind from other parishioners, Mrs Mothersole was found guilty and condemned to die. She was hanged a week after the trial, with five or six more unhappy creatures, at Bury St Edmunds.

Sir Matthew Fell, then Deputy Sheriff, was present at the execution. It was a damp, drizzly March morning when the cart made its way up the rough grass hill outside Northgate, where the gallows stood. The other victims were apathetic or broken down with misery; but Mrs Mothersole was, as in life so in death, of a very different temper. Her "poysonous Rage," as a reporter of the time puts it, "did so work upon the Bystanders—yea, even upon the Hangman—that it was constantly affirmed of all that saw her that she presented the living Aspect of a mad Divell. Yet she offer'd no Resistance to the Officers of the Law; onely she looked upon those that laid Hands upon her with so direfull and venomous an Aspect that—as one of them afterwards assured me—the meer Thought of it preyed inwardly upon his Mind for six Months after."

However, all that she is reported to have said was the seemingly meaningless words: "There will be guests at the Hall." Which she repeated more than once in an undertone.

Sir Matthew Fell was not unimpressed by the bearing of the woman. He had some talk upon the matter with the vicar of his parish, with whom he travelled home after the assize business was over. His evidence at the trial had not been very willingly given; he was not specially infected with the witch-finding mania, but he declared, then and afterwards, that he could not give any other account of the matter than that he had given, and that he could not possibly have been mistaken as to what he saw. The whole transaction had been repugnant to him, for he was a man who liked to be on pleasant terms with those about him; but he saw a duty to be done in this business, and he had done it. That seems to have been the gist of his sentiments, and the Vicar applauded it, as any reasonable man must have done.

A few weeks after, when the moon of May was at the full, vicar and squire met again in the park, and walked to the Hall together. Lady Fell was with her mother, who was dangerously ill, and Sir Matthew was alone at home; so the vicar, Mr Crome, was easily persuaded to take a late supper at the Hall.

Sir Matthew was not very good company this evening. The talk ran chiefly on family and parish matters, and, as luck would have it, Sir Matthew made a memorandum in writing of certain wishes or intentions of his regarding his estates, which afterwards proved exceedingly useful.

When Mr Crome thought of starting for home, about half-past nine o'clock, Sir Matthew and he took a preliminary turn on the gravelled walk at the back of the house. The only incident that struck Mr Crome was this: they were in sight of the ash tree which I described as growing near the windows of the building, when Sir Matthew stopped and said:

"What is that that runs up and down the stem of the ash? It is never a squirrel? They will all be in their nests by now."

The vicar looked and saw the moving creature, but he could make nothing of its colour in the moonlight. The sharp outline, however, seen for an instant, was imprinted on his brain, and he could have sworn, he said, though it sounded foolish, that, squirrel or not, it had more than four legs.

Still, not much was to be made of the momentary vision, and the two men parted. They may have met since then, but it was not for a score of years.

Next day Sir Matthew Fell was not downstairs at six in the morning, as was his custom, nor at seven, nor yet at eight. Hereupon the servants went and knocked at his chamber door. I need not prolong the description of their anxious listenings and renewed batterings on the panels. The door was opened at last from the outside, and they found their master dead and black. So much you have guessed. That there were any marks of violence did not at the moment appear; but the window was open.

One of the men went to fetch the parson, and then by his directions rode on to give notice to the coroner. Mr Crome himself went as quick as he might to the Hall, and was shown to the room where the dead man lay. He has left some notes among his papers which show how genuine a respect and sorrow was felt for Sir Matthew, and there is also this passage, which I transcribe for the sake of the light it throws upon the course of events, and also upon the common beliefs of the time:

"There was not any the least Trace of an Entrance having been forc'd to the Chamber: but the Casement stood open, as my poor Friend would always have it in this Season. He had his Evening Drink of small Ale in a silver vessel of about a pint measure, and to-night had not drunk it out. This Drink was examined by the Physician from Bury, a Mr Hodgkins, who could not, however, as he afterwards declar'd upon his Oath, before the Coroner's quest, discover that any matter of a venomous kind was present in it. For, as was natural, in the great Swelling and Blackness of the Corpse, there was talk made among the Neighbours of Poyson. The Body was very much Disorder'd as it laid in the Bed, being twisted after so extream a sort as gave too probable Conjecture that my worthy Friend and Patron had expir'd in great Pain and Agony. And what is as yet unexplain'd, and to myself the Argument of some Horrid and Artfull Designe in the Perpetrators of this Barbarous Murther, was this, that the Women which were entrusted with the laying-out of the Corpse and washing it, being both sad Persons and very well Respected in their Mournfull Profession, came to me in a great Pain and Distress both of Mind and Body, saying, what was indeed confirmed upon the first View, that they had no sooner touch'd the Breast of the Corpse with their naked Hands than they were sensible of a more than ordinary violent Smart and Acheing in their Palms, which, with their whole Forearms, in no long time swell'd so immoderately, the Pain still continuing, that, as afterwards proved, during many weeks they were forc'd to lay by the exercise of their Calling; and yet no mark seen on the Skin.

"Upon hearing this, I sent for the Physician, who was still in the House, and we made as carefull a Proof as we were able by the Help of a small Magnifying Lens of Crystal of the condition of the Skinn on this Part of the Body: but could not detect with the Instrument we had any Matter of Importance beyond a couple of small Punctures or Pricks, which we then concluded were the Spotts by which the Poyson might be introduced, remembering that Ring of *Pope Borgia*, with other known Specimens of the Horrid Art of the Italian Poysoners of the last age.

"So much is to be said of the Symptoms seen on the Corpse. As to what I am to add, it is meerly my own Experiment, and to be left to Posterity to judge whether there be anything of Value therein. There was on the Table by the Beddside a Bible of the small size, in which my Friend—punctuall as in Matters of less Moment, so in this more weighty one—used nightly, and upon his First Rising, to read a sett Portion. And I taking it up—not without a Tear duly paid to him which from the Study of this poorer Adumbration was now pass'd to the contemplation of its great Originall—it came into my Thoughts, as at such moments of Helplessness we are prone to catch at any the least Glimmer that makes promise of Light, to make trial of that old and by many accounted Superstitious Practice of drawing the *Sortes*: of which a Principall Instance, in the case of his late Sacred Majesty the Blessed Martyr King *Charles* and my Lord *Falkland*, was now much talked of. I must needs admit that by my Trial not much Assistance was afforded me: yet, as the Cause and Origin of these Dreadfull Events may hereafter be search'd out, I set down the Results, in the case it may be found that they pointed the true Quarter of the Mischief to a quicker Intelligence than my own.

"I made, then, three trials, opening the Book and placing my Finger upon certain Words: which gave in the first these words, from Luke xiii. 7, *Cut it down;* in the second, Isaiah xiii. 20, *It shall never be inhabited;* and upon the third Experiment, Job xxxix. 30, *Her young ones also suck up blood.*"

This is all that need be quoted from Mr Crome's papers. Sir Matthew Fell was duly coffined and laid into the earth, and his funeral sermon, preached by Mr Crome on the following Sunday, has been printed under the title of "The Unsearchable Way; or, England's Danger and the Malicious Dealings of Antichrist," it being the vicar's view, as well as that most commonly held in the neighbourhood, that the squire was the victim of a recrudescence of the Popish Plot.

His son, Sir Matthew the second, succeeded to the title and estates. And so ends the first act of the Castringham tragedy. It is to be mentioned, though the fact is not surprising, that the new Baronet did not occupy the room in which his father had died. Nor, indeed, was it slept in by anyone but an occasional visitor during the whole of his occupation. He died in 1735, and I do not find that anything particular marked his reign, save a curiously constant mortality among his cattle and livestock in general, which showed a tendency to increase slightly as time went on.

Those who are interested in the details will find a statistical account in a letter to the *Gentleman's Magazine* of 1772, which draws the facts from the Baronet's own papers. He put an end to it at last by a very simple expedient, that of shutting up all his beasts in sheds at night, and keeping no sheep in his park. For he had noticed that nothing was ever attacked that spent the night indoors. After that the disorder confined itself to wild birds, and beasts of chase. But as we have no good account of the symptoms, and as all-night watching was quite unproductive of any clue, I do not dwell on what the Suffolk farmers called the "Castringham sickness."

The second Sir Matthew died in 1735, as I said, and was duly succeeded by his son, Sir Richard. It was in his time that the great family pew was built out on the north side of the parish church. So large were the squire's ideas that several of the graves on that unhallowed side of the building had to be disturbed to satisfy his requirements. Among them was that of Mrs Mothersole, the position of which was accurately known, thanks to a note on a plan of the church and yard, both made by Mr Crome.

A certain amount of interest was excited in the village when it was known that the famous witch, who was still remembered by a few, was to be exhumed. And the feeling of surprise, and indeed disquiet, was very strong when it was found that, though her coffin was fairly sound and unbroken, there was no trace whatever inside it of body, bones, or dust. Indeed, it is a curious phenomenon, for at the time of her burying no such things were dreamt of as resurrection-men, and it is difficult to conceive any rational motive for stealing a body otherwise than for the uses of the dissecting-room.

The incident revived for a time all the stories of witch trials and of the exploits of the witches, dormant for forty years, and Sir Richard's orders that the coffin should be burnt were thought by a good many to be rather foolhardy, though they were duly carried out.

Sir Richard was a pestilent innovator, it is certain. Before his time the Hall had been a fine block of the mellowest red brick; but Sir Richard had travelled in Italy and become infected with the Italian taste, and, having more money than his predecessors, he determined to leave an Italian palace where he had found an English house. So stucco and ashlar masked the brick; some indifferent Roman marbles were planted about in the entrance-hall and gardens; a reproduction of the Sibyl's temple at Tivoli was erected on the opposite bank of the mere; and Castringham took an entirely new, and, I must say, a less engaging, aspect. But it was much admired, and served as a model to a good many of the neighbouring gentry in after-years.

One morning (it was in 1754) Sir Richard woke after a night of discomfort. It had been windy, and his chimney had smoked persistently, and yet it was so cold that he must keep up a fire. Also something had so rattled about the window that no man could get a moment's peace. Further, there was the prospect of several guests of position arriving in the course of the day, who would expect sport of some kind, and the inroads of the distemper (which continued among his game) had been lately so serious that he was afraid for his reputation as a game-preserver. But what really touched him most nearly was the other matter of his sleepless night. He could certainly not sleep in that room again.

That was the chief subject of his meditations at breakfast, and after it he began a systematic examination of the rooms to see which would suit his notions best. It was long before he found one. This had a window with an eastern aspect and that with a northern; this door the servants would be always passing, and he did not like the bedstead in that. No, he must have a room with a western look-out, so that the sun could not wake him early, and it must be out of the way of the business of the house. The housekeeper was at the end of her resources.

"Well, Sir Richard," she said, "you know that there is but the one room like that in the house."

"Which may that be?" said Sir Richard.

"And that is Sir Matthew's—the West Chamber."

"Well, put me in there, for there I'll lie tonight," said her master. "Which way is it? Here, to be sure;" and he hurried off.

"Oh, Sir Richard, but no one has slept there these forty years. The air has hardly changed since Sir Matthew died there."

Thus she spoke, and rustled after him.

"Come, open the door, Mrs Chiddock. I'll see the chamber, at least."

So it was opened, and, indeed, the smell was very close and earthy. Sir Richard crossed to the window, and, impatiently, as was his wont, threw the shutters back, and flung open the casement. For this end of the house was one which the alterations had barely touched, grown up as it was with the great ash tree, and being otherwise concealed from view.

"Air it, Mrs Chiddock, all today, and move my bed-furniture in in the afternoon. Put the Bishop of Kilmore in my old room."

"Pray, Sir Richard," said a new voice, breaking in on this speech, "might I have the favour of a moment's interview?"

Sir Richard turned round and saw a man in black in the doorway, who bowed.

"I must ask your indulgence for this intrusion, Sir Richard. You will, perhaps, hardly remember me. My name is William Crome, and my grandfather was vicar here in your grandfather's time."

"Well, sir," said Sir Richard, "the name of Crome is always a passport to Castringham. I am glad to renew a friendship of two generations' standing. In what can I serve you? for your hour of call-ing—and, if I do not mistake you, your bearing—shows you to be in some haste."

"That is no more than the truth, sir. I am riding from Norwich to Bury St Edmunds with what haste I can make, and I have called in on my way to leave with you some papers which we have but just come upon in looking over what my grandfather left at his death. It is thought you may find some matters of family interest in them."

"You are mighty obliging, Mr Crome, and, if you will be so good as to follow me to the parlour, and drink a glass of wine, we will take a first look at these same papers together. And you, Mrs Chiddock, as I said, be about airing this chamber... Yes, it is here my grandfather died... Yes, the tree, perhaps, does make the place a little dampish... No; I do not wish to listen to any more. Make no difficulties, I beg. You have your orders—go. Will you follow me, sir?"

They went to the study. The packet which young Mr Crome had brought—he was then just become a Fellow of Clare Hall in Cambridge, I may say, and subsequently brought out a respectable edition of Polyænus—contained among other things the notes which the old Vicar had made upon the occasion of Sir Matthew Fell's death. And for the first time Sir Richard was confronted with the enigmatical *Sortes Biblicæ* which you have heard. They amused him a good deal.

"Well," he said, "my grandfather's Bible gave one prudent piece of advice—*Cut it down*. If that stands for the ash tree, he may rest assured I shall not neglect it. Such a nest of catarrhs and agues was never seen."

The parlour contained the family books, which, pending the arrival of a collection which Sir Richard had made in Italy, and the building of a proper room to receive them, were not many in number.

Sir Richard looked up from the paper to the bookcase.

"I wonder," says he, "whether the old prophet is there yet? I fancy I see him."

Crossing the room, he took out a dumpy Bible, which, sure enough, bore on the flyleaf the inscription: "To Matthew Fell, from his Loving Godmother, Anne Aldous, 2 September, 1659."

"It would be no bad plan to test him again, Mr Crome. I will wager we get a couple of names in the Chronicles. H'm! what have we here? "Thou shalt seek me in the morning, and I shall not be." Well, well! Your grandfather would have made a fine omen of that, hey? No more prophets for me! They are all in a tale. And now, Mr Crome, I am infinitely obliged to you for your packet. You will, I fear, be impatient to get on. Pray allow me—another glass."

So with offers of hospitality, which were genuinely meant (for Sir Richard thought well of the young man's address and manner) they parted.

In the afternoon came the guests—the Bishop of Kilmore, Lady Mary Hervey, Sir William Kentfield, etc. Dinner at five, wine, cards, supper, and dispersal to bed.

Next morning Sir Richard is disinclined to take his gun with the rest. He talks with the Bishop of Kilmore. This prelate, unlike a good many of the Irish bishops of his day, had visited his see, and, indeed, resided there, for some considerable time. This morning, as the two were walking along the terrace and talking over the alterations and improvements in the house, the Bishop said, pointing to the window of the West Room:

"You could never get one of my Irish flock to occupy that room, Sir Richard."

"Why is that, my lord? It is, in fact, my own."

"Well, our Irish peasantry will always have it that it brings the worst of luck to sleep near an ash tree, and you have a fine growth of ash not two yards from your chamber window. Perhaps," the Bishop went on, with a smile, "it has given you a touch of its quality already, for you do not seem, if I may say it, so much the fresher for your night's rest as your friends would like to see you."

"That, or something else, it is true, cost me my sleep from twelve to four, my lord. But the tree is to come down tomorrow, so I shall not hear much more from it."

"I applaud your determination. It can hardly be wholesome to have the air you breathe strained, as it were, through all that leafage."

"Your lordship is right there, I think. But I had not my window open last night. It was rather the noise that went on—no doubt from the twigs sweeping the glass—that kept me open-eyed."

"I think that can hardly be, Sir Richard. Here—you see it from this point. None of these nearest branches even can touch your casement unless there were a gale, and there was none of that last night. They miss the panes by a foot."

"No, sir, true. What, then, will it be, I wonder, that scratched and rustled so—ay, and covered the dust on my sill with lines and marks?"

At last they agreed that the rats must have come up through the ivy. That was the Bishop's idea, and Sir Richard jumped at it.

So the day passed quietly, and night came, and the party dispersed to their rooms, and wished Sir Richard a better night.

And now we are in his bedroom, with the light out and the squire in bed. The room is over the kitchen, and the night outside still and warm, so the window stands open.

There is very little light about the bedstead, but there is a strange movement there; it seems as if Sir Richard were moving his head rapidly to and fro with only the slightest possible sound. And now you would guess, so deceptive is the half-darkness, that he had several heads, round and brownish, which move back and forward, even as low as his chest. It is a horrible illusion. Is it nothing more? There! Something drops off the bed with a soft plump, like a kitten, and is out of the window in a flash; another—four—and after that there is quiet again.

"Thou shalt seek me in the morning, and I shall not be."

As with Sir Matthew, so with Sir Richard—dead and black in his bed!

A pale and silent party of guests and servants gathered under the window when the news was known. Italian poisoners, Popish emissaries, infected air—all these and more guesses were hazarded, and the Bishop of Kilmore looked at the tree, in the fork of whose lower boughs a white tom-cat was crouching, looking down the hollow which years had gnawed in the trunk. It was watching something inside the tree with great interest.

Suddenly it got up and craned over the hole. Then a bit of the edge on which it stood gave way, and it went slithering in. Everyone looked up at the noise of the fall.

It is known to most of us that a cat can cry; but few of us have heard, I hope, such a yell as came out of the trunk of the great ash. Two or three screams there were—the witnesses are not sure which—and then a slight and muffled noise of some commotion or struggling was all that came. But Lady Mary Hervey fainted outright, and the housekeeper stopped her ears and fled till she fell on the terrace.

The Bishop of Kilmore and Sir William Kentfield stayed. Yet even they were daunted, though it was only at the cry of a cat; and Sir William swallowed once or twice before he could say:

"There is something more than we know of in that tree, my lord. I am for an instant search."

And this was agreed upon. A ladder was brought, and one of the gardeners went up, and, looking down the hollow, could detect nothing but a few dim indications of something moving. They got a lantern, and let it down by a rope.

"We must get at the bottom of this. My life upon it, my lord, but the secret of these terrible deaths is there."

Up went the gardener again with the lantern, and let it down the hole cautiously. They saw the yellow light upon his face as he bent over, and saw his face struck with an incredulous terror and loathing before he cried out in a dreadful voice and fell back from the ladder—where, happily, he was caught by two of the men—letting the lantern fall inside the tree.

He was in a dead faint, and it was some time before any word could be got from him.

By then they had something else to look at. The lantern must have broken at the bottom, and the light in it caught upon dry leaves and rubbish that lay there, for in a few minutes a dense smoke began to come up, and then flame; and, to be short, the tree was in a blaze.

The bystanders made a ring at some yards' distance, and Sir William and the Bishop sent men to get what weapons and tools they could; for, clearly, whatever might be using the tree as its lair would be forced out by the fire.

So it was. First, at the fork, they saw a round body covered with fire—the size of a man's head—appear very suddenly, then seem to collapse and fall back. This, five or six times; then a similar ball leapt into the air and fell on the grass, where after a moment it lay still. The Bishop went as near as he dared to it, and saw—what but the remains of an enormous spider, veinous and seared! And, as the fire burned lower down, more terrible bodies like this began to break out from the trunk, and it was seen that these were covered with greyish hair.

All that day the ash burned, and until it fell to pieces the men stood about it, and from time to time killed the brutes as they darted out. At last there was a long interval when none appeared, and they cautiously closed in and examined the roots of the tree.

"They found," says the Bishop of Kilmore, "below it a rounded hollow place in the earth, wherein were two or three bodies of these creatures that had plainly been smothered by the smoke; and, what is to me more curious, at the side of this den, against the wall, was crouching the anatomy or skeleton of a human being, with the skin dried upon the bones, having some remains of black hair, which was pronounced by those that examined it to be undoubtedly the body of a woman, and clearly dead for a period of fifty years."

A VINE ON A HOUSE

Ambrose Bierce

Ambrose Bierce was a Civil War veteran turned writer known for his journalistic work, poetry and short stories. Bierce's "A Vine on a House" is a concise example of the latter, published in *Cosmopolitan* (New York), October 1905. The titular house in this story is an old, run-down building missing windows and doors which has become overgrown with foliage. Because of its dilapidated appearance it has gained an "evil reputation" and is an example of a monstrous vine in plant horror.

bout three miles from the little town of Norton, in Missouri, on the road leading to Maysville, stands an old house that was last occupied by a family named Harding. Since 1886 no one has lived in it, nor is anyone likely to live in it again. Time and the disfavour of persons dwelling thereabout are converting it into a rather picturesque ruin. An observer unacquainted with its history would hardly put it into the category of "haunted houses," yet in all the region round such is its evil reputation. Its windows are without glass, its doorways without doors; there are wide breaches in the shingle roof, and for lack of paint the weatherboarding is a dun-grey. But these unfailing signs of the supernatural are partly concealed and greatly softened by the abundant foliage of a large vine over-running the entire structure. This vine—of a species which no botanist has ever been able to name—has an important part in the story of the house.

The Harding family consisted of Robert Harding, his wife Matilda, Miss Julia Went, who was her sister, and two young children. Robert Harding was a silent, saturnine man who made no friends in the neighbourhood, and apparently did not care to. He was about forty years old, frugal and industrious, and made a living from the little farm which is now overgrown with brush and brambles. He and his sister-in-law were rather tabooed by their neighbours, who seemed to think that they were seen too frequently together—not entirely their fault, for at these times they evidently did not challenge observation. The moral code of rural Missouri is stern and exacting.

Mrs Harding was a well-mannered, sad-eyed woman, lacking a left foot.

At some time in 1884 it became known that Mrs Harding had gone to visit her mother in Iowa. That was what her husband said in reply to inquiries, and his manner of saying it did not encourage further questioning. She never came back, and two years later, without selling his farm or anything that was his, or appointing an agent to look after his interests, or removing his household goods, Harding, with the rest of the family, left the country. Nobody knew whither he went; nobody at that time cared. Naturally, whatever was movable about the place soon disappeared, and the deserted house became "haunted" in the manner of its kind.

One summer evening, four or five years later, the Rev. J. Gruber, of Norton, and a Maysville attorney named Hyatt met on horseback in front of the Harding place. Having some business matters to discuss, they hitched their animals and, going to the house, sat on the porch to talk. Some humorous reference to the sombre reputation of the place was made, and forgotten as soon as uttered, and they talked of their business affairs until it grew almost dark. The evening was oppressively warm, the air absolutely stagnant.

Suddenly both men started from their seats in surprise: a long vine that covered half the front of the house and dangled its branches from the edge of the porch above them was visibly and audibly agitated, shaking violently in every stem and leaf.

"We shall have a storm," Hyatt exclaimed.

Gruber said nothing, but silently directed the other's attention to the foliage of adjacent trees, which showed no movement; even the delicate tips of the boughs silhouetted against the clear sky were motionless. They hastily passed down the steps to what had been a lawn and looked upward to the vine, whose entire length was now visible. It continued in violent agitation, yet they could discern no disturbing cause.

"Let us leave," said the minister.

And leave they did. Forgetting that they had been travelling in opposite directions, they rode away together. They went to Norton, where they related their uncanny experience to several discreet friends. The next evening, at about the same hour, accompanied by two others whose names are not recalled by the writer, they were again on the porch of the Harding house, and again the mysterious phenomenon occurred: the vine was violently agitated while under the closest scrutiny from root to tip, nor did their combined strength applied to the trunk serve to still it. After an hour's observation they retreated, no less wise than when they had come.

No great time was required for these singular facts to rouse the curiosity of the entire neighbourhood. By day and by night crowds of persons assembled at the Harding house "seeking a sign." It does not appear that any found it, yet so credible were the witnesses mentioned that none doubted the reality of the "manifestations" to which they testified.

By either a happy inspiration or some destructive design, it was one day proposed—nobody appeared to know from whom the suggestion came—to dig up the vine, and after a good deal of debate this was done. Nothing was found but the root, yet nothing could have been more strange!

For five or six feet from the trunk, which had at the surface of the ground a diameter of several inches, it ran downward, single and straight, into a loose, friable earth; then it divided and subdivided into rootlets, fibres and filaments, most curiously interwoven. When carefully freed from soil, they showed a singular formation. In their ramifications and doublings back upon themselves they made a compact network, having in size and shape an amazing resemblance to the human figure. Head, body and limbs were there; even the fingers and toes were distinctly defined; and many professed to see in the distribution and arrangement of the fibres in the globular mass representing the head a grotesque suggestion of a face. The figure was horizontal; the single great root had begun to divide at the breast.

In point of resemblance to the human form this image was imperfect. At about ten inches from one of the knees, the *cilia* forming that leg had abruptly doubled backward and inward upon their course of growth. The figure lacked the left foot.

There was but one inference—the obvious one; but in the ensuing excitement as many courses of action were proposed as there were counsellors who did not know what to do. The matter was settled by the sheriff of the county, who, as the lawful custodian of the abandoned estate, ordered the root replaced and the excavation filled with the earth that had been removed.

Later inquiry brought out only one fact of relevancy and significance: Mrs Harding had never visited her relatives in Iowa, nor did they know that she was supposed to have done so. Of Robert Harding and the rest of his family nothing is known to this day. The house retains its evil reputation, but the replanted vine is as orderly and well-behaved a vegetable as a nervous person could wish to sit under of a pleasant summer night when the katydids grate out their immemorial revelation and the distant whippoorwill signifies his notion of what ought to be done about it.

PROFESSOR JONKIN'S CANNIBAL PLANT

Howard R. Garis

Howard R. Garis is best remembered as a children's author for his series revolving around the rabbit character "Uncle Wiggily". Despite his aptitude for children's literature, his short story "Professor Jonkin's Cannibal Plant", first published in the literary magazine *The Argosy*, is far from fluffy. In Garis's tale Professor Jonkin is an accomplished scientist who has succeeded in cultivating a tree which produces many kinds of fruit. He becomes dissatisfied with leaving his research there and decides to learn from and experiment on a pitcher plant. Professor Jonkin makes particular reference to Charles Darwin when speaking of his beloved plant, which highlights Darwin's profound influence in the botanical field but also the author's imagination, as the plant evolves. This story is the first in the collection to introduce the pitcher plant into the man-eating plant canon. By nature the pitcher plant represents not only a trap, but a visceral abyss with the accompanying fear of being devoured alive.

fter Professor Jeptha Jonkin had, by skilful grafting and care, succeeded in raising a single tree that produced, at different seasons, apples, oranges, pineapples, figs, cocoanuts, and peaches, it might have been supposed he would rest from his scientific labours. But Professor Jonkin was not that kind of a man.

He was continually striving to grow something new in the plant world. So it was no surprise to Bradley Adams, when calling on his friend the professor one afternoon, to find that scientist busy in his large conservatory.

"What are you up to now?" asked Adams. "Trying to make a rose-bush produce violets, or a honeysuckle vine bring forth pumpkins?"

"Neither," replied Professor Jonkin a little stiffly, for he resented Adams' playful tone. "Not that either of those things would be difficult. But look at that."

He pointed to a small plant with bright, glossy green leaves mottled with red spots. The thing was growing in a large earthen pot.

It bore three flowers, about the size of morning glories, and not unlike that blossom in shape, save, near the top, there was a sort of lid, similar to the flap observed on a jack-in-the-pulpit plant.

"Look down one of those flowers," went on the professor, and Adams, wondering what was to come, did so.

He saw within a small tube, lined with fine, hair-like filaments, which seemed to be in motion. And the shaft or tube went down to the bottom of the morning-glory-shaped part of the flower. At the lower extremity was a little clear liquid.

"Kind of a queer blossom. What is it?" asked Adams.

"That," said the professor with a note of pride in his voice, "is a specimen of the Sarracenia Nepenthis."

"What's that? French for sunflower, or Latin for sweet pea?" asked Adams irreverently.

"It is Latin for pitcher plant," responded the professor, drawing himself up to his full height of five feet three. "One of the most interesting of the South American flora."

"The name fits it pretty well," observed Adams. "I see there's water at the bottom. I suppose this isn't the pitcher that went to the well too often."

"The Sarracenia Nepenthis is a most wonderful plant," went on the professor in his lecture voice, not heeding Adams' joking remarks. "It belongs to what Darwin calls the carnivorous family of flowers, and other varieties of the same species are the Dionœa Muscipula, or Venus Fly-trap, the Darlingtonia, the Pinguicula and Aldrovandra, as well as—"

"Hold on, professor," pleaded Adams. "I'll take the rest on faith. Just tell me about this pitcher plant. It seems interesting."

"It *is* interesting," said Professor Jonkin. "It eats insects."

"Eats insects?"

"Certainly. Watch."

The professor opened a small wire cage lying on a shelf and took from it several flies. These he liberated close to the queer plant.

The insects buzzed about a few seconds, dazed with their sudden liberty.

Then they began slowly to circle in the vicinity of the strange flowers. Nearer and nearer the blossoms they came, attracted by some subtle perfume, as well as by a sweet syrup that was on the edge of the petals, put there by nature for the very purpose of drawing hapless insects into the trap.

The flies settled down, some on the petals of all three blooms. Then a curious thing happened.

The little hair-like filaments in the tube within the petals suddenly reached out and wound themselves about the insects feeding on the sweet stuff, which seemed to intoxicate them. In an instant the flies were pulled to the top of the flower shaft by a contraction of the hairs, and then they went tumbling down the tube into the miniature pond below, where they were drowned after a brief struggle. Their crawling back was prevented by spines growing with points down, as the wires in some rat-traps are fastened.

Meanwhile the cover of the plant closed down.

"Why, it's a regular fly-trap, isn't it?" remarked Adams, much surprised.

"It is," replied the professor. "The plant lives off the insects it captures. It absorbs them, digests them, and, when it is hungry again, catches more."

"Where'd you get such an uncanny thing?" asked Adams, moving away from the plant as if he feared it might take a sample bite out of him.

"A friend sent it to me from Brazil."

"But you're not going to keep it, I hope."

"I certainly am," rejoined Professor Jonkin.

"Maybe you're going to train it to come to the table and eat like a human being," suggested Adams, with a laugh that nettled the professor.

"I wouldn't have to train it much to induce it to be polite," snapped back the owner of the pitcher plant.

And then, seeing that his jokes were not relished, Adams assumed an interest he did not feel, and listened to a long dissertation on botany in general and carnivorous plants in particular.

He would much rather have been eating some of the queer hybrid fruits the professor raised. He pleaded an engagement when he saw an opening in the talk, and went away.

It was some months after that before he saw the professor again. The botanist was busy in his conservatory in the meantime, and the gardener he hired to do rough work noticed that his master spent much time in that part of the glasshouse where the pitcher plant was growing.

For Professor Jonkin had become so much interested in his latest acquisition that he seemed to think of nothing else. His plan for increasing strawberries to the size of peaches was abandoned for a time, as was his pet scheme of raising apples without any core.

The gardener wondered what there was about the South American blossoms to require such close attention.

One day he thought he would find out, and he started to enter that part of the conservatory where the pitcher plant was growing. Professor Jonkin halted him before he had stepped inside and sternly bade him never to appear there again.

As the gardener, crestfallen, moved away after a glimpse into the forbidden region he muttered:

"My, that plant has certainly grown! And I wonder what the professor was doing so close to it. Looked as if he was feeding the thing."

As the days went by the conduct of Professor Jonkin became more and more curious. He scarcely left the southern end of the conservatory, save at night, when he entered his house to sleep.

He was a bachelor, and had no family cares to trouble him, so he could spend all his time among his plants. But hitherto he had divided his attention among his many experiments in the floral kingdom.

Now he was always with his mysterious pitcher plant. He even had his meals sent into the greenhouse.

"Be you keepin' boarders?" asked the butcher boy of the gardener one day, passing on his return to the store, his empty basket on his arm.

"No. Why?"

"The professor is orderin' so much meat lately. I thought you had company."

"No, there's only us two. Mr Adams used to come to dinner once in a while, but not lately."

"Then you an' the professor must have big appetites."

"What makes you think so?"

"The number of beefsteaks you eat."

"Number of beefsteaks? Why, my lad, the professor and I are both vegetarians."

"What's them?"

"We neither of us eat a bit of meat. We don't believe it's healthy."

"Then what becomes of the three big porterhouse steaks I deliver to the professor in the greenhouse every day?"

"Porterhouse steaks?" questioned the gardener, amazed.

"Do you feed 'em to the dog?"

"We don't keep a dog."

But the butcher boy questioned no further, for he saw a chum and hastened off to join him.

"Three porterhouse steaks a day!" mused the gardener, shaking his head. "I do hope the professor has not ceased to be a vegetarian. Yet it looks mighty suspicious. And he's doing it on the sly, too, for there's been no meat cooked in the house, of that I'm sure."

And the gardener, sorely puzzled over the mystery, went off, shaking his head more solemnly than before.

He resolved to have a look in the place the professor guarded so carefully. He tried the door when he was sure his master was in another part of the conservatory, but it was locked, and no key the gardener had would unfasten it.

A month after the gardener had heard of the porterhouse steaks, Adams happened to drop in to see the professor again.

"He's in with the Sarracenia Nepenthis," said the gardener in answer to the visitor's inquiry. "But I doubt if he will let you enter."

"Why won't he?"

"Because he's become mighty close-mouthed of late over that pitcher plant."

"Oh, I guess he'll see me," remarked Adams confidently, and he knocked on the door that shut off the locked section of the greenhouse from the main portion.

"Who's there?" called the professor.

"Adams."

"Oh," in a more conciliatory tone. "I was just wishing you'd come along. I have something to show you."

Professor Jonkin opened the door, and the sight that met Adams' gaze startled him.

The only plant in that part of the conservatory was a single specimen of the Sarracenia Nepenthis. Yet it had attained such enormous proportions that at first Adams thought he must be dreaming.

"What do you think of that for an achievement in science?" asked the professor proudly.

"Do you mean to say that is the small, fly-catching plant your friend sent you from Brazil?"

"The same."

"But—but—"

"But how it's grown, that's what you want to say, isn't it?"

"It is. How did you do it?"

"By dieting the blossoms."

"You mean—?"

"I mean feeding them. Listen. I reasoned that if a small blossom of the plant would thrive on a few insects, by giving it larger meals I might get a bigger plant. So I made my plans.

"First I cut off all but one blossom, so that the strength of the plant would nourish that alone. Then I made out a bill of fare. I began feeding it on chopped beef. The plant took to it like a puppy. It seemed to beg for more. From chopped meat I went to small pieces, cut up. I could fairly see the blossom increase in size. From that I went to choice mutton chops, and, after a week of them, with the plant becoming more gigantic all the while, I increased its meals to a porterhouse steak a day. And now—"

"Well, now?" questioned Adams.

"Now," went on the professor proudly, "my pitcher plant takes three big beefsteaks every day—one for breakfast, one for dinner, and one for supper. And see the result."

Adams gazed at the immense plant. From a growth about as big as an Easter lily it had increased until the top was near the roof of the greenhouse, twenty-five feet above.

About fifteen feet up, or ten feet from the top, there branched out a great flower, about eight feet long and three feet across the bell-shaped mouth, which, except for the cap or cover, was not unlike the opening of an immense morning glory.

The flower was heavy, and the stalk on which it grew was not strong enough to support it upright. So a rude scaffolding had been constructed of wood and boards, and on a frame the flower was held upright.

In order to see it to better advantage, and also that he might feed it, the professor had a ladder by which he could ascend to a small platform in front of the bell-shaped mouth of the blossom.

"It is time to give my pet its meal," he announced, as if he were speaking of some favourite horse. "Want to come up and watch it eat?"

"No, thank you," responded Adams. "It's too uncanny."

The professor took a large steak, one of the three which the butcher boy had left that day. Holding it in his hand, he climbed up the ladder and was soon on the platform in front of the plant.

Adams watched him curiously. The professor leaned over to toss the steak into the yawning mouth of the flower.

Suddenly Adams saw him totter, throw his arms wildly in the air, and then, as if drawn by some overpowering force, he fell forward, lost his balance, and toppled into the maw of the pitcher plant!

There was a jar to the stalk and blossom as the professor fell within. He went head first into the tube or eating apparatus of the strange plant, his legs sticking out for an instant, kicking wildly. Then he disappeared entirely.

Adams didn't know whether to laugh or be alarmed.

He mounted the ladder, and stood in amazement before the result of the professor's work as he looked down into the depth of the gigantic flower, increased a hundred times in size.

He was aware of a strange, sickish-sweet odour that seemed to steal over his senses. It was lulling him to sleep, and he fought against it. Then he looked down and saw that the huge hairs or filaments with which the tube was lined were in violent motion.

He could just discern the professor's feet about three feet below the rim of the flower. They were kicking, but with a force growing less every second. The filaments seemed to be winding about the professor's legs, holding him in a deadly embrace.

Then the top cover or flap of the plant closed down suddenly. The professor was a prisoner inside.

The plant had turned cannibal and eaten the man who had grown it!

For an instant, fear deprived Adams of reason. He did not know what to do. Then the awful plight of his friend brought back his senses.

"Professor!" he shouted. "Are you alive? Can you hear me?"

"Yes," came back in faint and muffled tones. "This beast has me, all right."

Then followed a series of violent struggles that shook the plant.

"I'll get you out. Where's an axe? I'll chop the cursed plant to pieces!" cried Adams.

"Don't! Don't!" came in almost pleading tones from the imprisoned professor.

"Don't what?"

"Don't hurt my pet!"

"Your pet!" snorted Adams angrily. "Nice kind of a pet you have! One that tries to eat you alive! But I've got to do something if I want to save you. Where's the axe?"

"No! No!" begged the professor, his voice becoming more and more muffled. "Use chloroform."

"Use what?"

"Chloroform! You'll find some in the closet."

Then Adams saw what the professor's idea was. The plant could be made insensible, and the imprisoned man released with no harm to the blossom.

He raced down the ladder, ran to a closet where he had seen the professor's stock of drugs and chemicals stowed away on the occasion of former visits, and grabbed a big bottle of chloroform. He caught up a towel and ran back up the ladder.

Not a sign of the professor could be seen. The plant had swallowed him up, but by the motion and swaying of the flower Adams knew his friend was yet alive.

He was in some doubt as to the success of this method, and would rather have taken an axe and chopped a hole in the side of the blossom, thus releasing the captive. But he decided to obey the professor.

Saturating the towel well with the chloroform, and holding his nose away from it, he pressed the wet cloth over the top of the blossom where the lid touched the edge of the bloom.

There was a slight opening at one point, and Adams poured some of the chloroform down this. He feared lest the fumes of the anaesthetic might overpower the professor also, but he knew they would soon pass away if this happened.

For several minutes he waited anxiously. Would the plan succeed? Would the plant be overcome before it had killed the professor inside?

Adams was in a fever of terror. Again and again he saturated the towel with the powerful drug. Then he had the satisfaction of seeing the lid of the pitcher plant relax.

It slowly lifted and fell over to one side, making a good-sized opening. The strong filaments, not unlike the arms of a devil fish, Adams thought, were no longer in uneasy motion. They had released their grip on the professor's legs and body.

The spines which had pointed downward, holding the plant's prey, now became limber.

Adams leaned over. He reached down, grasped the professor by the feet, and, being a strong man, while his friend was small and light, he pulled him from the tube of the flower, a little dazed from the fumes of the chloroform the plant had breathed in, but otherwise not much the worse for his adventure.

He had not reached the water at the bottom of the tube, which fact saved him from drowning.

"Well, you certainly had a narrow squeak," observed Adams as he helped the professor down the ladder.

"I did," admitted the botanist. "If you had not been on hand I don't know what would have happened. I suppose I would have been eaten alive."

"Unless you could have cut yourself out of the side of the flower with your knife," observed Adams.

"What! And killed the plant I raised with such pains?" ejaculated the professor. "Spoil the largest Sarracenia Nepenthis in the world? I guess not. I would rather have let it eat me."

"I think you ought to call it the cannibal plant instead of the pitcher plant," suggested Adams.

"Oh, no," responded the professor dreamily, examining the flower from a distance to see if any harm had come to it. "But to punish it, I will not give it any supper or breakfast. That's what it gets for being naughty," he added as if the plant were a child.

"And I suggest that when you feed it hereafter," said Adams, "you pass the beefsteaks in on a pitch-fork. You won't run so much danger then."

"That's a good idea. I'll do it," answered the professor heartily.

And he has followed that plan ever since.

THE VOICE IN THE NIGHT

William Hope Hodgson

This tale by essayist, novelist and short story writer William Hope Hodgson first appeared in *Blue Book* magazine's November 1907 issue. Known for his nautical themes, he drew upon his own experiences at sea from a young age as a cabin boy. As an accomplished horror writer, his short story "The Voice in the Night" is one of the eeriest in the collection. The story begins one night as a schooner is approached by a small rowboat in distress but it is too dark to see the man inside. He tells them of his tragic tale and pleas for some supplies to take back for his fiancée. This story is different to the others as it features fungi and not a flower, vine or tree. However, in terms of man-eating/parasitic plant horror and science fiction, fungi are part of the same narrative and share symbolism as the immobile become mobile and the food sources become the hunters. The all-consuming fungus stems from the same fear of contagion and infection as the modern zombie narrative, including cannibalistic elements as the victims of the fungus experience insatiable and indiscriminate hunger.

t was a dark, starless night. We were becalmed in the Northern Pacific. Our exact position I do not know; for the sun had been hidden during the course of a weary, breathless week, by a thin haze which had seemed to float above us, about the height of our mastheads, at whiles descending and shrouding the surrounding sea.

With there being no wind, we had steadied the tiller, and I was the only man on deck. The crew, consisting of two men and a boy, were sleeping forrard in their den; while Will—my friend, and the master of our little craft—was aft in his bunk on the port side of the little cabin.

Suddenly, from out of the surrounding darkness, there came a hail:

"Schooner, ahoy!"

The cry was so unexpected that I gave no immediate answer, because of my surprise.

It came again—a voice curiously throaty and inhuman, calling from somewhere upon the dark sea away on our port broadside:

"Schooner, ahoy!"

"Hullo!" I sung out, having gathered my wits somewhat. "What are you? What do you want?"

"You need not be afraid," answered the queer voice, having probably noticed some trace of confusion in my tone. "I am only an old—man."

The pause sounded oddly; but it was only afterwards that it came back to me with any significance.

"Why don't you come alongside, then?" I queried somewhat snappishly; for I liked not his hinting at my having been a trifle shaken.

"I—I—can't. It wouldn't be safe. I—" The voice broke off, and there was silence.

"What do you mean?" I asked, growing more and more astonished. "Why not safe? Where are you?"

I listened for a moment; but there came no answer. And then, a sudden indefinite suspicion, of I knew not what, coming to me, I stepped swiftly to the binnacle, and took out the lighted lamp. At the same time, I knocked on the deck with my heel to waken Will. Then I was back at the side, throwing the yellow funnel of light out into the silent immensity beyond our rail. As I did so, I heard a slight, muffled cry, and then the sound of a splash, as though someone had dipped oars abruptly. Yet I cannot say that I saw anything with certainty; save, it seemed to me, that with the first flash of the light, there had been something upon the waters, where now there was nothing.

"Hullo, there!" I called. "What foolery is this!"

But there came only the indistinct sounds of a boat being pulled away into the night.

Then I heard Will's voice, from the direction of the after scuttle: "What's up, George?"

"Come here, Will!" I said.

"What is it?" he asked, coming across the deck.

I told him the queer thing which had happened. He put several questions; then, after a moment's silence, he raised his hands to his lips, and hailed:

"Boat, ahoy!"

From a long distance away, there came back to us a faint reply, and my companion repeated his call. Presently, after a short period of silence, there grew on our hearing the muffled sound of oars; at which Will hailed again.

This time there was a reply:

"Put away the light."

"I'm damned if I will," I muttered; but Will told me to do as the voice bade, and I shoved it down under the bulwarks.

"Come nearer," he said, and the oar-strokes continued. Then, when apparently some half-dozen fathoms distant, they again ceased.

"Come alongside," exclaimed Will. "There's nothing to be frightened of aboard here!"

"Promise that you will not show the light?"

"What's to do with you," I burst out, "that you're so infernally afraid of the light?"

"Because—" began the voice, and stopped short.

"Because what?" I asked, quickly.

Will put his hand on my shoulder.

"Shut up a minute, old man," he said, in a low voice. "Let me tackle him."

He leant more over the rail.

"See here, Mister," he said, "this is a pretty queer business, you coming upon us like this, right out in the middle of the blessed Pacific. How are we to know what sort of a hanky-panky trick you're up to? You say there's only one of you. How are we to know, unless we get a squint at you—eh? What's your objection to the light, anyway?"

As he finished, I heard the noise of the oars again, and then the voice came; but now from a greater distance, and sounding extremely hopeless and pathetic.

"I am sorry—sorry! I would not have troubled you, only I am hungry, and—so is she."

The voice died away, and the sound of the oars, dipping irregularly, was borne to us.

"Stop!" sung out Will. "I don't want to drive you away. Come back! We'll keep the light hidden, if you don't like it."

He turned to me:

"It's a damned queer rig, this; but I think there's nothing to be afraid of?"

There was a question in his tone, and I replied.

"No, I think the poor devil's been wrecked around here, and gone crazy."

The sound of the oars drew nearer.

"Shove that lamp back in the binnacle," said Will; then he leaned over the rail, and listened. I replaced the lamp, and came back to his side. The dipping of the oars ceased some dozen yards distant.

"Won't you come alongside now?" asked Will in an even voice. "I have had the lamp put back in the binnacle."

"I—I cannot," replied the voice. "I dare not come nearer. I dare not even pay you for the—the provisions."

"That's all right," said Will, and hesitated. "You're welcome to as much grub as you can take—" Again he hesitated.

"You are very good," exclaimed the voice. "May God, who understands everything, reward you—" It broke off huskily.

"The—the lady?" said Will, abruptly. "Is she—"

"I have left her behind upon the island," came the voice.

"What island?" I cut in.

"I know not its name," returned the voice. "I would to God—!" it began, and checked itself as suddenly.

"Could we not send a boat for her?" asked Will at this point.

"No!" said the voice, with extraordinary emphasis. "My God! No!" There was a moment's pause; then it added, in a tone which seemed a merited reproach:

"It was because of our want I ventured— Because her agony tortured me."

"I am a forgetful brute," exclaimed Will. "Just wait a minute, whoever you are, and I will bring you up something at once."

In a couple of minutes he was back again, and his arms were full of various edibles. He paused at the rail.

"Can't you come alongside for them?" he asked.

"No—I *dare not*," replied the voice, and it seemed to me that in its tones I detected a note of stifled craving—as though the owner hushed a mortal desire. It came to me then in a flash, that the poor old creature out there in the darkness, was *suffering* for actual need of that which Will held in his arms; and yet, because of some unintelligible dread, refraining from dashing to the side of our little schooner, and receiving it. And with the lightning-like conviction, there came the knowledge that the Invisible was not mad; but sanely facing some intolerable horror.

"Damn it, Will!" I said, full of many feelings, over which predominated a vast sympathy. "Get a box. We must float off the stuff to him in it."

This we did—propelling it away from the vessel, out into the darkness, by means of a boathook. In a minute, a slight cry from the Invisible came to us, and we knew that he had secured the box.

A little later, he called out a farewell to us, and so heartful a blessing, that I am sure we were the better for it. Then, without more ado, we heard the ply of oars across the darkness.

"Pretty soon off," remarked Will, with perhaps just a little sense of injury.

"Wait," I replied. "I think somehow he'll come back. He must have been badly needing that food."

"And the lady," said Will. For a moment he was silent; then he continued:

"It's the queerest thing ever I've tumbled across, since I've been fishing."

"Yes," I said, and fell to pondering.

And so the time slipped away—an hour, another, and still Will stayed with me; for the queer adventure had knocked all desire for sleep out of him.

The third hour was three parts through, when we heard again the sound of oars across the silent ocean.

"Listen!" said Will, a low note of excitement in his voice.

"He's coming, just as I thought," I muttered.

The dipping of the oars grew nearer, and I noted that the strokes were firmer and longer. The food had been needed.

They came to a stop a little distance off the broadside, and the queer voice came again to us through the darkness:

"Schooner, ahoy!"

"That you?" asked Will.

"Yes," replied the voice. "I left you suddenly; but—but there was great need."

"The lady?" questioned Will.

"The—lady is grateful now on earth. She will be more grateful soon in—in heaven."

Will began to make some reply, in a puzzled voice; but became confused, and broke off short. I said nothing. I was wondering at the curious pauses, and, apart from my wonder, I was full of a great sympathy.

The voice continued:

"We—she and I, have talked, as we shared the result of God's tenderness and yours—"

Will interposed; but without coherence.

"I beg of you not to—to belittle your deed of Christian charity this night," said the voice. "Be sure that it has not escaped His notice."

It stopped, and there was a full minute's silence. Then it came again:

"We have spoken together upon that which—which has befallen us. We had thought to go out, without telling any, of the terror which has come into our—lives. She is with me in believing that tonight's happenings are under a special ruling, and that it is God's wish that we should tell to you all that we have suffered since—since—"

"Yes?" said Will, softly.

"Since the sinking of the *Albatross*."

"Ah!" I exclaimed, involuntarily. "She left Newcastle for 'Frisco some six months ago, and hasn't been heard of since."

"Yes," answered the voice. "But some few degrees to the North of the line she was caught in a terrible storm, and dismasted. When the day came, it was found that she was leaking badly, and, presently, it falling to a calm, the sailors took to the boats, leaving—leaving a young lady—my fiancée—and myself upon the wreck.

"We were below, gathering together a few of our belongings, when they left. They were entirely callous, through fear, and when we came up upon the decks, we saw them only as small shapes afar off upon the horizon. Yet we did not despair, but set to work and constructed a small raft. Upon this we put such few matters as it would hold, including a quantity of water and some ship's biscuit. Then, the vessel being very deep in the water, we got ourselves onto the raft, and pushed off.

"It was later, when I observed that we seemed to be in the way of some tide or current, which bore us from the ship at an angle; so that in the course of three hours, by my watch, her hull became invisible to our sight, her broken masts remaining in view for a somewhat longer period. Then, towards evening, it grew misty, and so through the night. The next day we were still encompassed by the mist, the weather remaining quiet.

"For four days, we drifted through this strange haze, until, on the evening of the fourth day, there grew upon our ears the murmur of breakers at a distance. Gradually it became plainer, and, somewhat after midnight, it appeared to sound upon either hand at no very great space. The raft was raised upon a swell several times, and then we were in smooth water, and the noise of the breakers was behind.

"When the morning came, we found that we were in a sort of great lagoon; but of this we noticed little at the time; for close before us, through the enshrouding mist, loomed the hull of a large sailing-vessel. With one accord, we fell upon our knees and thanked God; for we thought that here was an end to our perils. We had much to learn.

"The raft drew near to the ship, and we shouted on them, to take us aboard; but none answered. Presently, the raft touched against the side of the vessel, and, seeing a rope hanging downwards, I seized it and began to climb. Yet I had much ado to make my way up, because of a kind of grey, lichenous fungus, which had seized upon the rope, and which blotched the side of the ship, lividly.

"I reached the rail, and clambered over it, on to the deck. Here, I saw that the decks were covered, in great patches, with the grey masses, some of them rising into nodules several feet in height; but at the time, I thought less of this matter than of the possibility of there being people aboard the ship. I shouted; but none answered. Then I went to the door below the poop-deck. I opened it, and peered in. There was a great smell of staleness, so that I knew in a moment that nothing living was within, and with the knowledge, I shut the door quickly; for I felt suddenly lonely.

"I went back to the side, where I had scrambled up. My—my sweetheart was still sitting quietly upon the raft. Seeing me look down, she called up to know whether there were any aboard of the ship. I replied that the vessel had the appearance of having been long deserted; but that if she would wait a little, I would see whether there was anything in the shape of a ladder, by which she could ascend to the deck. Then we would make a search through the vessel together. A little later, on the opposite side of the decks, I found a rope side-ladder. This I carried across, and a minute afterwards, she was beside me.

"Together, we explored the cabins and apartments in the after-part of the ship; but nowhere was there any sign of life. Here and there, within the cabins themselves, we came across odd patches of that queer fungus; but this, as my sweetheart said, could be cleansed away.

"In the end, having assured ourselves that the after-portion of the vessel was empty, we picked our ways to the bows, between the ugly grey nodules of that strange growth; and here we made a further search, which told us that there was indeed none aboard but ourselves.

"This being now beyond any doubt, we returned to the stern of the ship, and proceeded to make ourselves as comfortable as possible. Together, we cleared out and cleaned two of the cabins; and, after that, I made examination whether there was anything eatable in the ship. This I soon found was so, and thanked God in my heart for His goodness. In addition to this, I discovered the whereabouts of the freshwater pump, and having fixed it, I found the water drinkable, though somewhat unpleasant to the taste.

"For several days, we stayed aboard the ship, without attempting to get to the shore. We were busily engaged in making the place habit-able. Yet even thus early, we became aware that our lot was even less to be desired than might have been imagined; for though, as a first step, we scraped away the odd patches of growth that studded the floors and walls of the cabins and saloon, yet they returned almost to their original size within the space of twenty-four hours, which not only discouraged us, but gave us a feeling of vague unease.

"Still, we would not admit ourselves beaten, so set to work afresh, and not only scraped away the fungus, but soaked the places where it had been, with carbolic, a can-full of which I had found in the pantry. Yet, by the end of the week, the growth had returned in full strength, and, in addition, it had spread to other places, as though our touching it had allowed germs from it to travel elsewhere.

"On the seventh morning, my sweetheart woke to find a small patch of it growing on her pillow, close to her face. At that, she came to me, so soon as she could get her garments upon her. I was in the galley at the time, lighting the fire for breakfast.

"'Come here, John,' she said, and led me aft. When I saw the thing upon her pillow, I shuddered, and then and there we agreed to go right out of the ship, and see whether we could not fare to make ourselves more comfortable ashore.

"Hurriedly, we gathered together our few belongings, and even among these, I found that the fungus had been at work; for one of her shawls had a little lump of it growing near one edge. I threw the whole thing over the side, without saying anything to her.

"The raft was still alongside; but it was too clumsy to guide, and I lowered down a small boat that hung across the stern, and in this we made our way to the shore. Yet, as we drew near to it, I became gradually aware that here the vile fungus, which had driven us from the ship, was growing riot. In places it rose into horrible, fantastic mounds, which seemed almost to quiver, as with a quiet life, when the wind blew across them. Here and there, it took on the forms of vast fingers, and in others it just spread out flat and smooth and treacherous. Odd places, it appeared as grotesque stunted trees, seeming extraordinarily kinked and gnarled— the whole quaking vilely at times.

"At first, it seemed to us that there was no single portion of the surrounding shore which was not hidden beneath the masses of the hideous lichen; yet, in this, I found we were mistaken; for somewhat later, coasting along the shore at a little distance, we descried a smooth white patch of what appeared to be fine sand, and there we landed. It was not sand. What it was, I do not know. All that I have observed, is that upon it, the fungus will not grow; while everywhere else, save where the sand-like earth wanders oddly, path-wise, amid the grey desolation of the lichen, there is nothing but that loathsome greyness.

"It is difficult to make you understand how cheered we were to find one place that was absolutely free from the growth, and here we deposited our belongings. Then we went back to the ship for such things as it seemed to us we should need. Among other matters, I managed to bring ashore with me one of the ship's sails, with which I constructed two small tents, which, though exceedingly rough-shaped, served the purposes for which they were intended. In these, we lived and stored our various necessities, and thus for a matter of some four weeks, all went smoothly and without particular unhappiness. Indeed, I may say with much of happiness—for—for we were together.

"It was on the thumb of her right hand, that the growth first showed. It was only a small circular spot, much like a little grey mole. My God! how the fear leapt to my heart when she showed me the place. We cleansed it, between us, washing it with carbolic and water. In the morning of the following day, she showed her hand to me again. The grey warty thing had returned. For a little while, we looked at one another in silence. Then, still wordless, we started again to remove it. In the midst of the operation, she spoke suddenly.

"'What's that on the side of your face, dear!' Her voice was sharp with anxiety. I put my hand up to feel.

173

"'There! Under the hair by your ear.—A little to the front a bit.' My finger rested upon the place, and then I knew.

"'Let us get your thumb done first,' I said. And she submitted, only because she was afraid to touch me until it was cleansed. I finished washing and disinfecting her thumb, and then she turned to my face. After it was finished, we sat together and talked awhile of many things; for there had come into our lives sudden, very terrible thoughts. We were, all at once, afraid of something worse than death.We spoke of loading the boat with provisions and water, and making our way out on to the sea; yet we were helpless, for many causes, and—and the growth had attacked us already. We decided to stay. God would do with us what was His will. We would wait.

"A month, two months, three months passed, and the places grew somewhat, and there had come others. Yet we fought so strenuously with the fear, that its headway was but slow, comparatively speaking.

"Occasionally, we ventured off to the ship for such stores as we needed. There, we found that the fungus grew persistently. One of the nodules on the main deck became soon as high as my head.

"We had now given up all thought or hope of leaving the island. We had realised that it would be unallowable to go among healthy humans, with the thing from which we were suffering.

"With this determination and knowledge in our minds, we knew that we should have to husband our food and water; for we did not know, at that time, but that we should possibly live for many years.

"This reminds me that I have told you that I am an old man. Judged by years this is not so. But—but—"

He broke off; then continued somewhat abruptly:

"As I was saying, we knew that we should have to use care in the matter of food. But we had no idea then how little food there was left, of which to take care. It was a week later, that I made the discovery that all the other bread tanks—which I had supposed full—were empty, and that (beyond odd tins of vegetables and meat, and some other matters) we had nothing on which to depend, but the bread in the tank which I had already opened.

"After learning this, I bestirred myself to do what I could, and set to work at fishing in the lagoon; but with no success. At this, I was somewhat inclined to feel desperate, until the thought came to me to try outside the lagoon, in the open sea.

"Here, at times, I caught odd fish; but so infrequently that they proved of but little help in keeping us from the hunger which threatened. It seemed to me that our deaths were likely to come by hunger, and not by the growth of the thing which had seized upon our bodies.

"We were in this state of mind when the fourth month wore out. Then I made a very horrible discovery. One morning, a little before midday, I came off from the ship, with a portion of the biscuits which were left. In the mouth of her tent, I saw my sweetheart sitting, eating something.

"'What is it, my dear?' I called out as I leapt ashore. Yet, on hearing my voice, she seemed confused, and, turning, slyly threw something towards the edge of the little clearing. It fell short, and, a vague suspicion having arisen within me, I walked across and picked it up. It was a piece of the grey fungus.

"As I went to her, with it in my hand, she turned deadly pale; then a rose red.

"I felt strangely dazed and frightened.

"'My dear! My dear!' I said, and could say no more. Yet, at my words, she broke down and cried bitterly. Gradually, as she calmed, I got from her the news that she had tried it the preceding day, and—and liked it. I got her to promise on her knees not to touch it again, however great our hunger. After she had promised, she told me that the desire for it had come suddenly, and that, until the moment of desire, she had experienced nothing towards it but the most extreme repulsion.

"Later in the day, feeling strangely restless, and much shaken with the thing which I had discovered, I made my way along one of the twisted paths—formed by the white, sand-like substance—which led among the fungoid growth. I had, once before, ventured along there; but not to any great distance. This time, being involved in perplexing thought, I went much further than hitherto.

"Suddenly, I was called to myself by a queer hoarse sound on my left. Turning quickly, I saw that there was movement among an extraordinarily shaped mass of fungus, close to my elbow. It was swaying uneasily, as though it possessed life of its own. Abruptly, as I stared, the thought came to me that the thing had a grotesque resemblance to the figure of a distorted human creature. Even as the fancy flashed into my brain, there was a slight, sickening noise of tearing, and I saw that one of the branch-like arms was detaching itself from the surrounding grey masses, and coming towards me. The head of the thing—a shapeless grey ball, inclined in my direction. I stood stupidly, and the vile arm brushed across my face. I gave out a frightened cry, and ran back a few paces. There was a sweetish taste upon my lips, where the thing had touched me. I licked them, and was immediately filled with an inhuman desire. I turned and seized a mass of the fungus. Then more, and—more. I was insatiable. In the midst of devouring, the remembrance of the morning's discovery swept into my mazed brain. It was sent by God. I dashed the fragment I held, to the ground. Then, utterly wretched and feeling a dreadful guiltiness, I made my way back to the little encampment.

"I think she knew, by some marvellous intuition which love must have given, so soon as she set eyes on me. Her quiet sympathy made it easier for me, and I told her of my sudden weakness; yet omitted to mention the extraordinary thing which had gone before. I desired to spare her all unnecessary terror.

"But, for myself, I had added an intolerable knowledge, to breed an incessant terror in my brain; for I doubted not but that I had seen the end of one of those men who had come to the island in the ship in the lagoon; and in that monstrous ending, I had seen our own.

"Thereafter, we kept from the abominable food, though the desire for it had entered into our blood. Yet, our drear punishment was upon us; for, day by day, with monstrous rapidity, the fungoid growth took hold of our poor bodies. Nothing we could do would check it materially, and so—and so—we who had been human, became— Well, it matters less each day. Only—only we had been man and maid!

"And day by day, the fight is more dreadful, to withstand the hunger-lust for the terrible lichen.

"A week ago we ate the last of the biscuit, and since that time I have caught three fish. I was out here fishing tonight, when your schooner drifted upon me out of the mist. I hailed you. You know the rest, and may God, out of His great heart, bless you for your goodness to a—a couple of poor outcast souls."

There was the dip of an oar—another. Then the voice came again, and for the last time, sounding through the slight surrounding mist, ghostly and mournful.

"God bless you! Goodbye!"

"Goodbye," we shouted together, hoarsely, our hearts full of many emotions.

I glanced about me. I became aware that the dawn was upon us.

The sun flung a stray beam across the hidden sea; pierced the mist dully, and lit up the receding boat with a gloomy fire. Indistinctly, I saw something nodding between the oars. I thought of a sponge—a great, grey nodding sponge— The oars continued to ply. They were grey—as was the boat—and my eyes searched a moment vainly for the conjunction of hand and oar. My gaze flashed back to the—head. It nodded forward as the oars went backward for the stroke. Then the oars were dipped, the boat shot out of the patch of light, and the—the thing went nodding into the mist.

THE PAVILION

Edith Nesbit

Edith Nesbit was a well-known English children's author who was friends with fellow writers such as H. G. Wells (who also features in this anthology) and George Bernard Shaw. Her short story "The Pavilion" was published in *The Strand* magazine in November 1915 and follows the story of Amelia, who is a typical wallflower outshone by her beautiful cousin Ernestine. Considered plain and often ignored, Amelia is not only the voice of reason in the tale but also the unexpected heroine when two men who have fallen for Ernestine dare each other to spend the night in an ominous vine-covered pavilion on the grounds.

"The Pavilion" has distinct feminist undertones as it puts male bravado under scrutiny and challenges preconceptions about women. Amelia is depicted as strikingly active and exhibits bravery and independence in a time when this was an undesirable mode of behaviour for women. Unlike other stories in the killer plant genre before this, Nesbit's story places women in the foreground by making Amelia the protagonist of this tale rather than a passive victim or villain.

here was never a moment's doubt in her own mind. So she said afterwards. And everyone agreed that she had concealed her feelings with true womanly discretion. Her friend and confidante, Amelia Davenant, was at any rate completely deceived. Amelia was one of those featureless blondes who seem born to be overlooked. She adored her beautiful friend, and never, from first to last, could see any fault in her, except, perhaps, on the evening when the real things of the story happened. And even in this matter she owned at the time that it was only that her darling Ernestine did not understand.

Ernestine was a prettyish girl with the airs, so irresistible and misleading, of a beauty; most people said that she was beautiful, and she certainly managed, with extraordinary success, to produce the illusion of beauty. Quite a number of plainish girls achieve that effect nowadays. The freedom of modern dress and coiffure and the increasing confidence in herself which the modern girl experiences aid her in fostering the illusion; but in the 'sixties, when everyone wore much the same sort of bonnet, when your choice in coiffure was limited to bandeaux or ringlets, and the crinoline was your only wear, something very like genius was needed to deceive the world in the matter of your personal charms. Ernestine had that genius; hers was the smiling, ringletted, dark-haired, dark-eyed sparkling type. Amelia had the blond bandeau and the appealing blue eyes, rather too small and rather too dull; her hands and ears were beautiful, and she kept them out of sight as much as possible. It was she who, at the age of fourteen, composed the remarkable poem beginning:

I know that am ugly: did I make
The face that is the laugh and jest of all?

and went on, after disclaiming any personal responsibility for the face, to entreat the kind earth to "cover it away from mocking eyes," and to "let the daisies blossom where it lies."

Amelia did not want to die, and her face was not the laugh and jest, or indeed the special interest, of anyone. Really life was a very good thing to Amelia, specially when she had a new dress and someone paid her a compliment. But she went on writing verses extolling the advantages of the Tomb, and grovelling metrically at the feet of One who was Another's. Until that summer when she was nineteen and went to stay with Ernestine at Doricourt. Then her muse took flight, scared, perhaps, by the possibility, suddenly and threateningly presented, of being asked to inspire verse about the real things of life.

At any rate, Amelia ceased to write poetry about the time when she and Ernestine and Ernestine's aunt went on a visit to Doricourt, where Frederick Doricourt lived with his aunt. It was not one of those hurried motor-led excursions which we have now and call weekends, but a long, leisurely visit, when all the friends of the static aunt called on the dynamic aunt, who returned the calls with much ceremony, a big barouche, and a pair of fat horses. There were croquet parties and archery parties and little dances, all pleasant informal gaieties arranged without ceremony among people who lived within driving distance of each other and knew each other's tastes and incomes and family history as well as they knew their own.

And at Doricourt life was delightful even on the days when there was no party. It was perhaps more delightful to Ernestine than to her friend, but even so, the one least pleased was Ernestine's aunt.

"I do think," she said to the other aunt whose name was Julia—"I dare say it is not so to you, being accustomed to Mr Frederick, of course from his childhood, but I always find gentlemen in the house so unsettling. Especially young gentlemen. And when there are young ladies also. One is always on the *qui vive* for excitement."

"Of course," said Aunt Julia, with the air of a woman of the world; "living as you and dear Ernestine do, with only females in the house—"

"We hang up an old coat and hat of my brother's on the hatstand in the hall," Aunt Emmeline protested.

"—the presence of gentlemen in the house must be a little unsettling. For myself, I am inured to it. Frederick has so many friends, Mr Thesiger perhaps the greatest. I believe him to be a most worthy young man, but peculiar." She leaned forward across her bright-tinted Berlin woolwork and spoke impressively, the needle with its trailing red poised in air. "You know, I hope you will not think it indelicate of me to mention such a thing—but dear Frederick—your dear Ernestine would have been in every way so suitable."

"Would have been?" Aunt Emmeline's tortoiseshell shuttle ceased its swift movement among the white loops and knots of her tatting.

"Well, my dear," said the other aunt, a little shortly, "you surely must have noticed—"

"You don't mean to suggest that Amelia — I thought Mr Thesiger and Amelia—"

"Amelia! I really must say! No, I was alluding to Mr Thesiger's attentions to dear Ernestine. Most marked. In dear Frederick's place I should have found some excuse for shortening Mr Thesiger's visit. But of course I cannot interfere. Gentlemen must manage these things for themselves. I only hope that there will be none of that trifling with the most holy affections of others which—"

The less voluble aunt cut in hotly with "Ernestine's incapable of anything so unladylike."

"Just what I was saying," the other rejoined blandly, got up, and drew the blind a little lower, for the afternoon sun was glowing on the rosy wreaths of the drawing-room carpet.

Outside in the sunshine Frederick was doing his best to arrange his own affairs. He had managed to place himself beside Miss Ernestine Meutys on the stone steps of the pavilion, but then Eugene Thesiger lay along the lower step at her feet, a good position for looking up into her eyes. Amelia was beside him, but then it never seemed to matter whom Amelia was beside.

They were talking about the pavilion on whose steps they sat, and Amelia, who often asked uninteresting questions, had wondered how old it was. It was Frederick's pavilion after all, and he felt this when his friend took the words out of his mouth and used them on his own account, even though he did give the answer the form of an appeal.

"The foundations are Tudor, aren't they" he said. "Wasn't it an observatory or laboratory or something of that sort in Fat Henry's time?"

"Yes," said Frederick; "there was some story about a wizard or an alchemist or something, and it was burned down, and then they rebuilt it in its present style."

"The Italian style, isn't it?" said Thesiger; "but you can hardly see what it is now, for the creeper."

"Virginia creeper, isn't it?" Amelia asked, and Frederick said, "Yes, Virginia creeper." Thesiger said it looked more like a South American plant, and Ernestine said Virginia was in South America, and that was why. "I know, because of the war," she said modestly, and nobody smiled or answered. There were manners in those days.

"There's a ghost story about it, surely?" Thesiger began again, looking up at the dark closed doors of the pavilion.

"Not that I ever heard of," said the pavilion's owner. "I think the country people invented the tale because there have always been so many rabbits and weasels and things found dead near it. And once a dog, my uncle's favourite spaniel. But, of course, that's simply because they get entangled in the Virginia creeper—you see how fine and big it is—and can't get out, and die as they do in traps. But the villagers prefer to think it's ghosts."

"I thought there was a real ghost story," Thesiger persisted.

Ernestine said, "A ghost story. How delicious! Do tell it, Mr Doricourt. This is just the place for a ghost story. Out of doors and the sun shining, so that we can't *really* be frightened."

Doricourt protested again that he knew no story.

"That's because you never read, dear boy," said Eugene Thesiger. "That library of yours—there's a delightful book—did you never notice it?—brown tree-calf with your arms on it; the head of the house writes the history of the house as far as he knows it. There's a lot in that book. It began in Tudor times—1515, to be exact."

"Queen Elizabeth's time." Ernestine thought that made it so much more interesting. "And was the ghost story in that?"

"It isn't exactly a ghost story," said Thesiger. "It's only that the pavilion seems to be an unlucky place to sleep in."

"Haunted?" Frederick asked, and added that he must look up that book.

"Not haunted exactly. Only several people who have slept the night there went on sleeping."

"Dead, he means," said Ernestine, and it was left for Amelia to ask:

"Does the book tell anything particular about how the people died, what killed them, or anything?"

"There are suggestions," said Thesiger; "but there, it *is* a gloomy subject. I don't know why I started it. Should we have time for a game of croquet before tea, Doricourt?"

"I wish *you'd* read the book and tell me the stories," Ernestine said to Frederick, apart, over the croquet balls.

"I will," he answered, fervently; "you've only to tell me what you want."

"Or perhaps Mr Thesiger will tell us another time—in the twilight. Since people like twilight for ghosts. Will you, Mr Thesiger?" She spoke over her blue muslin shoulder.

Frederick certainly meant to look up the book, but he delayed till after supper, when he went alone to the library, found the brown book, and took it to the circle of light made by the colza lamp.

"I can skim through it in half an hour," he said, and wound up the lamp and lighted his cigar.

The earlier part of the book was written in the beautiful script of the early sixteenth century, that looks so plain and is so impossible to read, and the later pages, though the handwriting was clear and Italian enough, left Frederick helpless, for the language was Latin, and Frederick's Latin was limited to the particular passages he had "been through" at his private school. He recognised a word here and there—*mors*, for instance, and *pallidus* and *sanguinis* and *pavor* and *arcanum*, just as you or I might; but to read the complicated stuff and make sense of it! Frederick replaced the book on the shelf, closed the shutters, and turned out the lamp. He thought he would ask Thesiger to translate the thing, but then again he thought he wouldn't. So he went to bed wishing that he had happened to remember more of the Latin so painfully beaten into the best years of his boyhood.

And the story of the pavilion was, after all, told by Thesiger.

There was a little dance at Doricourt next evening, a carpet dance they called it. The furniture was pushed back against the walls, and the tightly stretched Axminster carpet was not so bad to dance on as you might suppose. And even in those far-off days there were conservatories.

It was on the steps of the conservatory, not the steps leading from the dancing-room, but the steps leading to the garden, that the story was told. The four young people were sitting together, the girls' crinolined flounces spreading round them like huge pale roses, the young men correct in their high-shouldered coats and white cravats. Ernestine had been very kind to both the men, a little too kind perhaps—who can tell? At any rate, there was in their eyes exactly that light which you may imagine in the eyes of rival stags in the mating season. It was Ernestine who asked Frederick for the story, and Thesiger who, at Amelia's suggestion, told it.

"It's quite a number of stories," he said, "and yet it's really all the same story. The first man to sleep in the pavilion slept there ten years after it was built. He was a friend of the alchemist or astrologer who built it. He was found dead in the morning. There seemed to have been a struggle. His arms bore the marks of cords. No; they never found any cords. He died from loss of blood. There were curious wounds. That was all the rude leeches of the day could report to the bereaved survivors of the deceased."

"How funny you are, Mr Thesiger!" said Ernestine, with that celebrated soft, low laugh of hers.

"And the next?" asked Amelia.

"The next was sixty years later. It was a visitor that time, too. And he was found dead, just the same marks, and the doctors said the same thing. And so it went on. There have been eight deaths alto-gether—unexplained deaths. Nobody has slept in it now for over a hundred years. People seem to have a prejudice against the place as a sleeping apartment. I can't think why."

"Isn't he simply killing?" Ernestine asked Amelia, who said:

"And doesn't anyone know how it happened?"

No one answered till Ernestine repeated the question in the form of "I suppose it was just an accident?"

"It was a curiously recurrent accident," said Thesiger, and Frederick, who throughout the conversation had said the right things at the right moment, remarked that it did not do to believe all these old legends. Most old families had them, he believed. Frederick had inherited Doricourt from an unknown great uncle of whom in life he had not so much as heard, but he was very strong on the family tradition. "I don't attach any importance to these tales myself."

"Of course not. All the same," said Thesiger, deliberately, "you wouldn't care to pass a night in that pavilion."

"No more would you," was all Frederick found on his lips.

"I admit that I shouldn't enjoy it," said Eugene; "but I'll bet you a hundred you don't *do* it."

"Done," said Frederick.

"Oh, Mr Doricourt!" breathed Ernestine, a little shocked at betting "before ladies."

"Don't!" said Amelia, to whom, of course, no one paid any attention; "don't do it!"

You know how, in the midst of flower and leafage, a snake sometimes will suddenly, surprisingly rear a head that threatens? So, amid friendly talk and laughter, a sudden fierce antagonism sometimes looks out and vanishes again, surprising most of all the antagonists. This antagonism spoke in the tones of both men, and after Amelia had said "Don't!" there was a curiously breathless little silence. Ernestine broke it. "Oh," she said, "I do wonder which of you will win! I should like them both to win, wouldn't you, Amelia? Only I suppose that's not always possible, is it?"

Both gentlemen assured her that in the case of bets it was very rarely possible.

"Then I wish you wouldn't," said Ernestine. "You could *both* pass the night there, couldn't you, and be company for each other? I don't think betting for such large sums is quite the thing, do you, Amelia?"

Amelia said no, she didn't, but Eugene had already begun to say:

"Let the bet be off, then, if Miss Meutys doesn't like it. That suggestion is invaluable. But the thing itself needn't be off. Look here, Doricourt. I'll stay in the pavilion from one to three and you from three to five. Then honour will be satisfied. How will that do?"

The snake had disappeared.

"Agreed," said Frederick, "and we can compare impressions afterwards. That will be quite interesting."

Then someone came and asked where they had all got to, and they went in and danced some more dances. Ernestine danced twice with Frederick and drank iced sherry and water, and they said good night and lighted their bedroom candles at the table in the hall.

"I do hope they won't," Amelia said, as the girls sat brushing their hair at the two large white muslin-frilled dressing-tables in the room they shared.

"Won't what?" said Ernestine, vigorous with the brush.

"Sleep in that hateful pavilion. I wish you'd ask them not to, Ernestine. They'd mind, if *you* asked them."

"Of course I will if you like, dear," said Ernestine, cordially. She was always the soul of good nature. "But I don't think you ought to believe in ghost stories, not really."

"Why not?"

"Oh, because of the Bible and going to church and all that," said Ernestine.

"What was that?" said Amelia,

"That" was a sound coming from the little dressing-room. There was no light in that room. Amelia went into the little room, though Ernestine said, "Oh, don't! How can you? It might be a ghost or a rat or something," and as she went she whispered, "Hush!"

The window of the little room was open and she leaned out of it. The stone sill was cold to her elbows through her print dressing jacket.

Ernestine went on brushing her hair. Amelia heard a movement below the window and listened. "Tonight will do," someone said.

"It's too late," said someone else.

"If you're afraid it will always be too late or too early," said someone. And it was Thesiger.

"You know I'm not afraid," the other one, who was Doricourt, answered hotly.

"An hour for each of us will satisfy honour," said Thesiger, carelessly. "The girls will expect it. I couldn't sleep. Let's do it now and get it over. Let's see. Oh, hang it!"

A faint click had sounded.

"Dropped my watch. I forgot the chain was loose. It's all right, though; glass not broken even. Well, are you game?"

"Oh yes, if you insist. Shall I go first, or you?"

"I will," said Thesiger. "That's only fair, because I suggested it. I'll stay till half-past one or a quarter to two, and then you come on. See?"

"Oh, all right. I think it's silly, though," said Frederick.

Then the voices ceased. Amelia went back to the other girl.

"They're going to do it tonight."

"Are they, dear?" Ernestine was as placid as ever. "Do what?"

"Sleep in that horrible pavilion."

"How do you know?"

Amelia explained how she knew.

"Whatever can we do?" she added.

"Well, dear, suppose we go to bed?" suggested Ernestine, helpfully. "We shall hear all about it in the morning."

"But suppose anything happens?"

"What could happen?"

"Oh, *anything!*" said Amelia. "Oh, I do wish they wouldn't! I shall go down and ask them not to."

"*Amelia!*" The other girl was at last aroused. "You *couldn't!* I shouldn't *let* you dream of doing anything so unladylike. What would the gentlemen think of you?"

The question silenced Amelia, but she began to put on her so lately discarded bodice.

"I won't go if you think I oughtn't," she said.

"Forward and fast, auntie would call it," said the other. "I am almost sure she would."

"But I'll keep dressed. I shan't disturb you. I'll sit in the dressing-room. I *can't* go to sleep while he's running into this awful danger."

"Which he?" Ernestine's voice was very sharp. "And there isn't any danger."

"Yes, there is," said Amelia, sullenly, "and I mean *them*. Both of them."

Ernestine said her prayers and got into bed. She had put her hair in curl-papers, which became her like a wreath of white roses.

"I don't think auntie will be pleased," she said, "when she hears that, you sat up all night watching young gentlemen. Good night, dear!"

"Good night, darling," said Amelia. "I know you don't understand. It's all right."

She sat in the dark by the dressing-room window. There was no sound to break the stillness, except the little cracklings of twigs and rustlings of leaves as birds or little night-wandering beasts moved in the shadows of the garden, and the sudden creakings that furniture makes if you sit alone with it and listen in the night's silence.

Amelia sat on and listened, listened. The pavilion showed in broken streaks of pale grey against the wood that seemed to be clinging to it in dark patches. But that, she reminded herself, was only the creeper. She sat there for a very long time, not knowing how long a time it was. For anxiety is a poor chronometer, and the first ten minutes had seemed an hour. She had no watch. Ernestine had, and slept with it under her pillow. There was nothing to measure time's flight by, and she sat there rigid, straining her ears for a foot-fall on the grass, straining her eyes to see a figure come out of the dark pavilion and cross the dew-grey grass towards the house. And she heard nothing, saw nothing.

Slowly, imperceptibly, the grey of the dewy grass lightened, lightened; the grey of the sleeping trees took on faint dreams of colour. The sky turned faint above the trees, the moon perhaps was coming out. The pavilion grew more clearly visible. It seemed to Amelia that something moved among the leaves that surrounded it, and she looked to see him come out. But he did not come.

"I wish the moon would really shine," she told herself. And suddenly she knew that the sky was clear and that this growing light was not the moon's dead cold silver, but the growing light of dawn.

She went quickly into the other room, put her hand under the pillow of Ernestine, and drew out the little watch with the diamond "E" on it.

"A quarter to three," she said, aloud. Ernestine moved and grunted.

There was no hesitation about Amelia now. Without another thought for the ladylike and the really suitable, she lighted her candle and went quickly down the stairs, still dark, paused a moment in the hall, and so out through the front door into the grey of the new day. She passed along the terrace. The feet of Frederick protruded from the open French window of the smoking-room. She set down her candle on the terrace—it burned clearly enough in that clear air—went up to Frederick as he slept, his head between his shoulders and his hands loosely hanging, and shook him.

"Wake up!" she said. "Wake up! Something's happened! It's a quarter to three and he's not come back."

"Who's not what?" Frederick asked, sleepily.

"Mr Thesiger. The pavilion."

"Thesiger?—the— *You*, Miss Davenant? I beg your pardon. I must have dropped off."

He got up unsteadily, gazing dully at this white apparition still in evening dress with pale hair now no longer wreathed.

"What is it?" he said; "is anybody ill?"

Briefly and very urgently Amelia told him what it was, imploring him to go at once and see what had happened. If he had been fully awake, her voice and her eyes would have told him many things.

"He said he'd come back," he said. "Hadn't I better wait? You go back to bed, Miss Davenant. If he doesn't come in half an hour—"

"If you don't go this minute," said Amelia, tensely, "I shall."

"Oh, well, if you insist," Frederick said. "He has simply fallen asleep as I did. Dear Miss Davenant, return to your room, I beg. In the morning, when we are all laughing at this false alarm, you will be glad to remember that Mr Thesiger does not know of your anxiety."

"I hate you," said Amelia, gently; "and I am going to see what has happened. Come or not, as you like."

She caught up the silver candlestick, and he followed its steady gleam down the terrace steps and across the grey dewy grass.

Halfway she paused, lifted the hand that had been hidden among her muslin flounces, and held it out to him with a big Indian dagger in it.

"I got it out of the hall," she said. "If there's any *real* danger—anything living, I mean. I thought—but I know I couldn't use it. Will you take it?"

He took it, laughing kindly.

"How romantic you are!" he said, admiringly, and looked at her standing there in the mingled gold and grey of dawn and candlelight. It was as though he had never seen her before.

They reached the steps of the pavilion and stumbled up them. The door was closed, but not locked. And Amelia noticed that the trails of creeper had not been disturbed; they grew across the doorway as thick as a man's finger, some of them.

"He must have got in by one of the windows," Frederick said. "Your dagger comes in handy, Miss Davenant."

He slashed at the wet, sticky green stuff and put his shoulder to the door. It yielded at a touch and they went in.

The one candle lighted the pavilion hardly at all, and the dusky light that oozed in through the door and windows helped very little. And the silence was thick and heavy.

"Thesiger!" said Frederick, clearing his throat. "Thesiger! Halloa! Where are you?"

Thesiger did not say where he was. And then they saw.

There were low stone seats to the windows, and between the windows low stone benches ran. On one of these something dark, something dark and in places white, confused the outline of the carved stone.

"Thesiger!" said Frederick again, in the tone a man uses to a room that he is almost sure is empty. "Thesiger!"

But Amelia was bending over the bench. She was holding the candle crookedly, so that it flared and guttered.

"Is he there?" Frederick asked, following her; "is that him? Is he asleep?"

"Take the candle," said Amelia, and he took it obediently. Amelia was touching what lay on the bench. Suddenly she screamed. Just one scream, not very loud. But Frederick remembers just how it sounded. Sometimes he hears it in dreams and wakes moaning, though he is an old man now, and his old wife says, "What is it, dear?" and he says, "Nothing, my Ernestine, nothing."

Directly she had screamed she said, "He's dead," and fell on her knees by the bench. Frederick saw that she held something in her arms.

"Perhaps he isn't," she said. "Fetch someone from the house—brandy—send for a doctor. Oh, go, go, go!"

"I can't leave you here," said Frederick. "Suppose he revives?"

"He will not revive," said Amelia, dully; "go, go, go! Do as I tell you. Go! If you don't go," she added, suddenly and amazingly, "I believe I shall kill you. It's all your doing."

The astounding sharp injustice of this stung Frederick into action.

"I believe he's only fainted or something," he said. "When I've roused the house and everyone has witnessed your emotion you will regret—"

She sprang to her feet and caught the knife from him and raised it, awkwardly, clumsily, but with keen threatening, not to be mistaken or disregarded. Frederick went.

When Frederick came back with the groom and the gardener—he hadn't thought it well to disturb the ladies—the pavilion was filled full of white revealing daylight. On the bench lay a dead man, and kneeling by him a living woman on whose warm breast his cold and

195

heavy head lay pillowed. The dead man's hands were full of green crushed leaves, and thick twining tendrils were about his wrists and throat. A wave of green seemed to have swept from the open window to the bench where he lay.

The groom and the gardener and the dead man's friend looked and looked.

"Looks like as if he'd got himself entangled in the creeper and lost 'is 'ead," said the groom, scratching his own.

"How'd the creeper get in, though? That's what I says." It was the gardener who said it.

"Through the window," said Doricourt, moistening his lips with his tongue.

"The window was shut, though, when I come by at five last night," said the gardener, stubbornly "'Ow did it get all that way side five?"

They looked at each other voicing, silently, impossible things.

The woman never spoke. She sat there in the white ring of her crinolined dress like a broken white rose. But her arms were round Thesiger, and she would not move them.

When the doctor came he sent for Ernestine, who came flushed and sleepy-eyed and very frightened and shocked.

"You're upset, dear," she said to her friend, "and no wonder. How brave of you to come out with Mr Doricourt to see what had happened! But you can't do anything now, dear. Come in and I'll tell them to get you some tea."

Amelia laughed, looked down at the face on her shoulder, laid the head back on the bench among the drooping green of the creeper, stooped over it, kissed it, and said to it quite quietly and gently, "Goodbye, dear; goodbye!" took Ernestine's arm, and went away with her.

The doctor made an examination and gave a death certificate. "Heart failure" was his original and brilliant diagnosis. The certificate said nothing, and Frederick said nothing of the creeper that was wound about the dead man's neck, nor of the little white wounds, like little bloodless lips half-open, that they found about the dead man's neck.

"An imaginative or uneducated person," said the doctor, "might suppose that the creeper had something to do with his death. But we mustn't encourage superstition. I will assist my man to prepare the body for its last sleep. Then we need not have any chattering women."

"Can you read Latin?" Frederick asked. The doctor could. And, later, did.

It was the Latin of that brown book with the Doricourt arms on it that Frederick wanted read. And when he and the doctor had been together with the book between them for three hours, they closed it and looked at each other with shy and doubtful eyes.

"It can't be true," said Frederick.

"If it is," said the more cautious doctor, "you don't want it talked about. I should destroy that book if I were you. And I should cut down the creeper and burn it and dig up the roots. It is quite evident, from what you tell me, that your friend believed that this creeper was a man-eater; that it fed, just before its flowering time, as the book tells us, at dawn; and that he fully meant that the thing, when it crawled into the pavilion seeking its prey, should find *you* and not him. It would have been so, I understand, if his watch had not stopped at one o'clock."

"He dropped it, you know," said Doricourt, like a man in a dream.

"All the cases in this book are the same," said the doctor; "the strangling, the white wounds. I have heard of such plants; I never believed." He shuddered. "Had your friend any spite against you? Any reason for wanting to get you out of the way?"

Frederick thought of Ernestine, of Thesiger's eyes on her smile at him over her blue muslin shoulder.

"No," he said, "none. None whatever. It must have been an accident. I am sure he did not know. He could not read Latin." He lied, being, after all, a gentleman; and Ernestine's name being sacred.

"The creeper seems to have been brought here and planted in Henry the Eighth's time. And then the thing began. It seems to have been at its flowering season that it needed the—that in short, it was dangerous. The little animals and birds found dead near the pavilion. But to move itself all that way, across the floor! The thing must have been almost conscient," he said, with a sincere shudder. "One would think," he corrected himself at once, "that it knew what it was doing, if such a thing were not plainly contrary to the laws of Nature."

"Yes," said Frederick, "one would. I think if I can't do anything more I'll go and rest. Somehow all this has given me a turn. Poor Thesiger!"

His last thought before he went to sleep was one of pity.

"Poor Thesiger," he said; "how violent and wicked! And what an escape for me! I must never tell Ernestine. And all the time there was Amelia. Ernestine would never have done *that* for *me!*" And on a little pang of regret for the impossible he fell asleep.

Amelia went on living. She was not the sort that dies even of such a thing as happened to her on that night, when for the first and last time she held her love in her arms and knew him for the murderer he was. It was only the other day that she died, a very old woman. Ernestine, who, beloved and surrounded by children and grand-children, survived her, spoke her epitaph. "Poor Amelia," she said; "nobody ever looked the same side of the road where she was. There was an indiscretion when she was young. Oh, nothing disgraceful, of course. She was a lady. But people talked. It was the sort of thing that stamps a girl, you know."

THE GREEN DEATH

H. C. McNeile

"The Green Death" was published in *The Strand* magazine in 1920 in two parts by Herman Cyril McNeile, also known as "Sapper". McNeile was a British Soldier turned author who used his experience in the trenches as material for his writing. He became known for thrillers and his most famous series was *Bulldog Drummond*, featuring a dashing ex-army captain's adventures. In a similar theme and in keeping with his military background, "The Green Death" centres around the character of Major Bob Seymour, who finds himself at a dinner party which ends with a mysterious killing. Major Seymour's keen intellect and experience in foreign climes and exotic flora become invaluable in finding out the true culprit of the crime.

I

" ND why, Major Seymour, do they call you Old Point of Detail'?"

The tall, spare man, with a face tanned by years in the tropics, turned at the question, and glanced at the girl beside him. At the time when most boys are still at school, force of circumstances had sent him far afield into strange corners of the earth—a wanderer, and picker-up of odd jobs. He had done police work in India; he had been on a rubber plantation in Sumatra. The Amazon knew him and so did the Yukon, while his knowledge of the customs of tribes of Africa—the very names of which were unknown to most people— was greater than the average Londoner has of his native city. In fact, before the war it would have been difficult to sit for an evening in one of those clubs which spring into being in all corners where Englishmen guard their far-flung inheritance without Bob Seymour's name cropping up.

Then had come the war, and in the van of the great army from the mountains and the swamps which trekked home as the first shot rang out, he came. As his reward he got a DSO and one leg permanently shortened by two inches. He also met a girl—the girl who had just asked him the question.

He'd met her just a year after the Armistice; when he was won-dering whether there was any place for a cripple in the lands that he knew. And from that day everything had changed. Even to himself he wouldn't admit it; the thought of asking such a glorious bit of loveli-ness to tie herself to a useless has-been like himself was out of the question. But he let the days slip by, content to meet her occasionally at dinner—to see her, in the distance, at a theatre. And now, for the first time, he found himself staying under the same roof. When he'd arrived the preceding day and had seen her in the hall, just for a moment his heart had stopped beating, and then had given a great bound forward. She, of course, knew nothing of his feelings; of that he felt sure. And she must never know; of that he was determined. The whole thing was out of the question.

Of course—naturally. And the only comment which a mere narrator of facts can offer on the state of affairs is to record the remark made by Ruth Brabazon to a very dear friend of hers after Bob Seymour had limped upstairs to his room.

"That's the man, Delia," she said, with a little smile. "And if he doesn't say something soon, I shall have to."

"He looks a perfect darling," remarked the other.

"He is," sighed Ruth. "But he *won't* give me the chance of telling him so. He thinks he's a cripple."

With which brief insight into things as they really were, we can now return to things as Bob Seymour thought they were. Beside him, on a sofa in the hall, sat the girl who had kept him in England through long months, and she had just asked him a question.

"The Old, I trust, is a term of endearment," he answered, with a smile, "and not a brutal reflection on my tale of years. The Point of Detail refers to a favourite saying of mine with which my reprobate subalterns—of whom your brother was quite the worst—used to mock me."

"Bill is the limit," murmured the girl. "What was the saying?"

"I used to preach the importance of Points of Detail to 'em," he grinned. "One is nothing; two are a coincidence; three are a moral certainty. And they're very easy to see if you have eyes to see them with."

"I suppose they are, Old Point of Detail," she replied, softly.

Was it his imagination or did she lay a faint stress on the Old?

"It was certainly a term of endearment," she continued, deliberately, "if what Bill says is to be believed."

"Oh! Bill's an ass," said Seymour, sheepishly.

"Thank you," she remarked, and he noticed her eyes were twinkling. "I've always been told I'm exactly like Bill. I know we always used to like the same things when we were children." She rose and crossed the hall. "Time to dress for dinner, I think."

In the dim light he could not see her face clearly: he only knew his heart was thumping wildly. Did she mean—? And then from half-way up the stairs she spoke again.

"Two are certainly a coincidence," she agreed, thoughtfully. "But the third would have to be pretty conclusive before you could take it as a certainty."

II

"Well, Major Seymour, hitting 'em in the beak?" The Celebrated Actor mixed himself a cocktail with that delicate grace for which he was famed on both sides of the Atlantic.

"So-so, Mr Trayne," returned the other. "All the easy ones came my way."

The house-party were in the hall waiting for dinner to be announced, but the one member of it who mattered to Bob Seymour had not yet appeared.

"Rot, my dear fellow," said his host, who had come up in time to hear his last remark. "Your shooting was magnificent—absolutely magnificent. You had four birds in the air once from your guns."

"Personally," murmured the Celebrated Actor, "it fails to appeal to me. Apart from my intense fright at letting off lethal weapons, I have never yet succeeded in hitting anything except a keeper or—more frequently—a guest. I abhor violence—except at rehearsals." He broke off as a heavy, bull-necked man came slowly down the stairs. "And who is the latest addition to our number, Sir Robert?"

"A man who did me a good turn a few weeks ago," said the owner of the house, shortly. "Name of Denton. Arrived half an hour ago."

He moved away to introduce the newcomer, and the Actor turned to Bob Seymour.

"One wonders," he remarked, "whether it would be indiscreet to offer Mr Denton a part in my new play. Nothing much to say. He merely drinks and eats. In effect, a publican of unprepossessing aspect. One wonders—so suitable." He placed his empty glass on the table and drifted charmingly away towards his hostess, leaving Bob Seymour smiling gently. Undoubtedly a most suitable part for Mr Denton.

And then, quite suddenly, the smile died away. Bill Brabazon, who was standing near the fireplace, had turned round and come face to face with the newcomer. For a moment or two they stared at one another—a deadly loathing on their faces; then with ostentatious rudeness Denton turned his back and walked away.

"My God! Bob," muttered Bill, coming up to Seymour. "How on earth did that swine-emperor get here?"

His jaw was grim and set, his eyes gleaming with rage; and the hand that poured out the cocktail shook a little.

"What's the matter, Bill?" said Seymour, quietly. "For heaven's sake, don't make a scene, old man!"

"Matter?" choked Bill Brabazon. "Matter! Why—"

But any further revelations were checked by the announcement of dinner, and the party went in informally. To his delight, Bob Seymour found himself next to Ruth, and the little scene he had just witnessed passed from his mind. It was not until they were halfway through the meal that it was recalled to him by Ruth herself.

"Who is that dreadful-looking man talking to Delia Morrison?" she whispered.

"Denton is his name," replied Seymour, and every vestige of colour left her face.

"Denton," she muttered. "Good heavens! It can't be the same." She glanced round the table till she found her brother, who was answering the animated remarks of his partner with morose mono-syllables. "Has Bill—"

"Bill has," returned Seymour, grimly. "And he's whispered to me on the subject. What's the trouble?"

"They had the most fearful row—over a girl," she explained, a little breathlessly. "Two or three months ago. I know they had a fight, and Bill got a black eye. But he broke that other brute's jaw."

"Holy smoke!" muttered Seymour. "The meeting strikes the casual observer as being, to put it mildly, embarrassing. Do you know how the row started?"

"Only vaguely," she answered. "That man Denton got some girl into trouble, and then left her in the lurch—refused to help her at all. A poor girl—the daughter of someone who had been in Bill's platoon. And he came to Bill."

"I see," said Seymour, grimly. "I see. Bill would."

"Of course he would!" she cried, "Why, of course. Just the same as you would."

"I suppose that isn't pretty conclusive?" he said, with a grin. "As a third point, I mean."

But Ruth Brabazon had turned to the Celebrated Actor on her other side. He had already said, "My dear young lady" five times without avail, and he was Very Celebrated.

Neglected for the moment by both his neighbours, Bob proceeded to study the gentleman whose sudden arrival seemed so inopportune. He was a coarse-looking specimen, and already his face was flushed with the amount of wine he had drunk. Every now and then his eyes sought Bill Brabazon vindictively, and Seymour frowned as he saw it. Denton belonged to a type he had met before, and it struck him there was every promise of trouble before the evening was out. When men of Denton's calibre get into the condition of "drink-taken," such trifles as the presence of other guests in the house do not deter them from being offensive. And Bill Brabazon, though far too well-bred to seek a quarrel in such surroundings, was also far too hot-tempered to take any deliberate insult lying down.

Suddenly a coarse, over-loud laugh from Denton sounded above the general conversation, and Ruth Brabazon looked round quickly.

"Ugh! what a horrible man!" she whispered to Bob. "How I hate him!"

"I don't believe a word of it," he was saying, harshly. "Fraud by knaves for fools. For those manifestations that have been seen there is some material cause. Generally transparent trickery." He laughed again sneeringly.

For a second or two there was an uncomfortable silence. It was not so much what the man had said, as the vulgar, ill-bred manner in which he had said it, and Sir Robert hastily intervened to relieve the tension.

"Ghosts?" he remarked. "As impossible a subject to argue about as religion or politics. Incidentally, you know," he continued, addressing the table at large, "there's a room in this house round which a novelist might weave quite a good ghost story."

"Tell us, Sir Robert." A general chorus assailed him, and he smiled.

"I'm not a novelist," he said, "though for what it's worth I'll tell you about it. The room is one in the new wing which I used to use as a smoking-room. It was the part built on to the house by my predecessor—a gentleman, from all accounts, of peculiar temperament. He had spent all his life travelling to obscure places of the world; and I don't know if it was liver or what, but his chief claim to notoriety when he did finally settle down appears to have been an intense hatred of his fellow-men. There are some very strange stories of the things which used to go on in this house, where he lived the life of an absolute recluse, with one old man to look after him. He died about forty years ago."

Sir Robert paused and sipped his champagne.

"However, to continue. In this smoking-room in the new wing there is an inscription written in the most amazing jumble of letters by the window. It is written on the wall, and every form of hiero-glyphic is used. You get a letter of Arabic, then one of Chinese, then an ordinary English one, and perhaps a German. Well, to cut a long story short, I took the trouble one day to copy it out, and replaced the foreign letters—there are one or two Greek letters as well—by their corresponding English ones. I had to get somebody else to help me over the Chinese and Arabic, but the result was, at any rate, sense. It proved to be a little jingling rhyme, and it ran as follows:—

> When 'tis hot, shun this spot.
> When 'tis rain, come again.
> When tis day, all serene.
> When 'tis night, death is green."

Sir Robert glanced round the table with a smile.

"There was no doubt who had written this bit of doggerel, as the wing was actually built by my predecessor—and I certainly didn't. That's a pretty good foundation to build a ghost story on, isn't it?"

"But have you ever seen anything?" inquired one of the guests.

"Not a thing," laughed his host. "But"—he paused mysteriously— "I've smelt something. And that's the reason why I don't use the room any more.

"It was a very hot night—hotter even than this evening. There was thunder about—incidentally, I shouldn't be surprised if we had a storm before tomorrow—and I was sitting in the room after dinner, reading the paper. All of a sudden I became aware of a strange and most unpleasant smell: a sort of fetid, musty, rank smell, like you get sometimes when you open up an old vault. And at the same moment I noticed that the paper I held in my hand had gone a most peculiar green colour and I could no longer see the print clearly. It seemed to have got darker suddenly, and the smell became so bad that it made me feel quite faint.

"I walked over to the door and left the room, meaning to get a lamp. Then something detained me, and I didn't go back for half an hour or so. When I did the smell was still there, though so faint that one could hardly notice it. Also the paper was quite white again." He laughed genially. "And that's the family ghost; a poor thing, but our own. I'll have to get someone to take it in hand and bring it up to date."

"But surely you don't think there is any connection between this smell and the inscription?" cried Denton.

"I advance no theory at all." Sir Robert smiled genially. "All I can tell you is that there is an inscription, and that the colour green is mentioned in it. It seemed to me most certainly that my paper went green, through it is even more certain that I did not die. Also there is at times in the room this rather unpleasant smell. I told you it was a poor thing in the ghost line."

The conversation became general, and Ruth Brabazon turned to Bob, who was thoughtfully staring at his plate.

"Why so preoccupied, Major Seymour?"

"A most interesting yarn," he remarked, coming out of his reverie. "Have a salted almond, before I finish the lot."

III

To have two hot-tempered men who loathe one another with a bitter loathing in a house-party is not conducive to its happiness. And when one of them is an outsider of the first water, slightly under the influence of alcohol, the situation becomes even more precarious. For some time after dinner was over Bill Brabazon avoided Denton as unostentatiously as he could, though it was plain to Bob Seymour and Ruth that he was finding it increasingly difficult to control his temper. By ten o'clock it was obvious, even to those guests who knew nothing about the men's previous relations, that there was trouble brewing; and Sir Robert, who had been told the facts of the case by Bob, was at his wits' end.

"If only I'd known," he said, irritably. "If only someone had told me. I know Denton is a sweep, but he did me a very good turn in the City the other day, and, without thinking, I asked him to come and shoot some time. And when he suggested coming now, I couldn't in all decency get out of it. I hope to heaven there won't be a row."

"If there's going to be, Sir Robert, you can't prevent it," said Seymour. "I'm sure Bill will do all he can to avoid one."

"I know he will," answered his host. "But there are limits, and that man Denton is one of 'em. I wish I'd never met the blighter."

"Come and have a game of billiards, anyway," said the other. "It's no use worrying about it. If it comes, it comes."

When they had been playing about twenty minutes, Ruth Brabazon and Delia Morrison joined them, the billiard-room being, as they affirmed, the coolest room in the house.

"We'll have rain soon," said Sir Robert, bringing off a fine losing hazard off the red. "That'll clear the air."

And shortly afterwards his prophecy proved true. Heavy drops began to patter down on the glass skylight, and the girls heaved a sigh of relief.

"Thank goodness," gasped Ruth. "I couldn't have stood—" She broke off abruptly and stared at the door, which had just opened to admit her brother. "Bill," she cried, "what's the matter?"

Bob Seymour looked up quickly at her words; then he rested his cue against the table. Something very obviously was the matter. Bill Brabazon, his tie undone, with a crumpled shirt, and a cut under his eye on the cheek-bone, came into the room and closed the door.

"I must apologise, Sir Robert," he said, quietly, "for what has happened. It's a rotten thing to have to admit in another man's house, but the fault was not entirely mine. I've had the most damnable row with that fellow Denton—incidentally he was half-drunk—and I've laid him out. An unpardonable thing to do to one of your guests, but—well—I'm not particularly slow-tempered, and I couldn't help it. He went on and on and on—asking for trouble: and finally he got it."

"Damnation!" Sir Robert replaced his cue in the rack. "When did it happen, Bill?"

"About half an hour ago. I've been outside since. Meaning to avoid him I went to the smoking-room in the new wing, and I found him there examining that inscription by the window. I couldn't get away—without running away. I suppose I ought to have." An uncomfortable silence settled on the room, which was broken at length by Sir Robert.

"Where is the fellow now, Bill?"

"I haven't seen him—not since I socked him one on the jaw. I'm deucedly sorry about it," he continued, miserably, "and I feel the most awful sweep, but—"

He stopped suddenly as the door was flung open and the Celebrated Actor rushed in. The magnificent repose which usually stamped his features was gone: it was an agitated and frightened man who stood by the billiard table, pouring out his somewhat incoherent story. And as his meaning became clear Bill Brabazon grew white and leaned against the mantelpiece for support.

Dead—Denton dead! That was the salient fact that stood out from the Actor's disjointed sentences.

"To examine the inscription," he was saying. "I went in to examine it—and there—by the window…"

"He can't be dead," said Bill, harshly. "He's laid out, that's all."

"Quick! Which is the room?" Bob Seymour's steady voice served to pull everyone together. "There's no good standing here talking—"

In silence they crossed the hall, and went along the passage to the new wing.

"Here we are," said Sir Robert, nervously. "This is the door."

The room was in darkness and in the air there hung a rank, fetid smell. The window was open, and outside the rain was lashing down with tropical violence. Bob Seymour fumbled in his pocket for a match; then he turned up to the lamp and lit it. Just for a moment he stared at it in surprise, then Ruth, from the doorway, gave a little stifled scream.

"Look," she whispered. "By the window—"

A man was lying across the windowsill, with his legs inside the room and his head and shoulders outside.

"Good heavens," muttered Sir Robert, touching the body with a shaking hand. "I suppose—I suppose—he *is* dead?"

But Seymour apparently failed to hear the remark.

"Do you notice this extraordinary smell?" he said, at length.

"Damn the smell," said his host, irritably. "Give me a hand with this poor fellow."

Seymour pulled himself together and stepped forward as the other bent down to take hold of the sagging legs.

"Leave him alone, Sir Robert," he said, quickly. "You must leave the body till the police come. We'll just see that he's dead, and then—"

He picked up an electric torch from the table and leant out of the window. And after a while he straightened up again with a little shudder.

It was not a pretty sight. In the light of the torch the face seemed almost black, and the two arms, limp and twisted, sprawled in the sodden earth of the flower-bed. The man was quite dead, and they both stepped back into the middle of the smoking-room with obvious relief.

"Well," said Brabazon, "Is he—?"

"Yes—he's dead," said Seymour, gravely.

"But it's impossible," cried the boy, wildly. "Why, that blow I gave him couldn't have—have killed the man."

"Nevertheless he's dead," said Seymour, staring at the motionless body, thoughtfully. Then his eyes narrowed, and he bent once more over the dead man. Ruth, sobbing hysterically, was trying to comfort her brother, while the rest of the house-party had collected near the door, talking in low, agitated whispers.

"Bob—Bob," cried Bill Brabazon, suddenly. "I've just remembered.

I couldn't have done it when I laid him out. I told you I was walking up and down the lawn. Well, the light from this room was streaming out, and I remember seeing his shadow in the middle of the window. He must have been standing up. The mark of the window-sash was clear: on the lawn."

Seymour glanced at him thoughtfully. "But the light was out, Bill. How do you account for that?"

"It wasn't," said the other, positively. "Not then. It must have gone out later."

"We'll have to send for the police, Sir Robert," said Seymour, laying a reassuring hand on the boy's arm. "Tell them everything when they come."

"I've got nothing to hide," said the youngster, hoarsely. "I swear to Heaven I didn't do that."

"We'd better go," cried Sir Robert. "Leave everything as it is. I'll ring the police up."

With quick, nervous steps he left the room, followed by his guests, until only Seymour was left standing by the window with its dreadful occupant. For a full minute he stood there, while the rain still lashed down outside, sniffing as he had done when he first entered. And, at length, with a slight frown on his face, as if some elusive memory escaped him, he followed the others from the room, first turning out the light and then locking the door.

IV

It was half an hour before the police came, in the shape of Inspector Grayson and a constable. During that time the rain had stopped for a period of about twenty minutes; only to come on again just before a ring announced their arrival.

The house-party were moving aimlessly about in little scattered groups, obsessed with the dreadful tragedy. In the billiard-room Ruth sat with her brother in a sort of stunned silence; only Bob Seymour seemed unaffected by the general strain. Perhaps it was because in a life such as his death by violence was no new spectacle: perhaps it was that there was something he could not understand.

Who had blown the light out? That was the crux. Blown—not turned. The Celebrated Actor was very positive that the light had not been on when he first entered the room. It might have been the wind, but there was no wind. A point of detail—one. And then the smell—that strange, fetid smell. It touched a chord of memory, but try as he would he could not place it.

His mind started on another line. If the boy, in his rage, had struck the dead man a fatal blow, how had the body got into such a position? It would have been lying on the floor.

"Weak heart," he argued. "Hot night—gasping for breath—rushed to window—collapsed. That's what they'd say."

He frowned thoughtfully; on the face of it quite plausible. Not only plausible—quite possible.

"Major Seymour!" Ruth's voice beside him made him look up. "What can we do? Poor old Bill's nearly off his head."

"There's nothing to do, Miss Brabazon—but tell the truth," said Seymour, gravely. "What I mean is," he explained, hurriedly, "you've got to impress on Bill the vital necessity of being absolutely frank with the police."

"I know he didn't do it, Bob," she cried, desperately. "I know it."

Bob! she'd called him Bob. And such is human nature that for a moment the dead man was forgotten.

"So do I, Ruth," he whispered, impulsively. "So do I."

"And you'll prove it?" she cried.

"I'll prove it," he promised her. Which was no rasher than many promises made under similar conditions.

"Thank goodness you've come, Inspector." Sir Robert had met the police at the door. "A dreadful tragedy."

"So I gather, Sir Robert," answered the other. "One of your guests been murdered?"

"I didn't say so on the 'phone," said Sir Robert. "I said—killed."

The inspector grunted. "Where's the body?"

"In the smoking-room." He led the way towards the door.

"I've got the key in my pocket," said Seymour; and the inspector looked at him quickly.

"May I ask your name, sir?" he remarked.

"Seymour—Major Seymour?" returned the other. "I turned out the light and locked the door while Sir Robert was telephoning for you, to ensure that nothing would be moved."

The inspector grunted again, as Seymour opened the door and struck a light.

"Over in that window, Inspector—" began Sir Robert, only to stop and gape foolishly across the room.

"I don't quite understand, gentlemen," said Inspector Grayson, testily.

"No more do I," muttered Bob Seymour, with a puzzled frown.

The window-sill was empty; the body was gone.

"I left him lying, as we found him, half in and half out of the window," said Seymour. "His legs were inside, his head and shoulders from the waist upwards were outside."

It was the constable who interrupted him. While the others were standing by the door he had crossed to the window and leaned out.

"Here's the body, sir," he cried. "Outside in the flower-bed."

*

215

The inspector went quickly to the window and peered out; then he turned and confronted Sir Robert and Seymour.

"He's dead right enough *now*," he said, gravely. "It seems a pity that you gentlemen didn't take a little more trouble to find out if he was dead in the first place. You might have saved his life."

"Hang it, man!" exploded Seymour, angrily, "do you suppose I don't know a dead man when I see one?"

"I don't know whether you do or don't," answered the other, shortly. "But I've never yet heard of a dead man getting up and moving to an adjacent flower-bed. And you say yourself that you left him lying over the window-sill."

For a moment an angry flush mounted on the soldier's face; then, with an effort, he controlled himself. On the face of it, the inspector was perfectly justified in his remark: dead men do not move. The trouble was that Bob Seymour had felt the dead man's heart and his pulse; had turned the light of his torch from close range into his eyes. And he *knew* that he had made no mistake; he *knew* that the man was dead when he turned out the light and left the room. He *knew* it; but—dead men do not move. What had happened in the room during the time they were waiting for the police? The key had been in his pocket: who had moved the body? And why? Not Bill Brabazon: that he knew.

With a puzzled frown he crossed slowly towards the two policemen, who were hauling the limp form through the open window. And once again he paused and sniffed.

"That smell again, Sir Robert," he remarked.

"What smell?" demanded the inspector, as they laid the dead man on the floor.

"Don't you notice it? A strange, fetid, rank smell."

The inspector sniffed perfunctorily. "I smell the ordinary smell of rain on dead leaves," he remarked. "What about it?"

"Nothing, except that there are no dead leaves in June," returned Seymour, shortly.

"Well, sir," snorted the inspector, "whether there are dead leaves or not, we've got a dead man on the floor. And I take it he wasn't killed by a smell, anyway."

In the full light of the room Denton was an even more unpleasant sight than when he had lain sprawling over the window-sill. The water dripped from his sodden clothing and ran in little pools on the floor; the dark, puffy face was smeared with a layer of wet earth. But it was not at these details that Bob Seymour was staring: it was an angry-looking red weal round the neck just above the collar that riveted his attention. The inspector, taking no further notice of the two spectators, was proceeding methodically with his examination. First he turned out all the pockets, laying the contents neatly on the table; then, with the help of the constable, he turned the body over on its face. A little fainter, but still perfectly discernible, the red weal could be traced continuously round the neck; and after a while the inspector straightened up and turned to Sir Robert.

"It looks as if he had been strangled, sir," he remarked, professionally. "I should imagine from the size of the mark that a fairly thin rope was used. Have you any idea whether anyone had a grudge against him? The motive was obviously not robbery."

"Strangled!" cried Sir Robert, joining the other three. "But I don't understand." He turned perplexedly to Bob Seymour, who was standing near the window absorbed in thought. Then, a little haltingly, he continued: "Unfortunately there was a very severe row between him and another of my guests earlier in the evening."

"Where did the row take place?"

"Er—in this room."

"Was anyone else present?"

"No. No one heard them quarrelling. But Mr Brabazon, the guest in question, made no secret about it—afterwards. He told us in the billiard-room that—that they had come to blows in here."

"I would like to see Mr Brabazon, Sir Robert," said the inspector. "Perhaps you would be good enough to send for him."

"I will go and get him myself," returned the other, leaving the room.

"A very remarkable affair," murmured Seymour, as the door closed behind his host. "Don't you agree with me, Inspector?"

"In what way?" asked the officer, guardedly.

But the soldier was lighting a cigarette, and made no immediate answer. "May I ask," he remarked at length, "if you've ever tried to strangle a man with a rope? Because," he continued, when the other merely snorted indignantly, "I have. During the war—in German East Africa. And it took me a long while. You see, if you put a slipknot round a man's neck and pull, he comes towards you. You've got to get very close to him and kneel on him, or wedge him in some way, so that he can't move, before you can do much good in the strangling line."

"Quite an amateur detective, Major Seymour," said the other, condescendingly. "If you will forgive my saying so, however, it might have been better had you concentrated on seeing whether the poor fellow was dead."

He turned as the door opened, and Bill Brabazon came in, followed by Sir Robert.

"This is Mr Brabazon, Inspector," said the latter.

The officer eyed the youngster keenly for a moment before he spoke. Then he pointed to a chair, so placed that the light of the lamp would fall on the face of anyone sitting in it.

"Will you tell me everything you know, Mr Brabazon? And I should advise you not to attempt to conceal anything?"

"I've got nothing to conceal," answered the boy, doggedly. "I found Denton in here about half-past ten, and we started quarrelling. I'd been trying to avoid him the whole evening, but there was no getting away from him this time. After a while we began to fight, and he hit me in the face. Then I saw red, and really went for him. And I laid him out. That's all I know about it."

"And what did you do after you laid him out?"

"I went out into the garden to cool down. Then when the rain came on, I went to the billiard-room and told Sir Robert. And the first thing I knew about this," with a shudder he looked at the dead body, "was when Mr Trayne came into the billiard-room and told us."

"Mr Trayne! Who is he, Sir Robert?"

"Another guest stopping in the house. Do you wish to see him?"

"Please." The inspector paced thoughtfully up and down the room.

"The light was on, wasn't it, Bill, when you left the room?" said Seymour.

"It was. Why, I saw his shadow on the lawn, as I told you."

"Did you?" said the inspector, watching him narrowly. "Would you be surprised to hear, Mr Brabazon, that this unfortunate man was strangled?"

"Strangled?" Bill Brabazon started up from his chair. "Strangled! Good God! Who by?"

"That is precisely what we want to find out," said the inspector.

"But good heavens, man," cried the boy, excitedly, "don't you see that that exonerates me. I didn't strangle him: I only hit him on the jaw. And that shadow I saw," he swung round on Seymour, "must have been the murderer."

"You wish to see me, Inspector?" Trayne's voice from the doorway interrupted him, and he sat back in his chair again. And Seymour, watching the joyful look on Bill's face, knew that he spoke the truth.

His amazement at hearing the cause of death had been too spontaneous not to be genuine. In his own mind Bill Brabazon regarded himself as cleared: the trouble was that other people might not. The majority of murderers have died, still protesting their innocence.

"I understand that it was you, Mr Trayne, who first discovered the body," said the inspector.

"It was. I came in and found the room in darkness. I wished to study an inscription by the window to which Sir Robert had alluded at dinner. I struck a match, and then—I saw the body lying half in half out over the sill. It gave me a dreadful shock—quite dreadful. And I at once went to the billiard-room for assistance."

"So whoever did it turned out the light," said the inspector, musingly. "What time was it, Mr Trayne, when you made the discovery?"

"About half-past eleven, I should think."

"An hour after the quarrel. And in that hour someone entered this room either by the window or the door, and committed the deed. He, further, left either by the window or the door. How did you leave, Mr Brabazon?"

"By the door," said the youngster. "The flower-bed outside the window is too wide to jump."

"Then if the murderer entered by the window, he will have left footmarks. If he entered by the door and left by it the presumption is that he is a member of the house. No one who was not would risk leaving by the door after committing such an act."

"Most ably reasoned," murmured Seymour, mildly.

But the inspector was far too engrossed with his theory to notice the slight sarcasm in the other's tone. With a powerful electric torch he was searching the ground outside the window for any trace of footprints. The mark in the ground where the body had lain was clearly defined; save for that, however, the flower-bed revealed nothing. It was at least fifteen feet wide; to cross it, leaving no trace, appeared a physical impossibility. And after a while the inspector turned back into the room and looked gravely at Sir Robert Deering.

"I should like to have every member of the house-party and all your servants in here, Sir Robert, one by one," he remarked.

"Then you think it was done by someone in the house, Inspector?" Sir Robert was looking worried.

"I prefer not to say anything definite at present," answered the official, guardedly. "Perhaps we can start with the house-party."

With a shrug of his shoulder, Sir Robert left the room, and the inspector turned to the constable.

"Lend a hand here, Murphy; we'll put the body behind the screen before any of the ladies come in."

"Great Scot, man," cried Seymour. "What do you want the ladies for? You don't suggest that a woman could have strangled him?"

"You will please allow me to know my own business best," said the other, coldly. "Shut and bolt the windows, Murphy."

The rain had stopped as the policeman crossed the room to carry out his orders. And it was as he stood by the open window, with his hands upraised to the sash, that he suddenly stepped back with a startled exclamation.

"Something 'it me in the face, sir," he muttered. Then he spat disgustedly. "Gaw! What a filthy taste!"

But the inspector was not interested—he was covering the dead man's face with a pocket handkerchief, and after a moment's hesitation, the constable again reached up for the sash, and pulled it down. Only the soldier had noticed the little incident, and he was staring like a man bereft of his senses at a point just above the policeman's head.

"Don't move," he ordered, harshly. "Stand still, constable."

With a startled look the policeman obeyed, and Seymour stepped over to him. And then he did a peculiar thing. He lit a match and turned to the inspector.

"Just look at this match, Inspector," he murmured. "Burning brightly, isn't it?" He moved it a little, and suddenly the flame turned to a smoky orange colour. For a moment or two it spluttered; then it went out altogether.

"You can move now, constable," he said. "I didn't want any draught for a moment." He looked at Inspector Grayson with a smile. "Interesting little experiment that—wasn't it?"

Grayson snorted. "If you've quite finished your conjuring tricks, I'll get on with the business," he remarked. "Come along over here, Murphy."

"What is it, Bob?" Bill Brabazon cried, excitedly.

"The third point, Bill," answered the other. "Great Scot! What a fool I've been. Though it's the most extraordinary case I've ever come across."

"Think you can reconstruct the crime?" sneered the inspector.

"I don't think—I know," returned the other quietly. "But not tonight. There's the rain again."

"And might I ask what clues you possess?"

"Only one more than you, and that you can get from Sir Robert. I blush to admit it, but until a moment ago I attached no importance to it. It struck me as being merely the foolish jest of a stupid man. Now it does not strike me quite in that light. Ask him," he continued, and his voice was grim, "for the translation of that inscription under the window. And when you've got that, concentrate for a moment on the other end of the dead man—his trousers just above his ankles."

"They're covered with dirt," said the inspector, impressed, in spite of himself, by the other's tone.

"Yes—but what sort of dirt? Dry, dusty, cobwebby dirt—not the caked mud on his knees. Immense amount of importance in dirt, Inspector."

But Mr Grayson was recovering his dignity. "Any other advice?" he sneered.

"Yes. Hire a man and practise strangling him. Then buy a really good encyclopædia and study it. You'll find a wealth of interesting information in it." He strolled towards the door. "If you want me I shall be in the billiard-room. And, by the way, with regard to what I said about strangling, don't forget that the victim cannot come towards you if his feet are off the ground."

"Perhaps you'll have the murderer for me in the billiard-room," remarked the inspector, sarcastically.

"I'm afraid not," answered the other. "The real murderer, unfortunately, is already dead. I'll look for his accomplice in the morning."

With a slight smile he closed the door and strolled into the hall. The house-party were being marshalled by Sir Robert preparatory to their inquisition; the servants stood huddled together in sheepish groups under the stern eye of the butler.

"Have you found out anything, Major Seymour?" With entreaty in her eyes, Ruth Brabazon came up to him.

"Yes, Miss Brabazon, I have," answered the man, reassuringly. "You can set your mind absolutely at rest."

"You know who did it?" she cried, breathlessly.

"I do," he answered. "But unfortunately I can't prove it tonight. And you mustn't be alarmed at the attitude taken up by the inspector. He's not in a very good temper, and I'm afraid I'm the cause."

"But what does he think?"

"I should hesitate to say what great thoughts were passing through his brain," said Seymour. "But I have a shrewd suspicion that he has already made up his mind that Bill did it."

"And who did do it, Bob?" She laid her hand beseechingly on his arm as she spoke.

"I think it's better to say nothing at the moment," he answered, gently. "There are one or two points I've got to make absolutely certain of first. Until then—won't you trust me, Ruth?"

"Trust you! Why, my dear—" She turned away as she spoke, and Bob Seymour barely heard the last two words. But he did *just* hear them. And once again the dead man was forgotten.

V

"May I borrow your car, Sir Robert? I want to go to London and bring back a friend of mine—Sir Gilbert Strangways." Bob Seymour approached his host after breakfast the following morning. "I'll have to be back by three, in time for the inquest, and it's very important."

"Strangways—the explorer! Certainly, Seymour; though I'm not keen on adding to the house-party at present."

"It's essential, I'm afraid. They can only bring in one verdict this afternoon—Murder. That ass Grayson was nosing round this morning, and he, at any rate, is convinced of it."

"What—that Bill did it?" muttered the other.

"He's outside there now, making notes."

"You don't think the boy did it, do you, Seymour?"

"I *know* he didn't, Sir Robert. But to prove it is a different matter. May I order the car?"

"Yes, yes, of course. Anything you like. Why on earth did I ever ask the poor fellow down here?" Sir Robert walked agitatedly up and down the hall. "And anyway, who did do it?" He threw out his hands in despair. "He can't have done it himself."

"All in good time, Sir Robert," said the other, gravely. "The lucky thing for you is that you have practically never used that room."

"What do you mean?" muttered his host, going a little white.

"If you had, the chances are that this house-party would never have taken place," answered Seymour. "At least, not with you as the host."

"My God!" cried the other. "You don't mean to say that there's anything in that inscription?"

"It's the key to everything," returned the other, shortly. "To put it mildly, your predecessor had a peculiar sense of humour."

Ten minutes later he was getting into the car, when Inspector Grayson appeared round the comer.

"You won't forget the inquest is at three, Major Seymour?" he said, a trifle sharply.

"I shan't miss it," answered the soldier.

"Found the murderer yet?" asked the detective.

"Yes—this morning," returned the other. "Haven't you?"

And the officer was still staring thoughtfully down the drive long after the car had disappeared round a bend. This confounded soldier seemed so very positive, and Grayson, who was no fool, had been compelled to admit to himself that there were several strange features about the case. The inscription on the wall he had dismissed as childish; from inquiries made in the neighbourhood, Sir Robert Deering's predecessor had obviously been a most peculiar specimen. Not quite all there, if reports were to be believed. To return to the case, however, a complete alibi had been proved by every single member of the household, save one kitchen-maid, Mr Trayne, and—Bill Brabazon. The kitchen-maid and Mr Trayne could be dismissed—the former for obvious reasons, the latter owing to the impossibility of his having done the deed in the time between leaving the drawing-room and arriving in the billiard-room with the news. And that left—Bill Brabazon. Every single line of thought led ultimately to—Bill Brabazon. Motive, opportunity, capability from a physical point of view—all pointed to him. A further exhaustive search that morning of the flower-bed outside the window had revealed no trace of any footprint; it was impossible that the murderer should have entered by the window. Therefore—he shrugged his shoulders. The house-party again—and Bill Brabazon. Blind with fury, as he admitted himself, he had first knocked the dead man down and then strangled him, turning out the light lest anyone should see. Then, taking off the rope, he had left him, almost, but not quite, dead on the floor. In a last despairing gasp for air, Denton had staggered to the window and collapsed—still not quite dead. Finally, he had made one more con-vulsive effort, floundered on to the flower-bed, and had there died.

Such was the scene as Inspector Grayson reconstructed it, and yet he was far from satisfied. Why strangle? An un-English method of killing a man. Still—facts were facts—the man *had* been strangled. Un-English or not, that was the manner in which he had met his death; and since suicide could be ruled out, only murder remained. If the soldier could prove it was not young Brabazon—well and good. Until he did, Mr Grayson preferred to bank on facts which were capable of proof.

The result of the coroner's inquest was a foregone conclusion. Death after strangulation, with a rider to the effect that, had prompt assistance been given on the first discovery of the body, life might have been saved.

Bob Seymour, seated beside another lean, sun-tanned man, heard the verdict with an impassive face. He had given his evidence, con-fining it to the barest statement of fact; he had advanced no theory;

he had not attempted to dispute Inspector Grayson's deductions. Once he had caught Ruth's eyes fixed on him beseechingly, and he had given her a reassuring smile, And she—because she trusted him—knew that all was well; knew that the net which seemed to be closing so grimly round her brother would not be fastened. But why—why didn't he tell them now how it was done? That's what she couldn't understand.

And then, when it was all over, Bob and his friend had disappeared in the car again.

"There's no doubt about it, Bob," said Strangways. "What a diabolical old blackguard the man must have been."

"I agree," answered Seymour, grimly. "One wishes one could get at him now. As it is, the most we can do is to convince our mutton-headed friend Grayson. I owe the gentleman one for that rider to the verdict."

The car stopped first at a chemist's, and the two men entered the shop. It was an unusual request they made—cylinders of oxygen are generally required only for sick rooms. But after a certain amount of argument, the chemist produced one, and they placed it in the back of the car. Their next errand was even stranger, and consisted of the purchase of a rabbit. Finally, a visit to an ironmonger produced a rose such as is used on the end of a hosepipe for watering.

Then, their purchases complete, they returned to the house, stopping at the police station on the way. Grayson came out to see them, a tolerant smile on his face. Yes, he would be pleased to come up that evening after dinner.

"Do you want to introduce me to the murderer, Major?" he asked, maliciously.

"Something of the sort, Inspector," said Seymour. "Studied that encyclopædia yet?"

"I've been too busy on other matters—a little more important," answered the other, shortly.

"Good," cried Seymour, genially. "By the way, when you want to blow out a lamp what is the first thing you do?"

"Turn down the wick," said Grayson.

"Wise man. I wonder why the murderer didn't."

And for the second time that day, Inspector Grayson was left staring thoughtfully at a retreating motor-car.

It was not till after dinner that Bob Seymour reverted to the matter which was obsessing everyone's mind. Most of the house-party had left; only Mr Trayne and Ruth and her brother remained. And even the Celebrated Actor had been comparatively silent throughout the meal, while Bill had remained sunk in profound gloom. Everything at the inquest had pointed to him as the culprit; every ring at the bell and he had imagined someone arriving with a warrant for his arrest. And Bob had said nothing to clear him—not a word, in spite of his apparent confidence last night. Only Ruth still seemed certain that he would do something; but what *could* he do, exploded the boy miserably, when she tried to cheer him up. The evidence on the face of it was damning.

"About time our friend arrived, Gilbert." Bob Seymour glanced at his watch, and at that moment there came a ring at the bell.

"Who's that?" said Bill, nervously.

"The egregious Grayson, old boy," said Bob. "The experiment is about to begin."

"You mean—" cried Ruth, breathlessly.

"I mean that Sir Gilbert has kindly consented to take the place of Denton last night," said Bob, cheerfully. "He'll have one or two little props to help him, and I shall be stage-manager."

"But why have you put it off so long?" cried Bob, as the inspector came into the room.

228

"'When 'tis day. All serene,'" quoted Bob. "Good evening, Mr Grayson. Now that we are all here, we might as well begin."

"Just as well," agreed the inspector, shortly. "What do we begin with?"

"First of all a visit to the smoking-room," answered Seymour. "Then, except for Sir Gilbert Strangways, we shall all go outside into the garden."

In silence they followed him to the scene of the tragedy.

"I trust you will exonerate me from any charge of being theatrical," he began, closing the door. "But in this particular case the cause of Mr Denton's death is so extraordinary that only an actual reconstruction of what happened would convince such a pronounced sceptic as the inspector. Facts are facts, aren't they, Mr Grayson?"

The inspector grunted non-committally. "What's that on the floor?" he demanded.

"A cylinder of oxygen, and a rabbit in a cage," explained Seymour, pleasantly. "Now first to rearrange the room. The lamp was on this table—very possibly placed there by the dead man to get a better view of the inscription under the window. Otherwise, nothing needs moving; so that we may proceed to what happened.

"First, Inspector, Mr Brabazon entered the room, and, as he has already described, he and Mr Denton came to blows, with the result that he laid Denton out. Then Mr Brabazon left the room, as I propose we shall do shortly. And, after a while, Mr Denton came to his senses again, and went to the window for air, just as Sir Gilbert has done at the present moment."

"You can't prove it," snapped Grayson.

"True," murmured Seymour. "Just logical surmise—so far; from now onwards—irrefutable proof. The murderer is admirably trained, I assure you. Are you ready, Gilbert?"

"Quite," said Strangways, bending down and picking up the rabbit-cage, which he placed on the table by the lamp.

"Perhaps, Inspector, you would like to examine the rabbit?" remarked Seymour. "No! Well, if not, I would just ask you to notice Sir Gilbert's other preparations. A clip on his nose; the tube from the oxygen cylinder in his mouth."

"I don't understand all this, Major Seymour," cried Grayson, testily. "What's the rabbit for, and all this other tommy-rot?"

"I thought I'd explained to you that Sir Gilbert is taking the place of the murdered man last night: The tommy-rot is to prevent him sharing the same fate."

"Good God!" The inspector turned a little pale.

"Shall we adjourn to the garden?" continued Seymour, imperturbably. He led the way from the room. "I think we'll stand facing the window, so that we can see everything. Of course, I can't guarantee that the performance will be *exactly* the same; but it will be near enough, I think. Nor can I guarantee exactly when it will start." As he spoke they reached a point facing the window. The lamp was burning brightly in the room, outlining Sir Gilbert's figure as he stood facing them, and with a little shudder Ruth clutched her brother's arm.

"Even so did Denton stand last night." Seymour's even voice came out of the darkness. "You see his shadow on the grass, and the shadow of the sash; just as Mr Brabazon saw the shadow last night, Inspector."

Silence settled on the group; even the phlegmatic inspector seemed impressed. And then suddenly, when the tension was becoming almost unbearable, Sir Gilbert's voice came from the window.

"It's coming, Bob."

They saw him adjust his nose-clip and turn on the oxygen; then he stood up as before, motionless, in the window.

"Watch carefully, Inspector," said Seymour, "Do you see those dark, thin, sinuous feelers coming down outside the window? Like strands of rope. They're curling in underneath the sash towards Sir Gilbert's head. The lamp—look at the lamp—watch the colour of the flame. Orange—where before it was yellow. Look—it's smoking; thick black smoke; and the room is turning green. Do you see? Now the lamp again. It's going out—even as it went out last night. And, by this time last night, Inspector, Denton, I think, was dead; even as the rabbit on the table is dead now. Now watch Sir Gilbert's shirt front."

"Great heavens!" shouted Sir Robert. "It's going up."

"Precisely," said Bob. "At the present moment he is being lifted off his legs—as Denton was last night; and if at this period Denton was not already dead, he could not have lasted long. He would have been hanged."

"Oh, Bill, it's awful!" cried Ruth, hysterically.

"Then came the rain," continued Seymour. "I have here the hosepipe fitted with a rose." He dragged it nearer the window, and let it play on the side of the house as far up as the water would reach. Almost at once the body of Sir Gilbert ceased rising; it paused as if hesitating; then, with a little thud, fell downwards half in half out of the window, head and arms sprawling in the flower-bed.

"And thus we found Mr Denton last night, when it was still raining," said Seymour. "All right, Gilbert?"

"All right, old boy," came from the other.

"But if he's all right," said the inspector, wonderingly, "why wasn't the other?"

"Because Sir Gilbert, being in full possession of his senses when the hanging process started, used his hands to prevent strangulation. To continue—the rain ceased. We were out of the room waiting for your arrival, Mr Grayson, and while we were out—Look! look!"

Before their eyes the top part of Sir Gilbert's body was being raised till once again he stood straight up. Then steadily he was drawn upwards till his knees came about the level of the sill, when, with a sudden lurch, the whole body swung out and then back again, while the calves of his legs drummed against the outside of the house. "Do you remember the marks on the trousers, Inspector? And then the rain came again." Seymour turned on the hose. Once more the body paused, hesitated, and then crashed downwards into the flower-bed.

"All right, Gilbert?"

"All right," answered the other. "Merely uncomfortably wet." He rose and came towards them.

"And now, Inspector," murmured Seymour, mildly, "you know exactly how Mr Denton was killed."

"But, good Lord, gentlemen," said Grayson, feebly, "what was it that killed him?"

"A species of liana," said Sir Gilbert. "In my experience absolutely unique in strength and size—though I have heard stories from the Upper Amazon of similar cases. It's known amongst the natives as the Green Death."

"But is it an animal?" cried Grayson.

"You've asked me a question, Inspector," said Sir Gilbert, "that I find it very difficult to answer. To look at—it's a plant—a climbing plant, with long, powerful tendrils. But in habits—it's carnivorous, like the insect-eating variety in England. It's found in the tropical undergrowth, and is incidentally worshipped by some of the tribes. They give it human sacrifices, so the story goes. And now I can quite believe it."

"But, hang it, sir," exploded the inspector, "we aren't on the Upper Amazon. Do you mean to say that one of these things is here?"

"Of course. Didn't you see it? It's spread from the wall to the branches of that old oak."

"If you remember, Inspector, I pointed it out to you this morning," murmured Seymour, mildly. "But you were so engrossed with the flower-bed."

"But why did the lamp go out?" asked Ruth, breathlessly.

"For the same reason that the rabbit died," said Bob, "For the same reason that the match went out last night, and gave me the third clue. From each of the tendrils a green cloud is ejected, the principal ingredient of which is carbon dioxide—which is a gas that suffocates. The plant holds the victim, and they suffocate him. Hence the oxygen and the nose-clip; otherwise Sir Gilbert would have been killed tonight. By the way, would you like to see the rabbit, Inspector?"

"I'll take your word for it, sir," he grunted, shortly. "Only, why the devil you didn't tell me this last night I can't understand."

"For the very simple reason that you wouldn't have believed me," returned Bob. "I'd have shown you—only the rain had come on again. And you must admit I advised you to get an encyclopædia."

VI

"Bob, I don't understand how you did it," cried Ruth.

It was after breakfast the following morning, and the sound of axes came through the open window from the men who were already at work cutting down the old oak tree.

The other laughed. "Points of detail," he said, quietly. "At first, before the police arrived, I thought it possible that Bill had been responsible for his death. I thought he'd hit him so hard that the man's heart had given out, and that in a final spasm he'd staggered to the window and died. It struck me as just conceivable that Denton had himself blown out the lamp, thinking it made it hotter. But why not turn it out? And would he have had time if he was at his last gasp? Then the police came, and the body had moved. I *knew* the man was dead when he was lying over the sill, though I hadn't seen the mark round his neck. I therefore knew that some agency had moved the body. That agency must have been the murderer—anyone else would have mentioned the fact. Therefore it couldn't have been Bill, because he was in the billiard-room the whole time, and I'd locked the door of the smoking-room. Then I saw the mark round his neck—strangled. But you can't strangle a powerful man without a desperate struggle. And why should the strangler return after the deed was committed? Also there were no footmarks on the flower-bed. Then I noticed the grey dust on his trousers just below the knee, and underneath the window outside, kept dry by the sill, which stuck out, was ivy—dusty and cobwebby as ivy always is. How had his legs touched it? If they had—and there was nowhere else the dirt could have come from—he must have been lifted off the ground. Strangulation, certainly, of a type—hung. The dirt had not been there when we first found the body lying over the sill. And if he'd been hung—who did it? And why hang a dead man? What had happened between the time Bill left the room and the police found the body? A heavy shower of rain, during which we found the body; then clear again, while we were out of the room; then another shower, when the police found the body. And then I thought of the rhyme:

When 'tis hot, shun this spot;
When 'tis rain, come again.

Could it be possible that there was some diabolical agent at work, who stopped, or was frustrated, by rain? It was then I saw the green cloud itself over the constable's head—the cloud which extinguished my match.

"Incredible as it seemed, I saw at once that it was the only solution which fitted everything—the marks on the back of his trousers below the knee—everything. He'd been hung, and the thing that had hanged him had blown out the lamp—or extinguished it is a more accurate way of expressing it—even as it extinguished my match. The smell—I'd been searching my memory for that smell the whole evening, and it came to me when I saw that green gas—it's some rank discharge from the plant, mixed with the carbon dioxide. And I last saw it, and smelt it, on the Upper Amazon ten years ago. My native bearers dragged me away in their terror. There was a small animal, I remember, hanging from a red tendril, quite dead. The tendril was round its neck, exuding little puffs of green vapour. So I got Gilbert to make sure. That's all."

"But what a wicked old man be must have been who planted it!" cried the girl, indignantly.

"A distorted sense of humour, as I told our host," said Bob, briefly, starting to fill his pipe.

"Bill and I can never thank you enough, Major Seymour," said the girl, slowly, after a long silence. "If it hadn't been for you—" She gave a little shudder, and stared out of the window.

"Some advantages in wandering," he answered, lightly. "One does pick up odd facts. Suppose I'll have to push off again soon."

"Why?" she demanded.

"Oh, I dunno. Can't sit in England doing nothing."

"Going alone?" she asked, softly.

"Do you think anybody would be mug enough to accompany me?" he inquired, with an attempt at a grin. Dear heavens! If only he wasn't a cripple—

"I don't know, I'm sure," she murmured. "You'd want your three points of detail to make it a certainty, wouldn't you? We only reached the coincidence stage two nights ago."

"What do you mean, Ruth?" he whispered, staring at her.

"That for a clever man—you're an utter fool. With a woman one is a certainty. However, if you'll close your eyes, I'll pander to your feeble intellect. Tight, please."

And it was as the tree fell with a rending crash outside that Ruth Brabazon found that, at any rate as far as his arms were concerned, Bob Seymour was no cripple. And Bob—well, a kiss is pretty conclusive. At least, some kisses are.

THE WOMAN OF THE WOOD

Abraham Merritt

Abraham Merritt was an award-winning American fantasy and science fiction writer who experienced financial success and was inducted into the Science Fiction and Fantasy Hall of Fame in 1999 alongside the likes of Jules Verne, Mary Shelley, J. R. R. Tolkien and J. K. Rowling to name but a few. His piece of short fiction "The Woman of the Wood" is an interesting tale published in *Weird Tales* in 1926 and depicts a violent struggle between man and nature. McKay, a retired war pilot, is travelling in the French countryside when he finds an inn near a lake to stay for a while. Charmed by the beauty of the area, he is entranced and sees visions of beautiful tree women who seek his protection from a family in the forest.

Merritt's tale can be viewed as a prototypical EcoGothic short story as it depicts deforestation as a war between humans and the trees. The forest itself is unique in that the trees have souls who reach out to McKay for help. This personification of the trees adds an element of sympathy for the "women of the wood" who are suffering at the hands of the destructive force of man and are in need of protective action.

cKay sat on the balcony of the little inn that squatted like a brown gnome among the pines that clothed the eastern shore of the lake.

It was a small and lonely lake high up on the Vosges; and yet the word "lonely" is not just the one to tag its spirit; rather was it aloof, withdrawn. The mountains came down on every side, making a vast tree-lined bowl that seemed filled, when McKay first saw it, with a still wine of peace.

McKay had worn the wings with honour in the World War. And as a bird loves the trees, so did McKay love them. They were to him not merely trunks and roots, branches and leaves; they were personalities. He was acutely aware of character differences even among the same species—that pine was jolly and benevolent; that one austere, monkish; there stood a swaggering bravo and there a sage wrapped in green meditation; that birch was a wanton—the one beside her virginal, still a-dream.

The war had sapped McKay, nerve, brain and soul. Through all the years that had passed the wound had kept open. But now, as he slid his car down the side of the great green bowl, he felt its peace reach out to him; caress and quiet him; promise him healing. He seemed to drift like a falling leaf through the cathedraled woods; to be cradled by the hands of the trees.

McKay had stopped at the little gnome of the inn; and there he had lingered, day after day, week after week.

The trees had nursed him; soft whisperings of the leaves, slow chant of the needled pines, had first deadened, then driven from him the re-echoing clamour of the war and its sorrow. The open wound of this spirit had closed under their healing; had closed and become scars; and then even the scars had been covered and buried, as the scars on Earth's breast are covered and buried beneath the falling leaves of autumn. The trees had laid healing hands upon his eyes. He had sucked strength from the green breasts of the hills.

As that strength flowed back to him, McKay grew aware that the place was—troubled; that there was ferment of fear within it.

It was as though the trees had waited until he himself had become whole before they made their own unrest known to him. But now they were trying to tell him something; there was a shrillness as of apprehension, of anger, in the whispering of the leaves, the needled chanting of the pines.

And it was this that had kept McKay at the inn—a definite consciousness of appeal. He strained his ears to catch words in the rustling branches, words that trembled on the brink of his human understanding.

Never did they cross that brink.

Gradually he had focused himself, so he believed, to the point of the valley's unease.

On all the shores of the lake there were but two dwellings. One was the inn, and around the inn the trees clustered protectively; confidingly; friendly. It was as though they had not only accepted it, but had made it part of themselves.

Not so was it of the other habitation. Once it had been the hunting lodge of long-dead lords; now it was half-ruined, forlorn. It lay across the lake almost exactly opposite the inn and back upon the slope a half-mile from the shore. Once there had been fat fields around it and a fair orchard.

The forest had marched down upon fields and lodge. Here and there scattered pines and poplars stood like soldiers guarding some outpost; scouting parties of saplings lurked among the gaunt, broken fruit trees. But the forest had not had its way unchecked; ragged stumps showed where those who dwelt in the old house had cut down the invaders; blackened patches showed where they had fired the words.

Here was the centre of the conflict. Here the green folk of the forest were both menaced and menacing; at war.

The lodge was a fortress beleaguered by the trees, a fortress whose garrison sallied forth with axe and torch to take their toll of their besiegers.

Yet McKay sensed a slow, inexorable pressing on of the forest; he saw it as an army ever filling the gaps in its enclosing ranks, shooting its seeds into the cleared places, sending its roots out to sap them; and armed always with a crushing patience. He had the impression of constant regard, of watchfulness, as though night and day the forest kept myriads of eyes upon the lodge; inexorably, not to be swerved from its purpose. He had spoken of this impression to the innkeeper and his wife, and they had looked at him, oddly.

"Old Polleau does not love the trees, no," the old man had said. "No, nor do his two sons. They do not love the trees—and very certainly the trees do not love them."

Between the lodge and the shore, marching down to the verge of the lake was a singularly beautiful little coppice of silver birches and firs. This coppice stretched for perhaps a quarter of a mile; it was not more than a hundred feet or two in depth, and not alone the beauty of its trees but their curious grouping vividly aroused McKay's interest. At each end were a dozen or more of the glistening, needled firs, not clustered but spread out as though in open marching order;

at widely spaced intervals along its other two sides paced single firs. The birches, slender and delicate, grew within the guard of these sturdier trees, yet not so thickly as to crowd one another.

To McKay the silver birches were for all the world like some gay caravan of lovely demoiselles under the protection of debonair knights. With that odd other sense of his he saw the birches as delectable damsels, merry and laughing—the pines as lovers, troubadours in green-needled mail. And when the winds blew and the crests of the trees bent under them, it was as though dainty demoiselles picked up fluttering, leafy skirts, bent leafy hoods and danced while the knights of the firs drew closer round them, locked arms and danced with them to the roaring horns of the winds. At such times he almost heard sweet laughter from the birches, shouting from the firs.

Of all the trees in that place McKay loved best this little wood. He had rowed across and rested in its shade, had dreamed there and, dreaming, had heard again echoes of the sweet elfin laughter. Eyes closed, he had heard mysterious whisperings and the sound of dancing feet light as falling leaves; had taken dream-draft of that gaiety which was the soul of the little wood.

Two days ago he had seen Polleau and his two sons. McKay had lain dreaming in the coppice all that afternoon. As dusk began to fall he had reluctantly arisen and begun to row back to the inn. When he had been a few hundred feet from shore three men had come out from the trees and had stood watching him—three grim powerful men taller than the average French peasant.

He had called a friendly greeting to them, but they had not answered it; had stood there, scowling. Then as he bent again to his ours, one of the sons had raised a hatchet and had driven it savagely into the trunk of a slim birch. McKay thought he heard a thin, wailing cry from the stricken tree, a sigh from all the little wood.

He had felt as though the keen edge had bitten into his own flesh. "Stop that!" he had cried. "Stop it, damn you!"

For answer Polleau's son had struck again—and never had McKay seen hate etched so deep as on his face as he struck. Cursing, a killing rage in his heart, McKay had swung the boat around, raced back to shore. He had heard the hatchet strike again and again and, close now to shore, had heard a crackling and over it once more the thin, high wailing. He had turned to look.

The birch was tottering, was falling. Close beside it grew one of the firs, and, as the smaller tree crashed over, it dropped upon this fir like a fainting maid into the arms of her lover. And as it lay and trembled there, one of the branches of the other tree slipped from under it, whipped out and smote the hatchet-wielder a crushing blow upon the head, sending him to earth.

It had been, of course, only the chance blow of a bough, bent by pressure of the fallen trunk and then released as that had slipped down. Of course—yet there had been such suggestion of conscious action in the branch's recoil, so much of bitter anger in it; so much, in truth, had it been like a purposeful blow that McKay felt an eerie prickling of his scalp; his heart had missed its beat.

For a moment Polleau and the standing son had stared at the sturdy fir with the silvery birch lying upon its green breast. Folded in and shielded by its needled boughs as though—again the swift impression came to McKay—as though it were a wounded maid stretched on breast, in arms, of knightly lover. For a long moment father and son had stared.

Then, still wordless but with that same bitter hatred in both their faces, they had stooped and picked up the other and, with his arms around the neck of each, had borne him limply away.

*

243

McKay, sitting on the balcony of the inn that morning, went over and over that scene; realised more and more clearly the human aspect of fallen birch and clasping fir, and the conscious deliberateness of the later's blow. During the two days that had elapsed since then, he had felt the unease of the trees increase, their whispering appeal become more urgent.

What were they trying to tell him? What did they want him to do?

Troubled, he stared across the lake, trying to pierce the mists that hung over it and hid the opposite shore. And suddenly it seemed that he heard the coppice calling him, felt it pull the point of his attention toward it irresistibly, as the lodestone swings and holds the compass needle.

The coppice called him; it bade him come.

McKay obeyed the command; he arose and walked down to the boat landing; he stepped into his skiff and began to row across the lake. As his oars touched the water his trouble fell from him. In its place flowed peace and a curious exaltation.

The mists were thick upon the lake. There was no breath of wind, yet the mists billowed and drifted, shook and curtained under the touch of unfelt airy hands.

They were alive—the mists; they formed themselves into fantastic palaces past whose opalescent façades he flew; they built themselves into hills and valleys and circled plains whose floors were rippling silk. Tiny rainbows gleamed out among them, and upon the water prismatic patches shone and spread like spilled wine of opals. He had the illusion of vast distances—the hillocks of mist were real mountains, the valleys between them were not illusory. He was a colossus cleaving through some elfin world. A trout broke, and it was like Leviathan leaping from the fathomless deep. Around the arc of the fish's body rainbows interlaced and then dissolved into rain of softly gleaming gems—diamonds in dance with sapphires, flame-hearted rubies, pearls with shimmering souls of rose. The fish vanished, diving cleanly without sound; the jewelled bows vanished with it; a tiny irised whirlpool swirled for an instant where trout and flashing arcs had been.

Nowhere was there sound. He let his oars drop and leaned forward, drifting. In the silence, before him and around him, he felt opening the gateways of an unknown world.

And suddenly he heard the sound of voices, many voices; faint at first and murmurous. Louder they became, swiftly; women's voices sweet and lilting and mingled with them the deeper tones of men. Voices that lifted and fell in a wild, gay chanting through whose *joyesse* ran undertones both of sorrow and of anger—as though faery weavers threaded through silk spun of sunbeams, sombre strands dipped in the black of graves, and crimson strands stained in the red of wrathful sunsets.

He drifted on, scarce daring to breathe lest even that faint sound break the elfin song. Closer it rang and clearer; and now he became aware that the speed of his boat was increasing, that it was no longer drifting; as though the little waves on each side were pushing him ahead with soft and noiseless palms. His boat grounded, and as its keel rustled along over the smooth pebbles of the beach the song ceased.

McKay half arose and peered before him. The mists were thicker here but he could see the outlines of the coppice. It was like look-ing at it through many curtains of fine gauze, and its trees seemed shifting, ethereal, unreal. And moving among the trees were figures that threaded among the boles and flitted round them in rhyth-mic measures, like the shadows of leafy boughs swaying to some cadenced wind.

He stepped ashore. The mists dropped behind him, shutting off all sight of lake; and as they dropped McKay lost all sense of strangeness, all feeling of having entered some unfamiliar world. Rather was it as though he had returned to one he had once known well and that had been long lost to him.

The rhythmic flittings had ceased; there was now no movement as there was no sound among the trees—yet he felt the little wood full of watchful life. McKay tried to speak; there was a spell of silence on his mouth.

"You called me. I have come to listen to you—to help you if I can."

The words formed within his mind, but utter them he could not. Over and over he tried, desperately; the words seemed to die on his lips.

A pillar of mist whirled forward and halted, eddying half an arm-length away. Suddenly out of it peered a woman's face, eyes level with his own. A woman's face—yes; but McKay, staring into those strange eyes probing his, knew that, woman's though it seemed, it was that of no woman of human breed. They were without pupils, the irises deer-large and of the soft green of deep forest dells; within them sparkled tiny star-points of light like motes in a moonbeam. The eyes were wide and set far apart beneath a broad, low brow over which was piled braid upon braid of hair of palest gold, braids that seemed spun of shining ashes of gold. The nose was small and straight, the mouth scarlet and exquisite. The face was oval, tapering to a delicately pointed chin.

Beautiful was that face, but its beauty was an alien one; unearthly. For long moments the strange eyes thrust their gaze deep into his. Then out of the mist were thrust two slender white arms, the hands long, the fingers tapering. The tapering fingers touched his ears.

"He shall hear," whispered the red lips.

Immediately from all about him a cry arose; in it was the whispering and rustling of the leaves beneath the breath of the winds; the shrilling of the harpstrings of the boughs; the laughter of hidden brooks; the shoutings of waters flinging themselves down into deep and rocky pools—the voices of the forest made articulate.

"He shall hear!" they cried.

The long white fingers rested on his lips, and their touch was cool as bark of birch on cheek after some long upward climb through forest; cool and subtly sweet.

"He shall speak," whispered the scarlet lips of the wood woman.

"He shall speak!" answered the wood voices again, as though in litany.

"He shall see," whispered the woman, and the cool fingers touched his eyes.

"He shall see!" echoed the wood voices.

The mists that had hidden the coppice from McKay wavered, thinned and were gone. In their place was limpid, translucent, palely green *aether*, faintly luminous—as though he stood within some clear wan emerald. His feet pressed a golden moss spangled with tiny starry bluets. Fully revealed before him was the woman of the strange eyes and the face of unearthly beauty. He dwelt for a moment upon the slender shoulders, the firm, small, tip-tilted breasts, the willow litheness of her body. From neck to knees a smock covered her, sheer and silken and delicate as spun cobwebs; through it her body gleamed as though fire of the young spring moon ran in her veins.

He looked beyond her. There upon the golden moss were other women like her, many of them; they stared at him with the same wide-set green eyes in which danced the sparkling moonbeam motes; like her they were crowned with glistening, pallidly golden hair; like hers, too, were their oval faces with the pointed chins and perilous alien beauty. Only where she stared at him gravely, measuring him, weighing him—there were those of these her sisters whose eyes were mocking; and those whose eyes called to him with a weirdly tingling allure, their mouths athirst; those whose eyes looked upon him with curiosity alone; those whose great eyes pleaded with him, prayed to him.

Within that pellucid, greenly luminous *aether* McKay was abruptly aware that the trees of the coppice still had a place. Only now they were spectral indeed. They were like white shadows cast athwart a glaucous screen; trunk and bough, twig and leaf they arose around him and they were as though etched in air by phantom craftsmen—thin and unsubstantial; they were ghost trees rooted in another space.

He was aware that there were men among the women; men whose eyes were set wide apart as were theirs, as strange and pupilless as were theirs, but with irises of brown and blue; men with pointed chins and oval faces, broad-shouldered and clad in kirtles of darkest green; swarthy-skinned men, muscular and strong, with that same lithe grace of the women—and like them of a beauty that was alien and elfin.

McKay heard a little wailing cry. He turned. Close beside him lay a girl clasped in the arms of one of the swarthy, green-clad men. She lay upon his breast. His eyes were filled with a black flame of wrath, and hers were misted, anguished. For an instant McKay had a glimpse of the birch that old Polleau's son had sent crashing down into the boughs of the fir. He saw birch and fir as immaterial outlines around this man and this girl. For an instant girl and man and birch and fir seemed to be one and the same.

The scarlet-lipped woman touched his shoulder.

"She withers," sighed the woman, and in her voice McKay heard a faint rustling as of mournful leaves. "Now is it not pitiful that she withers—our sister who was so young, so slender and so lovely?"

McKay looked again at the girl. The white skin seemed shrunken; the moon radiance that gleamed through the bodies of the others was still in hers but dim and pallid; her slim arms hung listlessly; her body drooped. Her mouth was wan and parched; her long and misted green eyes dull. The palely golden hair was lustreless, and dry. He looked on a slow death—a withering death.

"May the arm that struck her down wither!" said the green-clad man who held her, and in his voice McKay heard a savage strumming as of winter winds through bleak boughs: "May his heart wither and the sun blast him! May the rain and the waters deny him and the winds scourge him!"

"I thirst," whispered the girl.

There was a stirring among the watching women. One came forward holding a chalice that was like thin leaves turned to green crystal. She paused beside the trunk of one of the spectral trees, reached up and drew down to her a branch. A slim girl with half-frightened, half-resentful eyes glided to her side and threw her arms around the ghostly bole. The woman cut the branch deep with what seemed an arrow-shaped flake of jade and held her chalice under it. From the cut a faintly opalescent liquid dripped into the cup. When it was filled the woman beside McKay stepped forward and pressed her own long hands around the bleeding branch. She stepped away and McKay saw that the stream had ceased to flow. She touched the trembling girl and unclasped her arms.

"It is healed," said the woman gently. "And it was your turn, little sister. The wound is healed. Soon you will have forgotten."

The woman with the chalice knelt and set it to the wan, dry lips of her who was—withering. She drank of it, thirstily, to the last drop. The misty eyes cleared; they sparkled; the lips that had been so parched and pale grew red, the white body gleamed as though the waning light within it had been fed with new.

"Sing, sisters," the girl cried, shrilly. "Dance for me, sisters!"

Again burst out that chant McKay had heard as he had floated through the mists upon the lake. Now, as then, despite his opened ears, he could distinguish no words, but clearly he understood its mingled themes—the joy of spring's awakening, rebirth, with green life streaming singing up through every bough, swelling the buds, burgeoning with tender leaves the branches; the dance of the trees in the scented winds of spring; the drums of the jubilant rain on leafy hoods; passion of summer sun pouring its golden flood down upon the trees; the moon passing with stately steps and slow, and green hands reaching up to her and drawing from her breast milk of silver fire; riot of wild gay winds with their mad pipings and strummings; soft interlacing of boughs; the kiss of amorous leaves—all these and more, much more that McKay could not understand since they dealt with hidden, secret things for which man has no images, were in that chanting.

And all these and more were in the rhythms of the dancing of those strange, green-eyed women and brown-skinned men; something incredibly ancient, yet young as the speeding moment; something of a world before and beyond man.

McKay listened; McKay watched, lost in wonder; his own world more than half forgotten.

The woman beside him touched his arm. She pointed to the girl.

"Yet she withers," she said. "And not all our life, if we poured it through her lips, could save her."

He saw that the red was draining slowly from the girl's lips; that the luminous life-tides were waning. The eyes that had been so bright were misting and growing dull once more. Suddenly a great pity and a great rage shook him. He knelt beside her, took her hands in his.

"Take them away! Take away your hands! They burn me!" she moaned.

"He tries to help you," whispered the green-clad man, gently. But he reached over and drew McKay's hands away.

"Not so can you help her or us," said the woman.

"What can I do?" McKay arose, looked helplessly from one to the other. "What can I do to help you?"

The chanting died, the dance stopped. A silence fell, and he felt upon him the eyes of all these strange people. They were tense—waiting. The woman took his hands. Their touch was cool and sent a strange sweetness sweeping through his veins.

"There are three men yonder," she said. "They hate us. Soon we shall all be as she is there—withering! They have sworn it, and as they have sworn so will they do. Unless—"

She paused. The moonbeam dancing motes in her eyes changed to tiny sparklings of red. They terrified him, those red sparklings.

"Three men?" In his clouded mind was dim memory of Polleau and his two strong sons. "Three men?" he repeated, stupidly. "But what are three men to you who are so many? What could three men do against those stalwart gallants of yours?"

"No," she shook her head. "No—there is nothing our—men—can do; nothing that we can do. Once, night and day, we were gay. Now we fear—night and day. They mean to destroy us. Our kin have warned us. And our kin can not help us. Those three are masters of blade and flame. Against blade and flame we are helpless."

"Blade and flame!" echoed the others. "Against blade and flame we are helpless."

"Surely will they destroy us," murmured the woman. "We shall wither—all of us. Like her there, or burn—unless—"

Suddenly she threw white arms around McKay's neck. She pressed her body close to him. Her scarlet mouth sought and found his lips and clung to them. Through all McKay's body ran swift, sweet flames, green fire of desire. His own arms went round her, crushed her to him.

"You shall not die!" he cried. "No—by God, you shall not!"

She drew back her head, looked deep into his eyes.

"They have sworn to destroy us," she said, "and soon. With blade and flame they will destroy us—those three—unless—"

"Unless?" he asked, fiercely.

"Unless you—slay them first!" she answered.

A cold shock ran through McKay, chilling the fires of his desire. He dropped his arm from around the woman; thrust her from him. For an instant she trembled before him.

"Slay!" he heard her whisper—and she was gone.

The spectral trees wavered; their outlines thickened out of immateriality into substance. The green translucence darkened. He had a swift vertiginous moment as though he swung between two worlds. He closed his eyes. The dizziness passed and he opened them, looked around him.

He stood on the lakeward skirts of the little coppice. There no shadows flitting, no sign of white women nor of swarthy, green-clad men. His feet were on green moss. Gone was the soft golden carpet with its bluets. Birches and firs clustered solidly before him.

At his left was a sturdy fir in whose needled arms a broken birch tree lay withering. It was the birch that Polleau's son had so wantonly slashed down. For an instant he saw within the fir and birch the immaterial outlines of the green-clad man and the slim girl who withered! For that instant birch and fir and girl and man seemed one and the same. He stepped back, and his hands touched the smooth, cool bark of another birch that rose close at his right.

Upon his hands the touch of that bark was like—was like what! Curiously was it like the touch of the long slim hands of the woman of the scarlet lips!

McKay stood there, staring, wondering, like a man who has but half awakened from dream. And suddenly a little wind stirred the leaves of the rounded birch beside him. The leaves murmured, sighed. The wind grew stronger and the leaves whispered.

"Slay!" he heard them whisper—and again. "Slay! Help us! Slay!"

And the whisper was the voice of the woman of the scarlet lips!

Rage, swift and unreasoning, sprang up in McKay. He began to run up through the coppice, up to where he knew was the old lodge in which dwelt Polleau and his sons. And as he ran the wind blew stronger about him, and louder and louder grew the whispering of the trees.

"Slay!" they whispered. "Slay them!" Save us! Slay!"

"I will slay! I will save you!" McKay, panting, hammer pulse heating in his ears, heard himself answering that ever more insistent command. And in his mind was but one desire—to clutch the throats of Polleau and his sons, to crack their necks. To stand by them then and watch them wither—wither like that slim girl in the arms of the green-clad men.

He came to the edge of the coppice and burst from it out into a flood of sunshine. For a hundred feet he ran, and then he was aware that the whispering command was stilled; that he heard no more the maddening rustling of wrathful leaves. A spell seemed to have been loosed from him, it was as though he had broken through some web of sorcery. McKay stopped, dropped upon the ground, buried his face in the grasses.

He lay there marshalling his thoughts into some order of sanity. What had he been about to do? To rush upon those three men who lived in the old lodge and—slay them! And for what? Because that unearthly, scarlet-lipped woman whose kisses he still could feel upon his month had bade him! Because the whispering trees of the little wood had maddened him with that same command!

For this he had been about to kill three men!

What were that woman and her sisters and the green-clad swarthy gallants of theirs? Illusions of some waking dream—phantoms born of the hypnosis of the swirling mists through which he had rowed and floated across the lake? Such things were not uncommon. McKay knew of those who by watching the shifting clouds could create and dwell for a time with wide-open eyes within some similar land of fantasy; knew others who needed but to stare at smoothly falling water to set themselves within a world of waking dreams; there were those who could summon dreams by gazing into a ball of crystal, others who found dream-life in saucers of shining ink.

Might not the moving mists have laid those same fingers of hypnosis upon his own mind?—and his love for the trees, the sense of appeal that he had felt so long, his memory of the wanton slaughter of the slim birch have all combined to paint upon his drugged consciousness the phantasms he had beheld?

McKay arose to his feet, shakily enough. He looked back at the coppice. There was no wind now; the leaves were silent, motionless. Reason with himself as he might, something deep within him stubbornly asserted the reality of his experience. At any rate, he told himself, the little wood was far too beautiful to be despoiled.

The old lodge was about a quarter of a mile away. A path led up to it through the ragged fields. McKay walked up the path, climbed rickety steps and paused, listening. He heard voices and knocked. The door was flung open and old Polleau stood there, peering at him through half-shut, suspicious eyes. One of the sons stood close behind him. They stared at McKay with grim, hostile faces.

He thought he heard a faint, far-off despairing whisper from the distant wood. And it was as though the pair in the doorway heard it too, for their gaze shifted from him to the coppice, and he saw hatred flicker swiftly across their grim faces. Their gaze swept back to him.

"What do you want?" demanded Polleau, curtly.

"I am a neighbour of yours, stopping at the inn—" began McKay, courteously.

"I know who you are," Polleau interrupted, brusquely, "but what is it that you want?"

"I find the air of this place good for me," McKay stifled a rising anger. "I am thinking of staying for a year or more until my health is fully recovered. I would like to buy some of your land and build me a lodge upon it."

"Yes, M'sieu?" There was acid politeness now in the old man's voice. "But is it permitted to ask why you do not remain at the inn? Its fare is excellent and you are well-liked there."

"I have desire to be alone," replied McKay. "I do not like people too close to me. I would have my own land, and sleep under my own roof."

"But why come to me?" asked Polleau. "There are many places upon the far side of the lake that you could secure. It is happy there and this side is not happy, M'sieu. But tell me, what part of my land is it that you desire?"

"That little wood yonder," answered McKay, and pointed to the coppice.

"Ah! I thought so!" whispered Polleau, and between him and his son passed a look of sombre understanding.

"That wood is not for sale, M'sieu," he said.

"I can afford to pay well for what I want," said McKay. "Name your price."

"It is not for sale," repeated Polleau, stolidly, "at any price."

"Oh, come," urged McKay, although his heart sank at the finality in that answer. "You have many acres and what is it but a few trees? I can afford to gratify my fancies. I will give you all the worth of your other land for it."

"You have asked what that place that you so desire is, and you have answered that it is but a few trees," said Polleau, slowly, and the tall son behind him laughed, abruptly, maliciously. "But it is more than that, M'sieu—oh, much more than that, and you know it, else why should you pay such a price as you offer? Yes, you know it—since you know also that we are ready to destroy it, and you would save it. And who told you all that, M'sieu?" he snarled.

There was such malignance, such black hatred in the face thrust suddenly close to McKay's, eyes blazing, teeth bared by uplifted lip, that involuntarily he recoiled.

"Only a few trees!" snarled old Polleau. "Then who told him what we mean to do—eh, Pierre?"

Again the son laughed. And at that laughter McKay felt within him resurgence of his own blind hatred as he had fled through the whispering wood. He mastered himself, turned away; there was nothing he could do—now. Polleau halted him.

"M'sieu," he said, "enter. There is something I would tell you; something, too, I would show you."

He stood aside, bowing with a rough courtesy. McKay walked through the doorway. Polleau with his son followed him. He entered a large, dim room whose ceiling was spanned with smoke-blackened beams. From these beams hung onion strings and herbs and smoke-cured meats. On one side was a wide fireplace. Huddled beside it sat Polleau's other son. He glanced up as they entered and McKay saw that a bandage covered one side of his head, hiding his left eye. McKay recognised him as the one who had cut down the slim birch. The blow of the fir, he reflected with a certain satisfaction, had been no futile one.

Old Polleau strode over to that son.

"Look, M'sieu," he said, and lifted the bandage.

McKay saw, with a tremor of horror, a gaping blackened socket, red-rimmed and eyeless.

"Good God, Polleau!" he cried. "But this man needs medical attention. I know something of wounds. Let me go across the lake and bring back my kit. I will attend him."

Old Polleau shook his head, although his grim face for the first time softened. He drew the bandages back in place.

"It heals," he said. "We have some skill in such things. You saw what did it. You watched from your boat as the cursed tree struck him. The eye was crushed and lay upon his cheek. I cut it away. Now he heals. We do not need your aid, M'sieu."

"Yet he ought not have cut the birch," muttered McKay, more to himself than to be heard.

"Why not?" asked old Polleau, fiercely; "since it hated him."

McKay stared at him. What did this old peasant know? The words strengthened his deep stubborn conviction that what he had seen and heard in the coppice had been actuality—no dream. And still more did Polleau's next words strengthen that conviction.

"M'sieu," he said, "you come here as ambassador—of a sort. The wood has spoken to you. Well, as ambassador I shall speak to you. Four centuries my people have lived in this place. A century we have owned this land. M'sieu, in all those years there has been no moment that the trees have not hated us—nor we the trees.

"For all those hundred years there have been hatred and battle between us and the forest. My father, M'sieu, was crushed by a tree; my elder brother crippled by another. My father's father, woodsman that he was, was lost in the forest—he came back to us with mind gone, raving of wood-women who had bewitched and mocked him, luring him into swamp and fen and tangled thicket, tormenting him. In every generation the trees have taken their toll of us—women as well as men—maiming or killing us."

"Accidents," interrupted McKay. "This is childish, Polleau. You can not blame the trees."

"In your heart you do not believe so," said Polleau. "Listen, the feud is an ancient one. Centuries ago it began when we were serfs, slaves of the nobles. To cook, to keep us warm in winter, they let us pick up the fagots, the dead branches and twigs that dropped from the trees. But if we cut down a tree to keep us warm, to keep our women and our children warm, yes if we but tore down a branch— they hanged us, or threw us into dungeons to rot, or whipped us till our backs were red lattices.

"They had their broad fields, the nobles—but we must raise our food in the patches where the trees disdained to grow. And if they did thrust themselves into our poor patches, then, M'sieu, we must let them have their way—or be flogged, or be thrown into the dungeons, or be hanged.

"They pressed us in—the trees," the old man's voice grew sharp with fanatic hatred. "They stole our fields and they took the food from the mouths of our children; they dropped their fagots to us like dole to beggars; they tempted us to warmth when the cold struck to our bones—and they bore us as fruit a-swing at the end of the foresters' ropes if we yielded to their tempting.

"Yes, M'sieu—we died of cold that they might live! Our children died of hunger that their young might find root space! They despised us—the trees! We died that they might live—and we were men!

"Then, M'sieu, came the Revolution and the freedom. Ah, M'sieu, then we took our toll! Great logs roaring in the winter cold—no more huddling over the alms of fagots. Fields where the trees had been—no more starving of our children that theirs might live. Now the trees were the slaves and we the masters.

"And the trees knew, and they hated us!

"But blow for blow, a hundred of their lives for each life of ours—we have returned their hatred. With axe and torch we have fought them—

"The trees!" shrieked Polleau, suddenly, eyes blazing red rage, face writhing, foam at the corners of his mouth and grey hair clutched in rigid hands. "The cursed trees! Armies of the trees creeping—creeping—closer, ever closer—crushing us in! Stealing our fields as they did of old! Building their dungeon round us as they built of old the dungeons of stone! Creeping—creeping! Armies of trees! Legions of trees! The trees! The cursed trees!"

McKay listened, appalled. Here was crimson heart of hate. Madness! But what was at the root of it? Some deep inherited instinct, coming down from forefathers who had hated the forest as the symbol of their masters—forefathers whose tides of hatred had overflowed to the green life on which the nobles had laid their taboo, as one neglected child will hate the favourite on whom love and gifts are lavished? In such warped minds the crushing fall of a tree, the maiming sweep of a branch, might appear as deliberate; the natural growth of the forest seem the implacable advance of an enemy.

And yet—the blow of the fir as the cut birch fell *had* been deliberate! And there *had* been those women of the wood—!

"Patience," the standing son touched the old man's shoulder. "Patience! Soon we strike our blow."

Some of the frenzy died out of Polleau's face.

"Though we cut down a hundred," he whispered, "by the hundred they return! But one of us, when they strike—he does not return, no! They have numbers and they have—time. We are now but three, and we have little time. They watch us as we go through the forest, alert to trip, to strike, to crush!

"But, M'sieu," he turned blood-shot eyes to McKay, "we strike our blow, even as Pierre has said. We strike at that coppice that you so desire. We strike there because it is the very heart of the forest. There the secret life of the forest runs at full tide. We know—and you know! Something that, destroyed, will take the heart out of the forest—will make it know us for its masters."

"The women!" The standing son's eyes glittered, malignantly. "I have seen the women there! The fair women with the shining skins who invite—and mock and vanish before hands can seize them."

"The fair women who peer into our windows in the night—and mock us!" muttered the eyeless son.

"They shall mock no more!" shouted old Polleau. "Soon they shall lie, dying! All of them—all of them! They die!"

He caught McKay by the shoulders and shook him like a child.

"Go tell them that!" he shouted. "Say to them that this very day we destroy them. Say to them it is *we* who will laugh when winter comes and we watch their bodies blaze in this hearth of ours and warm us! Go—tell them that!"

He spun McKay around, pushed him to the door, opened it and flung him staggering down the steps. He heard the tall son laugh, the door close. Blind with rage he rushed up the steps and hurled himself against the door. Again the tall son laughed. McKay beat at the door with clenched fists, cursing. The three within paid no heed. Despair began to dull his rage. Could the trees help him—counsel him? He turned and walked slowly down the field path to the little wood.

Slowly and ever more slowly he went as he neared it. He had failed. He was a messenger hearing a warrant of death. The birches were motionless; their leaves hung listlessly. It was as though they knew he had failed. He paused at the edge of the coppice. He looked at his watch, noted with faint surprise that already it was high noon. Short shrift enough had the little wood. The work of destruction would not be long delayed.

McKay squared his shoulders and passed in between the trees. It was strangely silent in the coppice. And it was mournful. He had a sense of life brooding around him, withdrawn into itself; sorrowing. He passed through the silent, mournful wood until he reached the spot where the rounded, gleaming-barked tree stood close to the fir that held the withering birch. Still there was no sound, no movement. He laid his hands upon the cool bark of the rounded tree.

"Let me see again!" he whispered. "Let me hear! Speak to me!"

There was no answer. Again and again he called. The coppice was silent. He wandered through it, whispering, calling. The slim birches stood, passive, with limbs and leaves adroop like listless arms and hands of captive maids awaiting in dull woe the will of conquerors. The firs seemed to crouch like hopeless men with heads in hands. His heart ached to the woe that filled the little wood, this hopeless submission of the trees.

When, he wondered, would Polleau strike? He looked at his watch again; an hour had gone by. How long would Polleau wait? He dropped to the moss, back against a smooth bole.

And suddenly it seeemed to McKay that he was a madman—as mad as Polleau and his sons. Calmly, he went over the old peasant's indictment of the forest; recalled the face and eyes filled with fanatic hate. They were all mad. After all, the trees were—only trees. Polleau and his sons—so he reasoned—had transferred to them the bitter hatred their forefathers had felt for those old lords who had enslaved them; had laid upon them too all the bitterness of their own struggle to exist in this high forest land. When they struck at the trees, it was the ghosts of those forefathers striking at the nobles who had oppressed them; it was themselves striking against their own destiny. The trees were but symbols. It was the warped minds of Polleau and his sons that clothed them in false semblance of conscious life, blindly striving to wreak vengeance against the ancient masters and the destiny that had made their lives one hard and unceasing battle against nature. The nobles were long dead, destiny can be brought to grips by no man. But the trees were here and alive. Clothed in mirage, through them the driving lust for vengeance could be sated. So much for Polleau and his sons.

And he, McKay: was it not his own deep love and sympathy for the trees that similarly had clothed them in that false semblance of conscious life? Had he not built his own mirage? The trees did not really mourn, could not suffer, could not—know. It was his own sorrow that he had transferred to them; only his own sorrow, that he felt echoing back to him from them. The trees were—only trees.

Instantly, upon the heels of that thought, as though it were answer, he was aware that the trunk against which he leaned was trembling; that the whole coppice was trembling; that all the little leaves were shaking tremulously.

McKay, bewildered, leaped to his feet. Reason told him that it was the wind—yet there was no wind!

And as he stood there, a sighing arose as though a mournful breeze were blowing through the trees—and again there was no wind!

Louder grew the sighing and within it now faint wailings.

"They come! They come! Farewell, sisters! Sisters—farewell."

Clearly he heard the mournful whispers.

McKay began to run through the trees to the trail that led out to the fields of the old ledge. And as he ran the wood darkened as though clear shadows gathered in it, as though vast unseen wings hovered over it. The trembling of the coppice increased; bough touched bough, clung to each other; and louder became the sorrowful crying: "Farewell sister! Sister—farewell!"

McKay burst out into the open. Halfway between him and the lodge were Polleau and his sons. They saw him; they pointed and lifted mockingly to him their bright axes. He crouched, waiting for them to come close, all fine-spun theories gone, and rising within him that same rage which hours before had sent him out to slay.

So crouching, he heard from the forested hills a roaring clamour. From every quarter it came, wrathful, menacing; like the voices of legions of great trees bellowing through the horns of tempest. The clamour maddened McKay; fanned the flame of rage of white heat.

If the three men heard it, they gave no sign. They came on steadily, jeering at him, waving their blades. He ran to meet them.

"Go back!" he shouted. "Go back, Polleau! I warn you!"

"He warns us!" jeered Polleau. "He—Pierre, Jean—he warns us!"

The old peasant's arm shot out and his hand caught McKay's shoulder with a grip that pinched to the bone. The arm flexed and hurled him against the unmaimed son. The son caught him, twisted him about and whirled him headlong a dozen yards, crashing through the brush at the skirt of the wood.

McKay sprang to his feet howling like a wolf. The clamour of the forest had grown stronger.

"Kill!" it roared. "Kill!"

The unmaimed son had raised his axe. He brought it down upon the trunk of a birch, half splitting it with one blow. McKay heard a wail go up from the little wood. Before the axe could be withdrawn he had crashed a fist in the axe-wielder's face. The head of Polleau's son rocked back; he yelped, and before McKay could strike again had wrapped strong arms around him, crushing breath from him. McKay relaxed, went limp, and the son loosened his grip. Instantly McKay slipped out of it and struck again, springing aside to avoid the rib-breaking clasp. Polleau's son was quicker than he, the long arm caught him. But as the arms tightened there was the sound of sharp splintering and the birch into which the axe had bitten toppled. It struck the ground directly behind the wrestling men. Its branches seemed to reach out and clutch at the feet of Polleau's son.

He tripped and fell backward, McKay upon him. The shock of the fall broke his grip and again McKay writhed free. Again he was upon his feet, and again Polleau's strong son, quick as he, faced him. Twice McKay's blows found their mark beneath his heart before once more the long arms trapped him. But the grip was weaker; McKay felt that now their strength was equal.

Round and round they rocked, McKay straining to break away. They fell, and over they rolled and over, arms and legs locked, each striving to free a hand to grip the other's throat. Around them ran Polleau and the one-eyed son, shouting encouragement to Pierre, yet neither daring to strike at McKay lest the blow miss and be taken by the other.

And all that time McKay heard the little wood shouting. Gone from it now was all mournfulness, all passive resignation. The wood was alive and raging. He saw the trees shake and bend as though torn by a tempest. Dimly he realised that the others could hear none of this, see none of it; as dimly wondered why this should be.

"Kill!" shouted the coppice—and ever over its tumult he was aware of the roar of the great forest.

"Kill! Kill!"

He saw two shadowy shapes—shadowy shapes of swarthy green-clad men, that pressed close to him as he rolled and fought.

"Kill!" they whispered. "Let his blood flow. Kill."

He tore a wrist free. Instantly he felt within his hand the hilt of a knife.

"Kill!" whispered the shadowy men.

"Kill!" shrieked the coppice.

"Kill!" roared the forest.

McKay's free arm swept up and plunged the knife into the throat of Polleau's son! He heard a choking sob; heard Polleau shriek; felt the hot blood spurt in face and over hand; smelt its salt and faintly acrid odour. The encircling arms dropped from him; he reeled to his feet.

As though the blood had been a bridge, the shadowy men leaped into materiality. One threw himself upon the man McKay had stabbed; the other hurled upon old Polleau. The maimed son turned and fled, howling with terror. A white woman sprang out from the shadow, threw herself at his feet, clutched them and brought him down. Another woman and another dropped upon him. The note of his shrieking changed from fear to agony; then died abruptly into silence.

And now McKay could see none of the trees, neither old Polleau nor his sons, for green-clad men and white women covered them!

He stood stupidly, staring at his red hands. The roar of the forest had changed to a deep triumphal chanting. The coppice was mad with joy. The trees had become thin phantoms etched in emerald translucent air as they had been when first the green sorcery had meshed him. And all around him wove and danced the slim, gleaming women of the wood.

They ringed him, their song bird sweet and shrill; jubilant. Beyond them he saw gliding toward him the woman of the misty pillar whose kisses had poured the sweet green fire into his veins. Her arms were outstretched to him, her strange wide eyes were rapt on his, her white body gleamed with the moon radiance, her red lips were parted and smiling, a scarlet chalice filled with the promise of undreamed ecstasies. The dancing circle, chanting, broke to let her through.

Abruptly, a horror filled McKay. Not of this fair woman, not of her jubilant sisters—but of himself.

He had killed! And the wound the war had left in his soul, the wound he thought had healed, had opened.

He rushed through the broken circle, thrust the shining woman aside with his blood-stained hands and ran, weeping, toward the lake shore. The singing ceased. He heard little cries; tender, appealing little cries of pity; soft voices calling on him to stop; to return. Behind him was the sound of little racing feet, light as the fall of leaves upon the moss.

McKay ran on. The coppice lightened, the beach was before him. He heard the fair woman call him, felt the touch of her hand upon his shoulder. He did not heed her. He ran across the narrow strip of beach, thrust his boat out into the water and wading through the shallows threw himself into it.

He lay there for a moment, sobbing; then drew himself up and caught at the oars. He looked back at the shore now a score of feet away. At the edge of the coppice stood the woman, staring at him with pitying, wise eyes. Behind her clustered the white faces of her sisters, the swarthy faces of the green-clad men.

"Come back!" the woman whispered, and held out to him slender arms.

McKay hesitated, his horror lessening in that clear, wise gaze. He half swung the boat around. But his eyes fell again upon his blood-stained hands and again the hysteria gripped him. One thought only was in his mind now—to get far away from where Polleau's son lay with his throat ripped open, to put the lake between him and that haunted shore. He dipped his oars deep, flung the boat forward. Once more the woman called to him and once again. He paid no heed. She threw out her arms in a gesture of passionate farewell. Then a mist dropped like a swift curtain between him and her and all the folk of the little wood.

McKay rowed on, desperately. After a while he slipped oars, and leaning over the boat's side he washed away the red on his hands and arms. His coat was torn and blood-stained; his shirt too. The latter he took off, wrapped it around the stone that was the boat's rude anchor and dropped it into the depths. His coat he dipped into the water, rubbing at the accusing marks. When he had lightened them all he could, he took up his oars.

His panic had gone from him. Upon its ebb came a rising tide of regret; clear before his eyes arose the vision of the shining woman, beckoning him, calling him... he swung the boat around to return. And instantly as he did so the mists between him and the farther shore thickened; around him they lightened as though they had withdrawn to make of themselves a barrier to him, and something deep within him whispered that it was too late.

He saw that he was close to the landing of the little inn. There was no one about; and none saw him as he fastened the skiff and slipped to his room. He locked the door, started to undress. Sudden sleep swept over him like a wave; drew him helplessly down into ocean depths of sleep.

A knocking at his door awakened McKay, and the innkeeper's voice summoning him to dinner. Sleepily he answered, and as the old man's footsteps died away he roused himself. His eyes fell upon his coat, dry now, and the poorly erased bloodstains splotching it. Puzzled, he stared at them for a moment—then full memory clicked back into place.

He walked to the window. It was dusk. A wind was blowing and the trees were singing, all the little leaves dancing; the forest hummed its cheerful vespers. Gone was all the unease, all the inarticulate trouble and the fear. The woods were tranquil and happy.

He sought the coppice through the gathering twilight. Its demoiselles were dancing lightly in the wind, leafy hoods dipping, leafy skirts a-blow. Beside them marched their green troubadours, carefree, waving their needled arms. Gay was the little wood, gay as when its beauty had first lured him to it.

McKay hid the stained coat shrewdly in his travelling trunk, bathed and put on a fresh outfit and sauntered down to dinner. He ate excellently. Wonder now and then crossed his mind that he felt no regret, no sorrow even for the man he had killed. Half he was inclined to believe it had all been only a dream—so little of any emotion did he feel. He had even ceased to think of what discovery might mean.

His mind was quiet; he heard the forest chanting to him that there was nothing he need fear; and when he sat for a time that night upon the balcony a peace that was half an ecstasy stole in upon him from the murmuring woods and enfolded him. Cradled by it he slept dreamlessly.

McKay did not go far from the inn that day. The little wood danced gaily and beckoned him, but he paid no heed. Something whispered to wait, to keep the lake between him and it until word came of what lay or had lain there. And the peace still was on him.

Only the old innkeeper seemed to grow uneasy as the hours went by. He went often to the landing, scanning the farther shore.

"It is strange," he said at last to McKay as the sun was dipping behind the summits. "Polleau was to see me here today. He never breaks his word, or if he could not come he would have sent one of his sons."

McKay nodded, carelessly.

"There is another thing I do not understand," went on the old man. "I have seen no smoke from the lodge all day. It is as though they were not there."

"Where could they be?" asked McKay indifferently.

"I do not know," the voice was more perturbed. "It all troubles me, M'sieu. Polleau is hard, yes; but he is my neighbour. Perhaps an accident—"

"They would let you know soon enough if there was anything wrong," McKay said.

"Perhaps, but—" the old man hesitated. "If he does not come tomorrow and again I see no smoke, I will go to him," he ended.

McKay felt a little shock run through him—tomorrow then he would know, definitely, what it was that had happened in the little wood.

"I would if I were you," he said. "I'd not wait too long, either."

"Will you go with me, M'sieu?" asked the old man.

"No!" whispered the warning voice within McKay. "No! Do not go!"

269

"Sorry," he said, aloud. "But I've some writing to do. If you should need me send back your man; I'll come."

And all that night he slept, again dreamlessly, while the crooning forest cradled him.

The morning passed without sign from the opposite shore. An hour after noon he watched the old innkeeper and his man row across the lake. And suddenly McKay's composure was shaken, his serene certainty wavered. He unstrapped his field glasses and kept them on the pair until they had beached the boat and entered the coppice. His heart was beating uncomfortably, his hands felt hot and his lips dry. How long had they been in the wood? It must have been an hour! What were they doing there? What had they found? He looked at his watch, incredulously. Less than five minutes had passed.

Slowly the seconds ticked by. And it was all of an hour indeed before he saw them come out upon the shore and drag their boat into the water. McKay, throat curiously dry, deafening pulse within his ears, steadied himself; forced himself to stroll leisurely down to the landing.

"Everything all right?" he called as they were near. They did not answer; but as the skiff warped against the landing they looked up at him on their faces were stamped horror and a great wonder.

"They are dead, M'sieu," whispered the innkeeper. "Polleau and his two sons—all dead!"

McKay's heart gave a great leap, a swift faintness took him.

"Dead!" he cried. "What killed them?"

"What but the trees, M'sieu?" answered the old man, and McKay thought that his gaze dwelt upon him strangely. "The trees killed them. See—we went up the little path through the wood, and close to its end we found it blocked by fallen trees. The flies buzzed round those trees, M'sieu, so we searched there. They were under them, Polleau and his sons. A fir had fallen upon Polleau and had crushed in his chest. Another son we found beneath a fir and upturned birches. They had broken his back, and an eye had been torn out—but that was no new wound, the latter."

He paused.

"It must have been a sudden wind," said his man. "Yet I never knew of a wind such as that must have been. There were no trees down except those that lay upon them. And of those it was as though they had leaped out of the ground! Yes, as though they had leaped out of the ground upon them. Or it was as though giants had torn them out for clubs. They were not broken—their roots were bare—"

"But the other son—Polleau had two?" Try as he might, McKay could not keep the tremor out of this voice.

"Pierre," said the old man, and again McKay felt that strange quality in his gaze. "He lay beneath a fir. His throat was torn out!"

"His throat torn out!" whispered McKay. His knife! The knife that had been slipped into his hand by the shadowy shapes!

"His throat was torn out," repeated the innkeeper. "And in it still was the broken branch that had done it. A broken branch, M'sieu, pointed like a knife. It must have caught Pierre as the fir fell, and ripping through his throat—been broken off as the tree crashed."

McKay stood, mind whirling in wild conjecture. "You said—a broken branch!" McKay asked through lips gone white.

"A broken branch, M'sieu." The innkeeper's eyes searched him. "It was very plain—what it was that happened. Jacques," he turned to his man, "go up to the house."

He watched until the man shuffled out of sight.

"Yet not all is so plain, M'sieu," he spoke low to McKay, "since in Pierre's hand I found—this."

He reached into a pocket and drew out a button from which hung a strip of cloth. They had once been part of that stained coat which McKay had hidden in his trunk. And as McKay strove to speak, the old man raised his hand. Button and cloth dropped from it, into the water. A wave took it and floated it away; another and another snatched it and passed it on. They watched it, silently, until it had vanished.

"Tell me nothing," said the keeper of the inn. "Polleau was a hard man and hard men were his sons. The trees hated them. The trees killed them. The—souvenir—is gone. Only M'sieu would better also—go."

That night McKay packed. When dawn had broken he stood at his window, looking long at the little wood. It too was awakening, stirring sleepily—like drowsy, delicate demoiselles. He thought he could see that one slim birch that was—what?

Tree or woman? Or both?

Silently, the old landlord and his wife watched him as he swung out his car—a touch of awe, a half-fear, in their eyes. Without a word they let him go.

And as McKay swept up the road that led over the lip of the green bowl he seemed to hear from all the forest a deep-toned, mournful chanting. It arose around him as he topped the rise in one vast whispering cloud—of farewell! And died.

Never, he knew, would that green door of enchantment be opened to him again. His fear had closed it—forever. Something had been offered to him beyond mortal experience—something that might have raised him to the level of the gods of Earth's youth. He had rejected it. And nevermore, he knew, would he cease.

THE MOANING LILY

Emma Vane

One of the lesser-known authors in this anthology, Emma Vane closes the volume with her tale of "The Moaning Lily" published in *Wonder Stories* in 1935. The story follows the botanist Carl Brense, who begins to enter flower shows with his marvellous creations of unusually coloured roses and sweet peas. A friend soon becomes concerned by Brense's obsession and unusual behaviour with a peculiar new lily. The titular flora is unique as it has developed a mouth and can moan. "The Moaning Lily" is unique in its body horror elements as it features lurid, feminine and erotic descriptions of the flower's mouth. Emma Vane's story blurs the lines between human and plant, and predator and prey. The lily is no longer something passive to be enjoyed and consumed by the human gaze.

hen Carl Brense, exponent superior of Harvard, Oxford, Heidelberg and what not, took up botany as his life profession, we, his class-mates, were not in the least surprised. There was something about the man's tall, very thin frame and lean sensitive face that suggested flowers and subjects idealistic. His grey eyes were big and soulful and his features sharply chiselled like those of a Dante. And when he smiled, it was only a fleeting condescension to the distressing materialness of the surrounding world.

For five years after our graduation, I never set eyes on Carl. Then, one day, I ran across him at a flower show in New York City. He was standing like a sober statue alongside some ravishing roses and sweet peas. I greeted him affectionately, and he was really glad to see me.

"Heavens, man," I enthused wholeheartedly, taking in the marvellous exhibits, "I never saw such exotic colours in flowers before. That purple rose there with its lemon leaves! And those silver sweet peas! No wonder they have won prizes! How *do* you do it!"

"Oh, everything is simple to him who knows how," said Brense, unruffled. "I have made an exhaustive study of plant-grafting and am compiling a book on the subject. I have won thousands in prizes."

"Well, well!" I ejaculated. "You *are* taking it seriously. Live here?"

"No," answered Brense. "I have a little stone cottage near the palisades in Jersey. There I grow a good-sized garden far removed from city confusion."

Then he took out of his pocket a card, pencilled his address thereon, and handed it to me.

"I would like to see more of you, Crale," he said. "I am very lonely."

So, from then on, Brense and I became close friends and I had ample opportunity for seeing how extremely intense he was in his devotion to rare floral specimens.

Then, one raw November day, the man suddenly disappeared. I went to his cottage only to find it shuttered and silent. An old caretaker, his man-servant, was mechanically puttering around Carl's garden and looked up listlessly as I approached.

"Ah, Mr Crale, glad to see yez," said the old man, hobbling toward me. "Mr Brense left a letter for you. Here it is."

I took the letter and proceeded to read it.

"I am going to Brazil," wrote Carl, "on the most exciting adventure of my life. The tropical blossoms down there are the most curious in the world, and I must study them. I will produce a flower that will shock mankind—just you see. This uncontrollable ambition has fired me consummately. God willing, I will return and exhibit a peerless super-specimen. Nothing else matters."

Well, that was that. Carl Brense had gone. So I left the stone cottage and returned to my bachelor quarters downtown. And thus a year passed.

Then, just as suddenly as Brense had left, he came back one day. Driving aimlessly around, I happened to wander on a Sunday to the familiar acorn road near the palisades and found myself, by force of habit, approaching the little stone cottage. It was May, and through the tall elms that shadowed Carl's place I could glimpse a sector of his garden already aglow with its multi-coloured blossoms.

I stopped my car in front of the low iron gate and cautiously walked up the gravelled path that led circuitously toward the cottage.

Bobbing tulips of riotous hues caressed my feet as I proceeded. I was feeling strangely tremulous because Carl's abode had always seemed like a sanctuary to me and I never entered his premises without being curiously affected.

Suddenly I paused in my tracks, for emerging upon the lawn at the right was a tall, dark apparition of most indefinite outline. The face that topped the spectre was that of Carl Brense, but his figure was swathed from neck to toe in a long voluminous black cape. And he moved along evenly over the grass without any visible means of locomotion, his ponderous robe dragging around him and completely enveloping his limbs.

"God, man," I called out huskily. "You give me the jitters. Are you turned into a monk or something? Why the long monasterial robe?"

Carl Brense just extended his right hand from the folds of his cape and tolerantly smiled. He evidently preferred to ignore my comment concerning his robe.

"And your face!" I continued persistently distressed. "You look like a ghost! You must be deathly sick!" And I was truly worried, for the features of the man were a saffron yellow with deep, dark crescents under his cavernous eyes. His left hand, which I saw for a fleeting second, was covered with varicose veins, brown instead of blue! The sight was startling.

"Come into the house," said Carl quietly. "It's good to see you again. Tell me about yourself."

"Tell me about *you*, you mean," I remonstrated. "If you have been studying the flowers of Brazil, your efforts certainly have been doing you no good. Gosh! I can't get over the picture you present!"

We were by then sitting in Carl's lounge. I lit a cigarette, but he would not smoke, and though it was a warm day, he kept his clumsy draperies still swathed closely around his body.

"I have found my flower, Crale," said he portentously, his eyes glittering. "It goes on exhibition tomorrow at the Flower Show. And, mark you, it will take the world by storm."

"You don't say!" I exclaimed. "Let me see it."

"Not now. You will see it tomorrow," said Brense firmly. "I am very sick, Crale, but I have succeeded in bringing back here the most remarkable of specimens. I call it 'the moaning lily'."

"Aw, Carl," I pleaded, "why in heck will you ruin yourself just to show a new flower! And gad, take off that unsightly cape. This isn't the medieval age. You're in New York, man."

But Carl did not respond. He just twitched nervously, his eyes dropping a little. Then he breathed heavily as if in pain while I thought I heard him moan. At the same time, he arose from his seat with a somewhat laboured motion and walked toward the door. I felt instinctively that he wanted me to depart.

"You must not fail to attend the show tomorrow," he said politely. "Be there at ten. I will be in booth twenty. Then you will see the moaning lily."

"All right, I'll be there, don't worry," I promised. "But, hang it all, Brense, snap out of it. Be yourself! I can't bear to see you looking like a Franciscan monk. A man of your brains falling for religion! Heavens!"

"I am falling for no religion," assured Carl solemnly. "I cannot explain now, Crale, but some day you will know what this is all about."

So, the next day, I repaired to the flower show and made straight for booth twenty. Brense was already there sitting in front of his exhibits down near the spectator line. Quite a few people had collected about him, and no wonder.

The sight of the tall, gaunt monk was enough to arouse anybody's curiosity, but that wasn't all. Hugged in the hollow of his left elbow, his long bony fingers gently holding the foliage, was a broad, dignified plant. There were three or four large scraggly leaves upon a thick stout stem, and growing out of the latter was a pale pink lily conical in shape like the Easter lily, but the curling lip of the petal was carmine instead of white and the centre was the same rich red. Also, the shoot coming up from the centre was red and looked for all the world like a long, attenuated tongue. It was a strange sight and all eyes were glued to the spot. I, too, gazed entranced. Never had I beheld such exotic colouring.

Carl's face was sternly immobile as the public gazed, and he just stared solemnly ahead as the barker at his right began orating on the new prodigy, chanting out in stereotyped phrases his dynamic description of the same.

"Here," he barked, "we have one of the strangest flowers of all time. Imagine a white lily with a red top and a red centre. It is dazzling! And that is not all! Step up closely and observe that the opening of the lily is remarkably like a human mouth! In fact, it *is* a human mouth! There are distinctly two red lips with a long tongue emerging between!"

The crowd pressed nearer and were properly impressed.

"And *now*," continued the barker, "come closer and *lis-ten* everybody, listen *intently*, and you will actually hear this lily *moan!*"

And surely enough!—from the depths of the flower's interior there issued a definite long drawn-out wail, and while it vibrated, Carl Brense still sat immobile, his sad eyes looking vaguely into space.

The spectators were spell-bound. There was something about the sight that was gruesome and uncanny. Why, the "lips" of the lily had certainly moved and the red "tongue" protruding from the centre had really quivered as the weird sound issued forth.

Repelled and awed, the public slowly drew back. The pallid ethereal-looking monk with his big sunken eyes looked like some long-suffering saint. His audience was hushed. It was as if the people were intruding on some sort of a shrine.

The barker, with proverbial callousness, invited the crowd to feel of the flower, but it seemed repulsive to them. They instinctively kept their distance like wide-eyed children. Only I approached and stroked the deep ivory petals and the over-hanging lips. They were softly bulbous like the bleeding-heart. A flower's petals had always to me seemed fleshly to the touch, but this lily was especially so.

But I was principally interested in Carl, so I edged toward him.

"Get out of there, Brense," I said almost fiercely in a tense undertone. "Leave your moaning lily and come home. You look as sick as a dog."

But Carl paid no attention to me. Then the barker continued:

"Mr Carl Brense here is the most renowned botanist of his age. His successful experiments in the grafting of flowers have made him pre-eminent in this field, and this last wonder of his is undoubtedly his crowning achievement. Therefore, ladies and gentlemen, this moaning lily has won first prize not only for its extremely beautiful colouring, but because of the strange inexplainable sound that comes from its centre. In fact, this flower is supernatural, and is so valuable that Mr Brense will never leave it. He takes it home with him every night and never allows it out of his sight."

Then the barker proceeded to sell photographs of the monk and the lily to the eager buyers. This ordeal over, Carl Brense arose and sidled toward the exit of the booth. He was thoroughly fatigued and anxious to get away, but I pressed in on him. His pathetic expression haunted me.

"Don't lug that clumsy plant home," I begged. "Let me take it to my apartment near here. It will be perfectly safe."

But Carl turned on me, a peculiarly wild look in his eyes, and drew himself up with all the dignity of his six-feet-eight.

"Don't interfere, Crale," he said severely. "I must take my plant with me. Don't worry about me. Thank you and good night."

So I left him. "Carl must be beside himself," I thought resentfully. "He is going too far. This is fanaticism."

That night the phone rang. It was the excited voice of Kito, Carl's man-servant. "Come quickly to Mr Brense!" cried the servant. "He is dying and is asking for you, Mr Crale."

"I'll be over right away," I answered.

It was a good forty minutes from my apartment across the George Washington Bridge to the little stone cottage near the palisades, but I managed to have patience and keep my wits clear. Brense had a secret to tell me, I knew, probably the mystery of the moaning lily.

Kito met me at the door, his hands twitching and his voice quavering.

"So glad you come!" he wailed.

"Well, what's happened?" I asked impatiently. "Accident?"

"I don't know," panted Kito. "When Mr Brense got back from the show, he looked like death. 'Kito,' says he, 'go to the butcher without delay and bring me a quart of blood.' As I hurried off, I saw Mr Brense excitedly writing a letter. Well, the butcher thought I was crazy, but I got the blood. Then when I got back to the cottage, Mr Brense put the blood into a long, black vase. Then he took the letter he wrote and stuck it in his bosom. Then he looked coldly at me, sir, and ordered me from the room. When I came in a few minutes later in answer to his call, I found him—but step in, Mr Crale, and see for yourself."

So I followed Kito into his master's bedroom. There on the table was a tall black vase, and in it towered the moaning lily, while Brense lay prone upon his bed. He had evidently flopped down upon it dressed as ever in his inevitable cape. Alarmed, I went over to him. There was no doubt that the man was dead, for his eyes stared up glassily at the ceiling. I gently closed them. I loosened his cape in front and the letter fell out. The latter was soiled with marks of blood coming obviously from a wound in his left arm. Eagerly I clutched the bit of paper. It was addressed to me, so I tore it open, and with a cold tremor permeating my body, I began to read its contents:

"And so, dear friend," said the letter, "I decided to study that strange carnivorous plant of Brazil, that plant that drags to itself insects or small animals and then sucks the blood out of them, a veritable animal bound to the soil. After I arrived at the spot and began to analyse the strange properties of the growth, I became suddenly inflamed, God help me, with a most odious impulse. I was obsessed. Graft! Graft! The word was forever running through my brain.

"I have always loved animals, so I did not have the heart to try my experiment on any one of them. Besides, they might die too soon. But I *must* graft that carnivorous plant on to another thing that was also carnivorous. The idea was burning me up, so I knew then that I would graft it onto myself. I had read of the amazing physical fortitude of certain men who were able to cut off their own limbs to save themselves from death after a poisonous snakebite. So, reasoned I, why should *I* not be able to endure extreme suffering likewise, for a remarkable cause?

"So, with grim determination and with the skill that years of experiment have given me, I grafted a stem of this carnivorous plant to my upper left arm. As the thing bulged rather inconveniently, I was obliged to conceal it from the public's view, so I covered myself with a voluminous black cape which was loose enough to enable the plant to breathe freely. Thus protected from prying eyes, I proceeded to await developments.

"Soon, with the accompaniment of a deep, dull ache, the roots began to take hold. The plant was actually going to live! And from then on, I was in the paradoxical state of physical suffering combined with intellectual ecstasy.

"Daily, I watched the stout roots spread under my thin transparent skin. They crawled along quite visibly, across my shoulder and under my arm, scrambling outwards like scrawny, greedy fingers. With a twiny, insidious grip, they embraced my left chest, and I knew positively that when they clutched at my lungs or heart, I would die. But I did not care. All I wanted was my new flower, and my only anxiety was that its sprouting stem might not have time to mature into a blossom before my death would end the experiment. But I was allowed to survive, and for that I was exceedingly thankful.

"Then, just two weeks before I knew the blossom would appear, I returned home, for I had timed the full florescence with the date of the Flower Show.

"And how zealously I watched my treasure unfold! The original flower resembled a lily somewhat, so I was not surprised at the *new* lily that finally materialised. But I *did* wince when I discovered that the opening of the lily was a perfect replica of a boneless human mouth. For months, I had moaned and groaned when no one was near, so it was only logical that the new flower should reflect in substance my most materially active organ. And there was the amazing carmine of the lips and the actual tongue bursting from the centre! I was thrilled beyond measure!

"Then, one day, when the lily trembled and actually moaned, well, my exhilaration knew no bounds. I hadn't expected anything like that! My fondest hopes were realised. I forgot my physical pains and the desperate impulses I had had to sever the growth from my body. Instead, I fondly nourished it and was terribly afraid to transplant the specimen for fear it might die before thousands could see it and gasp at its super-excellence.

"But my glory was soon to end, for today, when the bloom was at the apex of its beauty, I realised that my death was imminent, that it was only a matter of a few hours. My glorious parasite had sucked me dry! Also there seemed to be definitely ensuing a certain weakness on the part of the lily. Its fate, of course, was linked with my own. Therefore, I could hardly wait to get home and rejuvenate it.

"I quickly procured a quart of blood which I placed in the glass vase. Then I cut the basic stem of the plant from my arm and placed the twig in the vase. I chose glass because I wanted the observer to know that the lily was in blood instead of water. Thus nourished, the flower may last a week or so.

"So, my beloved friend, take it back to the show. I want thousands and thousands to behold it and sing its praises. Do not fail me, I beg of you. I am failing fast— it is the end."

Such was Carl's amazing revelation concluding with a pathetic apology for having caused me so much trouble. Trouble indeed! The least I could do now for my dear friend was to loyally carry out his last wish.

So, the next day, with heavy heart, I took the moaning lily back to the Grand Central Palace where I placed it in lone grandeur on a table, its majestic splendour flaring conspicuously from the tall, glass vase.

Heretofore, when the monk held the flower, some trick of ventriloquism had been suspected by some sceptical spectators. But now that the monk was dead, all were convinced that the lily really moaned all by itself. And just as Carl wished, thousands came to gaze upon it, to listen and to wonder.

Then, on the seventh day, the flower began to fade. It shrank rapidly in size and the observers drew close, as usual. Then suddenly, while they were watching, the "red lips" opened wide in one last spasm of life, synchronously emitting an unusually long moan, a miserable sound that could be heard for yards distant. The people recoiled, instantly drew back, frightened of they knew not what, some of the superstitious actually crossing themselves religiously.

Finally, the flower gave one last quiver and collapsed centrally into a crinkling mass of folds, its whole weight sagging down over its stout brown stalk. The miracle was no more.

But the fame of Carl Brense and his super-blossom spread all over the globe. But of what avail to him who had perished? The Indian fanaticist walking with bare feet over coals of fire and jagged knives had nothing on *him*, my poor demented friend who had plodded heavily about through long tortuous months in his stifling black mantle zealously guarding his precious moaning lily.

British Library Tales of the Weird collects a thrilling array of uncanny storytelling, from the realms of gothic, supernatural and horror fiction. With stories ranging from the nineteenth century to the present day, this series revives long-lost material from the Library's vaults to thrill again alongside beloved classics of the weird fiction genre.

We welcome any suggestions, corrections or feedback you may have, and will aim to respond to all items addressed to the following:

The Editor (Tales of the Weird),
British Library Publishing
The British Library
96 Euston Road
London, NW1 2DB

We also welcome enquiries through our Twitter account, @BL_Publishing.

ALSO AVAILABLE

Festive cheer turns to maddening fear in this new collection of seasonal hauntings, which includes the best Christmas ghost stories from the 1860s to the 1940s.

The traditional trappings of the holiday are turned upside down as restless spirits disrupt the merry games of the living, Christmas trees teem with spiteful pagan presences and the Devil himself treads the boards at the village pantomime.

As the cold night of winter closes in and the glow of the hearth begins to flicker and fade, the uninvited visitors gather in the dark in this distinctive assortment of Yuletide chillers.